ONLY TWO

"Nobody is going to come between us tonight," Matt murmured. His fingertips traced the collar of Gillian's shirt, slightly rough against the silk. He kissed her again, caressing her mouth, sending desire licking like flames along her veins. Rational thought was swallowed up as the sensation blossomed inside her.

"Nobody," Gillian echoed, her lips against his. She clung to him, exchanging kiss for kiss, breath for breath, caress for caress, until she could no longer tell where she left off and he began.

CELEBRATE
101 Days of Romance with
HarperMonogram

FREE BOOK OFFER!

See back of book for details.

Harper
Monogram

LEGACY OF DREAMS

Martha Johnson

HarperPaperbacks
A Division of HarperCollins*Publishers*

This is a work of fiction. The characters, incidents, and dialogues are products of the author's imagination and are not to be construed as real. Any resemblance to actual events or persons, living or dead, is entirely coincidental.

HarperPaperbacks   *A Division of* HarperCollins*Publishers*
10 East 53rd Street, New York, N.Y. 10022

Copyright © 1995 by Martha P. Johnson
All rights reserved. No part of this book may be used or reproduced in any manner whatsoever without written permission of the publisher, except in the case of brief quotations embodied in critical articles and reviews. For information address HarperCollins*Publishers,*
10 East 53rd Street, New York, N.Y. 10022.

Cover illustration by Jeff Cornell

First printing: June 1995

Printed in the United States of America

HarperPaperbacks, HarperMonogram, and colophon are trademarks of HarperCollins*Publishers*

❖ 10 9 8 7 6 5 4 3 2 1

In memory of Robin, who understood friendship.
One day we'll walk in the woods together again.
And, as always, for Brian.

LEGACY OF DREAMS

1

Gillian Lang's first impression of Lake House, that grand old lady of Victorian resorts in upstate New York, was of a massive stone pile, looming over her as if about to topple, crushing everything in its path.

Don't go hunting for ghosts, Gillian. You just might find them.

Her stepfather's words slid into her mind, sending a tremor along her nerves. She shrugged off the feeling. Ghosts hadn't brought her here, whatever her family thought. Just an ordinary job.

An ordinary job and a thirty-year-old question that needed an answer.

Gillian shivered as she stepped from her car into a chilly June evening. It had to be fifteen degrees colder here in the mountains than in New York City. She handed the car keys to the bellman and pulled on her navy suit jacket. No matter how late, she'd arrive at Lake House looking like a fitting representative of the Lockwood Hotel chain. For better or worse, she was here.

She passed under the massive, stone-arched portico and pushed open the door to Lake House.

The lobby was vaguely reminiscent of an English gentlemen's club, with dark wainscoting, burgundy carpet, and crystal chandeliers. A faint, pleasant scent of jasmine perfumed the air. Gillian's gaze was drawn to the massive mahogany staircase which soared upward from the lobby's center. Magnificent. She could almost see ladies in huge hats and leg-of-mutton sleeves descending it. Any guest who came looking for Victorian atmosphere would be awed.

But the staircase, like the lobby, was empty. Gillian glanced at her watch. It was not quite eleven. The guests must retire early, maybe tired out by hiking the mountain trails. Lake House owned the entire mountaintop, so there were thousands of acres to explore.

She took another step forward, then stopped as a rush of warmth surged to greet her. The air itself seemed filled with welcome, as if she were a long-awaited and cherished guest. It was like coming home for Thanksgiving, feeling her half sister's hug, hearing the twins battle over who got to carry her bags in, smelling the aroma of pumpkin pie wafting out the door.

Gillian shook her head. She must be more tired than she thought, or else Lake House had an ambiance they should bottle and sell.

The woman behind the reception desk wore a forest green blazer over a silk shirt, a step up from the windbreakers worn by the bell staff. Her glossy dark hair curved around her face, and perfectly outlined red lips pursed slightly before she smiled.

"You must be Gillian Lang. It's a pleasure to have you here at Lake House."

It was the sort of speech Gillian expected, yet the woman's tone sounded a bit too proprietary for an ordinary staff member. Gillian glanced at the brass name badge. Brenda Corvo, Assistant Manager, seemed to have adopted Lake House as her own, or maybe she was worried about losing her job, if the deal with Lockwood Hotels went through.

"Thank you. I'm sorry to arrive so late." Brenda Corvo might not find meeting her such a pleasure when she learned how thorough an assessment Gillian planned to do. As Assistant Manager, Brenda would probably be the person assigned to help her.

"Your key." Brenda slid it across the counter with a manicured nail and gave her another dazzling smile. "I know Mr. O'Donnell is looking forward to meeting with you tomorrow."

Gillian didn't doubt that. She represented the money that would bail Lake House out of the trouble Matt O'Donnell had gotten it into. That is, *if* she advised Frederick Lockwood that investing in Lake House was a sound idea.

"Thank you." Gillian reached for the key, but someone beat her to it.

"You're Gillian Lang. I'll show you up." The woman stood so close her muslin sleeve brushed Gillian's arm as she snatched the key.

Brenda Corvo looked dismayed for an instant, and then the perfect assistant mask slid back into place. "Of course, Miss O'Donnell." Her voice was as smooth as cream, but obviously Brenda didn't like this intervention. "Ms. Lang, this is Della O'Donnell. You couldn't have a better guide. She knows everything about Lake House."

The woman who took Gillian's arm might have been any age from forty to sixty. Her hair, which was a faded, indeterminate color, frizzed in a halo held back by a bright yellow scarf, and her dangling turquoise earrings touched the shoulders of her cream muslin dress. Her complexion was beautiful; her face unlined. With her wide, unfocused gaze, she looked like someone who should be behind the counter of a New Age health store.

Miss O'Donnell. That would make her the aunt of Matt O'Donnell, the hotel's owner, the man she had to deal with.

"I'm sure I can find the room, Miss O'Donnell." Gillian tried to pull her arm free, but the woman's grip was surprisingly strong. She towed Gillian toward the elevator, making it impossible to do anything but go along. They passed a massive stone fireplace, then a lounge evidently set up for a musical performance, with rows of empty chairs facing a grand piano.

"Call me Della. All the guests do." The woman tossed her head, setting her earrings dancing. "I'm part of the scenery here, like the lake and the cliffs." That should have been accompanied by a smile, but wasn't. "I've put you on the second floor of the old wing, near the family quarters. After all, any friend of Frederick's is a friend of ours." For an instant there was a malicious glint in Della's dark eyes. "Frederick's going to help us out of the hole we're in. Whether we want him to or not."

"I'm not a friend of Mr. Lockwood's, just an employee." She was an employee whose assignment might not be as clear-cut as she'd expected. Gillian would have assumed the whole O'Donnell family would welcome her with open arms, but Della O'Donnell sounded as if she didn't want this investment from Lockwood Hotels. Her nephew did, though, and his was the only opinion that counted.

The elevator, with its brocade wallpaper and velvet-covered bench, looked antique, but it whisked them soundlessly to the second floor. The doors slid open, and they stepped into a hallway, dimly lit by wall sconces. Gillian turned to the left and then stopped, uncertain.

"That's right." Della brushed past her. "This way." She set off down the hall, the key dangling from her hand. "You've been here before, haven't you?"

"No, I haven't." She hadn't. But the hallway, with its brocade wallpaper and wrought-iron lamp sconces, had a comfortable air of familiarity, almost like that sense of welcome she'd felt in the lobby. No, she was tired, that was all. A hotel was a hotel, and she'd seen plenty of them after eight years in the business.

"That's too bad. I've lived here all my life, you know." Della's dark eyes lost their vague look, growing bright with either passion or anger, Gillian wasn't sure which. Della turned to grip her arm with thin, strong fingers. "There have always been O'Donnells at Lake House. There always will be. Remember that."

"I'm sure you're right." Gillian shrugged herself free. What was wrong with the woman? She caught again the faint whiff of jasmine in the air. "About my room . . . "

"Here it is." Della paused in front of a door.

Gillian practically grabbed the key from her hand. She wanted, quite suddenly, to be alone. "Thank you." She made the words firm, pleasant, dismissive. "Good night."

Once Della had gone, Gillian unlocked the door. Alone, she could let herself sag, feeling the effects of the long drive and the strain of seeing Lake House at last.

The room was perfectly Victorian, with rose and green print wallpaper and a golden oak bed and dresser. The fireplace opposite the bed boasted an intricately carved oak mantelpiece, while a delicate lady's writing desk stood by the glass door to a tiny balcony. Gillian crossed the room to the bath, feeling fatigue seep into her. Maybe a warm shower before bed . . .

Her mind presented her with an image of an old-fashioned claw-footed tub and marble washstand. She shrugged off the thought. That would be carrying Victorian trappings to extremes. Modern hotel guests expected showers. She switched on the light and stiffened, staring at the claw-footed bathtub and marble washstand.

It was exactly as she'd pictured it in the instant before the light came on.

For a moment Gillian stood and stared, until common sense asserted itself. What else would she expect in a hotel that prided itself on Victorian atmosphere? She was tired, that was all. She'd better go to bed before she started seeing pink elephants dancing in the halls.

With her robe wrapped snugly around her, Gillian paused at the window and stared out, past her pale reflection superimposed on the dark bulk of the adjoining wing. Out there in the night was the lake for which Lake House was named. Out there also, somewhere, was the artist's cottage, and while she was here she had to find it.

Lake House had a reputation as a cultural center, providing concerts and summer theater productions along with boating and rock climbing. Thirty years ago that cultural interest had included an artist-in-residence: Alec McLeod. Her father. Alec McLeod had lived and worked in the artist's cottage, wherever it was, until the night he'd suddenly packed his bags and left. And vanished. Since that night, no one had ever heard from him again.

Gillian pulled the shade down abruptly, shutting out the night, wishing she could do the same with her thoughts. Alec McLeod had deserted his wife and infant daughter. Plenty of men did that, and plenty of girls grew into successful women without fathers in their lives. She'd had Mitch Lang, anyway, who'd probably enjoyed being a father a lot more than Alec McLeod would have, from what she knew of him. Artistic geniuses tended to be footloose.

This sudden need to know what happened to her birth father had surfaced, without warning, at the time of her thirtieth birthday. The amateur psychologists among her friends would make something of that, if they knew about it. Thirty was one of the watershed birthdays, when people assessed how their lives were going. And her father had been thirty when he walked out of Lake House and disappeared.

Now she was here. Gillian would never have done something so exotic, so impractical, as come to the last place he'd lived to try and find out about him. Never, if it hadn't been for Frederick Lockwood assigning her to do the evaluation of Lake House as a possible investment. Maybe fate had taken the unlikely form of the chairman of Lockwood Hotels. She could hardly come to Lake House, for whatever reason, and not look for answers.

Don't go hunting for ghosts, Gillian. You just might find them.

Again that faint tingle ran along her nerves; again she shrugged it off. More than likely she'd find nothing at all. It had been thirty years, after all. How could there be anything left of Alec McLeod at Lake House?

There'd be time enough to plan her strategy tomorrow. Now she'd better get some rest. Her first meeting with Matt O'Donnell would be crucial, and she couldn't afford to go into it at less than top form.

The bed was warm and comfortable. Gillian half-expected to be too keyed up to relax, but she tumbled into sleep as abruptly as if she'd fallen down a well.

Candle flames danced on a linen-covered table, dazzling her eyes, while music played in the background. It was familiar music, a movie theme Gillian couldn't quite place. The candle flames reflected in the wavy panes of French doors. Outside, moonlight glistened on water. She had a vague impression of people chatting near a fireplace, but the edges of the scene were blurred. Her attention focused on the other end of the room, where every detail was so sharp it almost hurt to look.

A man stood frowning down at the table. He was tall and dark, with a dramatic white streak in his black hair. His broad shoulders seemed tense under his dinner jacket.

He swung abruptly toward Gillian. Her breath caught, and for a moment she was afraid. His dark brown eyes glittered; a muscle twitched in his strong jaw. Whoever he was, he was angry, violently so. He picked up one of the china cups from the table, his fingers clenching it without regard for its fragility.

Feminine laughter rippled through the open doorway, and the room stirred in anticipation. On a wave of laughter and jasmine, a woman floated through the door.

Gorgeous. That was the only word that came to mind. Her black hair was swept up with jeweled combs in a style that was vaguely Grecian. Her dress was somehow

*classical, too, a floating green confection that crossed her
breasts and left her white arms bare. Diamond drops
glinted at her ears and a diamond pendant at her throat.*

"Darling." *Her voice was warm and throaty, but her
green eyes were as icy as the diamonds.* "So nice of you
to wait for me."

"Our guests have been here for an hour. Where the
hell have you been?"

*There was the briefest pause in the conversation at the
other end of the room, then it rose in volume, as if the
guests hoped to drown out his angry voice.*

"I had things to do in the city. Did you miss me?"

*When he didn't answer she moved closer, trailing her
fingers down his white shirt front.* "Well, Robert?" *Her
voice was edged with malice this time.* "Did you miss me?"

"Why should I? I've gotten used to it."

"Have you?" *The woman tilted her face up to his, sliding her arms around him.* "Have you really gotten used
to doing without me?"

*His hands closed on her shoulders, dark against her
white skin. For a moment they tightened as though to
pull her against him, and she smiled up at him, red lips
parting. Then he shoved her away.*

*The woman stumbled backward against the table, rat-
tling the china cups. There was a flicker of vulnerability
in her eyes, and then she laughed.* "That's my answer,
isn't it?"

"Who were you with?" *His words were spoken in a
furious undertone.* "Damn you, who was it? One of our
friends? Or some poor devil I don't even know? Who is
it you run off to New York to meet?"

The woman gave a smile of secret satisfaction.
"Darling, I can't imagine what you're talking about.

There's no one but you." The mocking words were an open invitation to anger.

"Liar!" The word wasn't loud, but the china cup soared across the room and shattered against the far wall. The people by the fireplace, unable to preserve the facade of polite disinterest, turned to stare.

"One day." He ground the words out, seeming to struggle for control. "One day you'll push me too far." Then he spun on his heel and stalked out of the room.

When the woman looked after him, Gillian would have sworn that was pain in her eyes. Then she turned to the people by the fireplace.

"Dear Robert. Such a temper. I must remind him that I'm supposed to be the one with the artistic temperament."

She moved toward her guests, and they laughed awkwardly with her. The figures seemed to waver. The scene faded, leaving behind only a faint scent of jasmine.

Gillian came awake gradually, aware first of the comfort of the bed, then of the sunlight around the edges of the shade. She lay still for a moment, staring at the ceiling, and the dream slid back into her conscious mind, whole, with none of the fragmentary transitions of her usual dreams. Gillian tried to will it away, but it refused to go. It had been so real. She could almost smell the perfume the woman wore. That was odd. She'd never been aware of smell in a dream before. Her subconscious had certainly been working overtime, embroidering the jasmine she smelled at Lake House into her dreams.

She shoved the sheet aside and stretched. Her talents were for facts and figures, concrete items that could be listed, tabulated, checked off. Not for anything remotely imaginative or artistic. The only traits she'd inherited from her father were the coppery hair and fair skin that had been the bane of her existence since she learned that freckles weren't generally considered beauty marks.

Gillian reached for her robe. A quick bath would wash away the lingering remnants of the dream.

An hour later Gillian stood at the window, bathed and dressed. It was a shame to wear a suit on such a gorgeous day, but business was business.

She could see now what she hadn't been able to the night before. The lake, a crystal blue gem, was so close she could almost jump from her balcony into it. On the wooded mountainside she could pick out trails, where a few early joggers wove through the trees. Directly across from her the jagged surface of a white limestone cliff rose from the water. It was both beautiful and starkly primitive, almost menacing.

She should take a walk later, just to get the feel of the place. Maybe she could find the artist's cottage today, although finding it wasn't likely to tell her anything about her father's disappearance.

A rap on the door interrupted her thoughts.

"Good, you're ready." Della's halo of curls was tied back with a bright red scarf this morning, and she wore an unusual necklace of twisted red thread. "You'll have breakfast with us. Come along, I'll show you the way. Then you and Matt can get on with this business of yours."

The sooner the better, her tone implied. Or maybe, *the sooner you're out of here, the better.*

"Are you against Mr. Lockwood's investment, Miss O'Donnell?"

"Della," the woman corrected immediately, then shot an unreadable glance at Gillian. "Against?" She shrugged. "The money has to come from somewhere. I suppose it might as well come from Frederick. If my brother were still running things, there'd be no need for outsiders poking in here. Matt isn't the man his father was."

As one of the outsiders in question, Gillian felt a stirring of pity for Matt O'Donnell. It didn't sound as if he had an easy time of it.

The hallway, with its twelve-foot ceilings, stretched on forever. They turned a corner, and guest rooms gave way to a small conference room, then a lounge that seemed the size of a football field. Gillian paused to stare at three huge fireplaces, a mahogany grand piano, and a Chinese vase taller than she was.

"The Parlor." Della's tone clearly capitalized it. "I'll show you around later."

Della led the way down another corridor and pushed open a carved, heavy door that looked as if it belonged on a church. "These are the family quarters. The family's lived in these rooms since Lake House was built."

Directly across the room, French doors opened onto a wooden porch, beyond which lay the lake, glittering in the sun. To Gillian's right was a fireplace, surrounded by blue and white Delft tiles. Gillian stopped dead and put her hand on a chair to steady herself.

It was the room she had dreamed about last night.

For an instant the room seemed to whirl around her. She clenched the chair back, her mind racing. There was an explanation for this. There had to be.

"Coffee or tea?" Della had already moved to the table. Gillian forced herself to follow.

"Coffee, please." Her voice actually sounded normal.

The last time she saw this table, it was set for a party. Gillian choked back an hysterical laugh. Ridiculous. Surely there was some logical explanation. Now, if only she could think of one. Gillian took a gulp of scalding black coffee, hoping it would clear her head.

"What a lovely room. I almost feel as if I've seen it before." She could hardly say she'd seen it in her dreams.

"I wouldn't be a bit surprised if you'd seen photographs of it," Della said. "It's been featured in magazines several times. Lake House is rather unique, you know."

"It certainly is." The words came out fervently. Okay, she wasn't going crazy. She'd seen photos of the place at one time or another, and stored the memory in her subconscious. There was nothing mysterious about it.

Gillian took a blueberry muffin from the basket Della handed her and broke it open, fragrant steam rising in her face. Only the scents of coffee and blueberries filled the room, not jasmine.

Della silently stared at her with that unfocused dark gaze, apparently feeling no need to talk. Gillian hoped that Matt O'Donnell was more down-to-earth than his aunt. The woman made her feel vaguely uneasy, as if everything in Della's presence was off-kilter.

"You've lived here at Lake House all your life?" Gillian asked. Lake House seemed to be Della's only topic of conversation.

"All my life," Della echoed. "O'Donnells belong at Lake House. That's what I tried to tell them when they took Matt away, but nobody would listen."

"Took him away?" What was the woman talking about?

"After his parents died." Della seemed to assume Gillian knew all about it. "He was only five when that grandfather of his took him away, clear out to Texas. He should have been raised here, raised to respect his family's traditions."

"Are you on that hobbyhorse again, Aunt Della?"

The deep male voice startled both of them, and Gillian looked up to receive a second shock. The man was tall, dark, broad-shouldered, and tension radiated from him. Gillian's breath caught. He was the man from her dream.

No, of course he wasn't. Common sense asserted itself immediately. This man was tall and broad-shouldered, with dark hair and dark eyes, but her imagination·did the rest. His strong face didn't have the lines of bitterness she'd seen in her dream. His thick charcoal brown hair was untouched by white. This man had a stubborn square jaw and eyes like rich Belgian chocolate.

Della didn't bother answering his question. "This is Gillian Lang. Frederick's friend."

"Ms. Lang." His voice was a husky bass rumble, with a trace of a Texas drawl. "Welcome to Lake House. I'm Matt O'Donnell." He thrust his hand out, and his fingers enveloped hers.

"I'm glad to meet you." Thank goodness her voice sounded cool and collected. His unexpected resemblance to the man in her dream left her off balance, and the way his eyes assessed her didn't help any.

He held her hand an instant too long, his grip warm and strong, then shot a look at his aunt, which suggested he hadn't expected to find Gillian here. "Business at the breakfast table?" His dark brows lifted slightly. "Frederick must be quite a boss to demand that kind of service—and get it."

"Certainly not." Gillian met his eyes. She wouldn't back away from a challenge, if that's what it was. She put down her muffin. Having butter dripping from her fingers was a disadvantage in a business situation. So was the fact that she wore a business suit when he had on faded jeans and a flannel shirt, the sleeves rolled back to reveal muscular forearms. "Miss O'Donnell invited me. If you prefer to talk later, I'll be glad to meet you in your office." She started to rise, but he stopped her with a firm hand on her wrist.

"Not at all." His dark gaze moved from her to his aunt. "Aunt Della meant it for the best. Let's get on the outside of some breakfast first. We can talk later."

O'Donnell sat down next to her, and the table suddenly seemed too small. The man generated a vibrant energy from the top of his glossy hair to the tips of his well-worn cowboy boots. His arm brushed hers as he reached for the coffee.

"Sleep well, Ms. Lang?" He smiled, and Gillian felt a jolt as tendrils of warmth crept along her skin, setting it tingling.

"Gillian," Della said. "Her name is Gillian."

"Ms. Lang will do," Gillian said. The more businesslike she could keep this, the better.

"Gillian." He repeated her name as if he hadn't heard her. No, as if he'd decided to ignore what she wanted. "Scottish, isn't it?"

"Yes, Mr. O'Donnell." She didn't intend to offer any explanations at this point. He might not have heard of Alec McLeod, and that suited her just fine.

"Call me Matt." His dark eyes held hers. "We're just one big happy family around here. Aren't we, Aunt Della?"

The jibe under the words made Gillian uncomfortable. If Matt had a problem with her presence, it would be better if he came right out with it.

"Family's family," Della said. She stared at Matt. "You should be more like your father."

His fingers tightened around the spoon, then relaxed. "Oh, I don't know." His drawl became more pronounced as he leaned back in his chair. His dark gaze seemed to dare Gillian, and she half-expected him to prop his boots on the table. "I reckon I'm a lot like him." He nodded to something behind Gillian. "Tell me what you think." She felt the challenge in his words. "Am I like my father, or not?"

A feather of uneasiness brushed along Gillian's skin. She turned, not sure what she was looking for. Her eyes caught the glint of a gold frame, then a white dinner jacket against a dark background. Bitter lines bracketed a strong mouth. A chill ran down her spine, and she had to force her gaze higher. She found herself looking, somehow without surprise, into the eyes of the man from her dream.

2

"*I think you're very like him.*" Gillian found it astonishing that her voice was so steady. "In appearance, anyway."

Did he share the same explosive temper? Now, wait a minute. This was ridiculous. She couldn't treat a dream as if it really happened. The man in her dream was a figment of her imagination.

"Hear that, Aunt Della? Gillian thinks I look like him."

Gillian stared at the place setting in front of her, unwilling to face those arrogant painted features again.

"Looks are one thing," Della said stubbornly. "Character's another."

Matt's long fingers tightened on the cup he held. "That how you see it, too? The kid can't live up to his old man?" he asked Gillian.

Bitterness laced his words. He was baiting her, trying

to make her take sides in this war he waged with his aunt. What did he mean by putting her in this awkward position?

"Your aunt knows you better than I do." Gillian regretted the words as soon as they were out. She was supposed to work with Matt O'Donnell, not antagonize him.

Anger flared in his eyes. She waited for an explosion, but it didn't come. No cups shattered against the wall. Matt went perfectly still for a moment, then he smiled.

"Too bad Grandpa Young's not here." One of his dark brows lifted ironically. "He always worries that I'm too much like my father. He'd be glad to hear I'm not." He pushed back his chair. "Excuse me. Seems I'm not hungry this morning. I've got things to do."

None of which, Gillian would guess, involved meeting with her. Well, he would have to, like it or not. "I'll need to discuss my evaluation plans with you sometime today. I find it helps if everyone involved understands just what I'll be doing."

"Fine," he said, though his tone made it clear that it was anything but fine. He tossed his napkin on the table, looking as if he wished the scrap of cloth were something breakable. "I'll see you in my office at eleven."

When he was gone, Gillian stared down at the muffin that lay crumbled on her plate. Like Matt, she no longer felt hungry. She glanced across the table. Della ate steadily, her appetite apparently unimpaired. Maybe she was used to fireworks at the breakfast table.

"I'll show you something." Della got up. "You'll understand about Lake House when you've seen this."

Della rummaged through the bottom shelves of the china closet. Gillian could see the china cups from her chair. If she counted them, would one be missing from the set? She tried telling herself again that it was ridiculous.

"There!" Della plopped a heavy scrapbook on the table, narrowly missing the butter dish. "Look at this." She flipped through the pages, past yellowed newspaper clippings and faded photographs. "I've got everything that's ever been published about Lake House in my scrapbooks."

Gillian paged through the book, pausing at a glossy magazine article on Lake House. The photographs of the living quarters showed every detail, including the dinnerware. Gillian let out a breath she hadn't realized she'd been holding. All right. She wasn't crazy. She just had a subconscious mind like a pack rat.

In one photograph an elegant, familiar figure stood laughing up at Matt's father. *Well-known artist Clarice Young shares a quiet moment with husband Robert O'Donnell at Lake House Inn,* Gillian read. *Miss Young's one-woman show will open in September at the prestigious Hawn Gallery in New York.*

Gillian realized that Della was looking at her expectantly. Did she wonder at Gillian's avid curiosity? Probably not. She seemed to think everyone shared her passion for Lake House. "It's a lovely article. I take it this is Matt's mother?"

"Clarice." Della sniffed. "She never did fit in here. Too busy with her painting to be the kind of wife Robert needed."

Gillian felt a pang of sympathy for Clarice. It couldn't have been easy to live up to what Della expected. She glanced at the byline on the article. "Henry Morrison. He was quite well-known."

Della nodded, turquoise earrings bouncing. "Henry

was always underfoot, always taking his pictures. Now that he's retired, he lives here at Lake House most of the year."

"I see." Lake House had a resident star, in other words. Henry Morrison had been noted for his photographs of the famous and the infamous during the sixties and seventies. Everyone who was anyone wanted to be photographed by him, even though his pictures often told more about their subjects than they wanted known.

"Thank you for showing me." Gillian closed the heavy album with relief. Being here at Lake House must have triggered her memory of this article or a similar one, letting it float to the surface in her dream. It was odd, but nothing more. She could tabulate it, explain it, forget it.

Gillian got up. The sooner she got on with things, the better. "If you'll excuse me, I think I'll take a look around before I meet with your nephew."

For a moment she thought Della would insist on going with her, but the woman had reopened the scrapbook and bent over it, nose almost touching the pages. "You go ahead," she murmured.

Della was certainly devoted to Lake House. Obsessed might be a better word. Gillian closed the heavy door, feeling she'd escaped from something. Still, it wasn't any of Gillian's concern, as long as it didn't affect the profit potential of the hotel. Maybe now that her dream had been satisfactorily explained, she could get her mind back onto business. Lockwood Hotels hadn't sent her here to let her imagination run wild.

Gillian walked down the massive mahogany staircase to the main floor, running her hand along a satiny railing polished by generations of hands. The lounges and public rooms seemed virtually deserted.

She paused in the lobby, glancing over the bulletin board. It listed incoming guests, but there weren't many of them. Lake House had four floors, several wings, and over a hundred guest rooms. It was operating at far below its capacity, and there didn't seem to be any obvious reason why.

The situation had sounded simple enough back in New York. Lake House was in financial trouble, and Frederick Lockwood was an old friend of the O'Donnell family. Gillian frowned, trying to remember some elusive detail of office gossip. She'd heard Lockwood owned a home in this area. In any event, there was a personal, as well as a business, reason for him to invest in Lake House.

Gillian ticked off the meager store of facts she had. Matt O'Donnell was the sole owner of Lake House, having inherited it from his father, who'd died when Matt was a child. He was evidently something of a stranger to the hotel, since Della said he'd been raised by a grandfather in Texas. Maybe that wasn't so surprising, if being raised by Della was the only other option. Matt had taken over management of the hotel eight months earlier, when the former manager died.

Gillian remembered Lockwood shaking his leonine head, that distinctive white mane waving around his aristocratic face. King Frederick, people called him, but not where he could hear.

"Matt was always a wild one." Lockwood had balanced a delicate Chinese bronze horse between his long fingers. "Too much like his mother for his own good. He spent the last ten years knocking around the globe, then came back and thought he'd walk in and run a hotel with no experience at all." To Lockwood, that was the ultimate heresy. "Run it into the ground, more likely." He seemed to catch himself. The king didn't show his feelings to so junior a subject. "The point is, he's the son of an old friend, and Lake House has been in the O'Donnell family for a long time. Naturally I'm interested. I don't want to see one of the finest Victorian resort hotels in the country deteriorate."

It was a match made in heaven, as far as Gillian could tell. Lockwood Hotels was known for buying up distinguished old establishments and refurbishing them under the Lockwood banner. This was a little different, in that Lockwood was considering going in as a partner, rather than buying outright. And in this case he seemed to have a personal interest.

"If you're familiar with the operation, Mr. Lockwood, I'm not sure . . . "

Lockwood smiled. ". . . why I want a report from you?" He leaned forward, long, elegant fingers caressing the smooth bronze. "This is still a business deal. Matt O'Donnell invited me to look at his operation before making a decision, so I'm sending you." Lockwood set the horse down. "You'll do a good job for me, I know. Take all the time you need."

The audience was evidently over. Gillian had left the office, still not sure why Frederick Lockwood had chosen her. She'd only been with the company six months. Still, Lockwood knew she had a good background, with experience in resort hotels on Hilton Head and in Palm Beach. She was certainly competent to do the job.

So she was here. If this went well . . . what was she saying? This had to go well. She wasn't going to blow her first big solo assignment for Lockwood Hotels, even if Matt O'Donnell proved less than cooperative. Even if she had bad dreams every night she was here.

A man emerged from the lounge, laden with cameras and a knapsack. Gillian knew he was Henry Morrison, though he looked younger than Gillian would have expected. She smiled, and he stopped, looking at her searchingly.

"Excuse me. Have we met?"

Gillian shook her head. "No, but of course I recognize you, Mr. Morrison."

Morrison smiled. He had a pleasant, smooth, unremarkable face and a diffident manner, as if he might blend into the wallpaper at any moment. "No 'of course' about it, my dear, but thank you for the kind thought." He held out his hand. "Henry Morrison. And you are . . . ?"

"Gillian Lang."

Awareness sharpened in his eyes. "Frederick Lockwood's sleuth. Come to ferret out all the little secrets of Lake House."

It was said with a smile, but Gillian sensed an edge under the words. "Nothing so exciting." She nodded toward the cameras. "What about you? Are you working on an assignment?"

"I am, thank goodness, retired." Morrison had an oddly formal manner and a slight British accent. He patted the cameras. "No, the sad truth is that these things are an addiction. I simply can't go any place without them."

"Miss O'Donnell showed me a photo essay you did of Lake House some years ago. It was lovely. I'm sure I've seen it before."

"No doubt." Morrison seemed to take it for granted that she'd seen his work. "I know the one you mean. That was a favorite piece of mine." A trace of sorrow moved across his face. "Clarice Young was a natural. It was impossible to get a bad picture of her."

"She was very lovely." Gillian remembered the vivid creature from her dream.

"Yes." Henry's voice softened. He looked up at the wide staircase. "She'd come floating down those stairs to greet you, and you'd swear her feet didn't touch the ground."

The aroma of jasmine teased Gillian's nostrils. She followed his gaze to the staircase and froze. Clarice came down the steps, smiling, her hands held out to them. She wore the same floating green dress she'd worn in Gillian's dream.

Gillian gasped, her hand clenching Henry's arm. She closed her eyes. When she opened them again, Clarice was gone.

Morrison looked at her strangely. "Ms. Lang? Is something wrong? You look quite pale."

It was a wonder he didn't ask her if she'd seen a ghost.

"No, I'm fine." Gillian managed a smile that she hoped didn't look as stiff as it felt. Fine. Sure, she was fine. She was dreaming about people she'd never met and seeing things that weren't there. She was fine.

Matt paused at his office door. Lately he'd found it harder and harder just to open the damn door. The frustration that dogged him everywhere at Lake House was strongest here, in the office that still seemed to belong to somebody else. He grabbed the knob with a quick angry movement and went inside.

The golden oak desk that had once been his father's was awash with papers. He looked at them for a moment, then swept them into a pile. He could go through them backwards and forwards, and nothing would change. Lake House was going under. The decline had started long before he took over, but Matt didn't kid himself. The months he'd spent at Lake House had been a disaster, a total disaster.

"A man oughta be big enough to admit his mistakes." He could almost hear his grandfather's raspy voice. The photo on his desk showed the old man leaning against a fence, with a dusty corral behind him. He looked like a character out of a Western movie, with his faded denims and Stetson. He was ninety years old now, but still as tough as a piece of aged rawhide.

An onlooker wouldn't guess that beyond the corral stretched some of the most oil-rich land in the country. Not that oil was the blessing it used to be, his grandfather would be quick to remind him.

"You were right, old man." Matt said it aloud. "I never should have come back."

He flung himself into the swivel chair, and it creaked in protest, yet another thing that needed to be replaced. The whole place was sucking up money as fast as he poured it in.

The chair had belonged to Reed Windom, the dry stick of a man who'd managed Lake House after his father's death. Matt had never been impressed with Windom at their yearly meetings. Fussy, precise, tied hand and foot by tradition . . . no, he and Windom hadn't had much in common.

Windom had started Lake House on its downward spiral, with his stubborn insistence on clinging to old ways of doing everything. But Matt's ideas and innovations had just speeded the decline, so maybe Windom had been right after all.

Matt tilted the chair back, propping his leather boots on the desktop, enjoying the defiant gesture. There was no point in crying over spilt milk. The thing to do now was bail the place out.

He looked again at the picture of his grandfather. No, he didn't figure he could do that. The old man would come up with the money quick enough, if Matt asked him. But knowing how his grandfather felt about Lake House and anything to do with the O'Donnell family, Matt didn't intend to ask him. So that left Frederick Lockwood's offer, and Gillian Lang.

She had fey, Scottish eyes. That was the first thing he'd noticed when he found her at his breakfast table. Deep blue eyes with a cluster of pure gold around the iris, like so many he'd seen among the Highland Scots, that year he'd worked a North Sea rig. She had fine-textured skin that begged to be touched and vivid red curls that would cling to your fingers if you got your hands in them. Her aloof, touch-me-not air was strangely at odds with the soft curves and creamy skin. He might enjoy getting to know Gillian Lang, if it weren't for the fact that every time he looked at her he was reminded of his own failure.

The no-nonsense rap on the door told him it was time for their meeting. Matt removed his boots from the desk, then propped them back up again. No, dammit. He might have to accept Lockwood's help, but he didn't have to like it.

"Come in." He shouted it casually, knowing it would annoy her. He could sense her irritation at the sight of a pair of worn cowboy boots on the desktop.

Matt hauled himself to his feet when she approached. The old man would have berated him for failure to rise when a lady approached. Old ways died hard in the West.

"Right on time, I see." He pulled a chair up close to

his. "Sit down, relax. Tell me all about how you're going to find out what's wrong with Lake House."

Gillian settled into the chair carefully. She obviously would have preferred a nice expanse of desk between them. "Mr. O'Donnell, I— "

"Matt, remember?" He smiled, letting his gaze wander over the soft curve of her breasts under her cream silk shirt. "Let's keep this as painless as possible, okay?"

He was making this difficult for her, and he knew it, but that was the only weapon he had. She'd probably gotten orders from Lockwood not to hurt his pride, but facts were facts. If he hadn't blown it, she wouldn't be here at Lake House.

Gillian Lang would obviously be more at home in midtown Manhattan, just as he'd be more at home in central Texas. Well, nobody got what they wanted in this deal, except maybe Lockwood.

"Mr. Lockwood asked me to tell you how much he appreciates your cooperation." She crossed her legs, then immediately uncrossed them. "I'm sure we can get this done quickly. And painlessly."

"Maybe not too quickly." He drawled the words as he looked from her delicate temple to the column of her throat. There was an answering glow of warmth to her skin. "Give us a chance to get to know each other." He paused. "You and Lake House, I mean."

"Of course." Gillian cleared her throat. "Was there anything you wanted to go over with me?"

"Well, now." Matt pulled a diagram toward her, his hand brushing hers. The brief touch sent a jolt sizzling up his arm. He saw in the sudden darkening of those blue-gold eyes that she felt it, too. "This will give you an idea of the extent of Lake House."

He leaned closer, until their heads nearly touched. The light floral scent she wore teased his senses. He traced the outline on the diagram with his finger. "This is what's included, besides the hotel itself. Sixty thousand acres, counting the land that's in the Preservation Trust."

Gillian studied the diagram, perhaps to avoid looking at him. "May I keep this?"

"Sure can." Matt slid it over to her. His hand grazed hers again. He might as well make sure that reaction wasn't an accident. It wasn't. "Anything to make your job more pleasant."

"Good of you to be so cooperative."

"You'll find I'm always . . . cooperative."

She had no choice but to take it at face value, but he saw feminine awareness lurking behind the businesslike exterior.

"Thank you." Gillian paused a moment. "I'll need access to the personnel in each department, of course. And to the financial records, if that's all right."

Matt leaned back in a movement he hoped looked relaxed.

"I don't exactly have a choice, do I?" When she didn't answer he stood up, took a few long strides to the window, and stared outside. Damn. He hadn't known this would hurt so much. It was like sitting in the dentist's chair, waiting for the probe to strike something else painful.

"Look at anything you want." It cost him to say it. "You'll find a trail of mistakes since the day I took over." He could taste bitterness in his mouth, and black rage rose in him. At himself, not at her. At his own failure.

"Things often don't look as bad to an outsider as they do when you're too close to them." Her voice was hesitant, as if she wasn't sure what it was safe to say.

He swung to face her. "Trying to make me feel better? Don't bother. Let's not kid ourselves. Della was right. I'm not the man my father was. Bumming around the world from oil rig to oil rig isn't exactly the best preparation for running a hotel."

"No, I guess not."

Gillian looked as if she wished she were anywhere else. She was a corporate type, the kind of person who'd spend her life working for someone else, never knowing the challenge of confronting something that was hers alone. She'd never know the heady jolt of satisfaction at her own success, or the gut-wrenching pain of failure.

"Forget it." He heard the edge in his voice and knew she heard it, too. He almost thought that was sympathy he saw in those clear-as-glass eyes.

"I know this is difficult."

"Difficult?" He covered the few feet between them in a few angry steps. "It's impossible." He glared down at her, then he shook his head. "And it's not your fault. Sorry."

The word was torn from him reluctantly. She probably expected a more gracious apology. She'd have to take what she got. He wasn't going to thank Lockwood's lackey for laying out the heart and soul of Lake House on a debit and credit sheet.

"Matt, I—"

A knock interrupted her.

He glared at the door. "Come in."

Brenda Corvo hesitated in the doorway. "Excuse me, Matt, but you did want me to meet with Ms. Lang, didn't you?"

Brenda Corvo seemed to be everywhere, questioning everything. She was always raising those elegant eyebrows as if to doubt his decisions. If she hadn't been at Lake House so long, he'd have gotten rid of her his first week.

"Brenda, I want you to help Ms. Lang in any way you can. She's to have access to all records, information, whatever she asks for. Is that clear?" He knew the words were brusque, and he didn't care. He'd had enough of this dissection of Lake House for one day.

"I'll be glad to do anything I can." Brenda gave a perfunctory smile.

"Good." Matt crossed the room in a sudden explosion of energy. He couldn't wait to get away from both of them. "You can use my office. I'm going out."

"But Matt . . . "

The door banged shut behind him. Brenda shrugged, turning to Gillian with a rueful smile.

The assistant manager must be devoted to Lake House to work such long hours, Gillian thought—on the desk until nearly midnight, then on duty again this morning. Today she wore a patterned silk scarf with the forest green blazer.

"There are things he really should take care of, but that's the way it always is. Poor Matt. I'm afraid he really isn't cut out to be a hotelier."

Well, well. Brenda certainly was blunt. In other words, she meant to align herself with the winning team. Gillian slid her papers together. Loyalty seemed to be in short supply around Lake House. "Would you like to work here, or would it be more convenient in your office?"

"Let's go to my office." Brenda looked around with an elaborate shudder. "This still seems like Mr. Windom's office to me. I can't quite believe he's gone."

"You worked with him for a long time?" Gillian followed her across the hall to a second office.

"Five years." Brenda indicated a chair and slid behind her desk. "He knew how to run a hotel. I learned a lot from Mr. Windom. Of course, it doesn't compare to working for somebody like Frederick Lockwood."

That was something Brenda planned to experience very soon, if Gillian understood her correctly.

"Didn't Mr. O'Donnell get involved in the operation while Mr. Windom was alive?"

Brenda's eyebrows lifted. "You must be joking. We didn't see him around here more than once a year, if that. O'Donnell might have the name, but he never showed any interest in Lake House until Mr. Windom died. Then he decided to take over, just like that." She leaned forward confidingly. "You and I both know hotel management is a complex business. You don't learn it on an oil rig."

Gillian decided she might as well be as blunt as Brenda. If the hotel's financial difficulties were due solely to bad management, Frederick Lockwood had a right to know that.

"So you think Lake House's problem is really Matt O'Donnell?"

"Well, of course the economic climate has been terrible. But I'm sorry to say Matt O'Donnell has been a disaster for Lake House."

Sorry? The woman wasn't sorry in the least. If Matt valued loyalty in his employees, he should have gotten rid of this one long ago.

"I appreciate your . . . " Gillian rejected several words that came to mind. ". . . candor. Now, I'll need an office and access to your computer system." Gillian slid a paper across the desk. "Here's a list of the records I'd like to see first."

Brenda's eyebrows went up as she looked at the list. "I didn't realize . . . but naturally, I'll get the things together for you. And find some office space. If Matt had told me in advance what you needed, it would be ready now."

So Brenda was surprised. Did she really think Gillian would just take her word for the situation? "You'll have it ready by this afternoon?"

Brenda's smile stiffened. "It'll take some time, but I'll do my best."

"Until later, then."

When she reached the corridor, Gillian glanced at her watch. It was time for lunch. She felt suddenly confident. The little exchange with Brenda had been good for her.

She'd seen plenty of Brendas in the last eight years—people whose eyes were fixed so firmly on their own goals they couldn't see anything else. She'd found it refreshing to deal with Brenda after the complexity that was Matt O'Donnell. His bitterness had startled and unsettled her.

She could handle this, all of it, including Matt O'Donnell, with his rough edges and that masculine magnetism that pulled at her every time they were together. She'd get something to eat and go out exploring. She might be able to find the artist's cottage right away. It probably wouldn't tell her anything, but it seemed important to see it. By the time she got back her office would be ready, and she could get to work.

The dining room had a huge fireplace dominating the wall opposite the door. Gillian paused as she entered, glancing around. To her left, a wall of windows overlooked the valley, which spread out below Lake House like a patchwork quilt. To her right, another wall of windows fronted on a manicured lawn that should have had women in long white dresses playing croquet.

A mammoth buffet table stretched down the center of the room, laden with soups, quiche, salads, even a roast beef and a ham. Gillian steered toward the salads. Even with the best of intentions, she couldn't resist a flaky, buttery croissant. Eating like this three times a day could have demoralizing results.

Matt O'Donnell stayed fit enough. For an instant she saw again the barely controlled energy of his walk, felt the charged tingle that accompanied his touch. She shoved the thought away. He was altogether too disturbing to her peace of mind.

An hour later Gillian had changed clothes and was walking on the path around the lake. The map, which she'd stuck in her jeans pocket, hadn't shown anything called an artist's cottage. Gillian frowned. If her mother and stepfather had been a little more forthcoming, it would help. Gillian had thought she'd prepared very well for telling them the unpalatable truth about her assignment.

"By the way, you'll never guess where Mr. Lockwood's sending me. He's considering investing in Lake House, and I'm doing an evaluation of the business for him."

She'd brought it out with just the right degree of casual, what-a-coincidence flair. Unfortunately nobody took it casually. Mitch Lang's open blue eyes clouded with instant concern, and he darted a look at his wife.

Gillian knew, just as the twins and Amy knew, that their mother always came first with Mitch. She might have attributed it to the fact that she was his stepdaughter, except that Mitch's own children, ten-year-old Amy and sixteen-year-old David and Derek, were treated exactly the same way. What was her mother's attraction, that two such diverse men as brilliant artist Alec McLeod and solid, dependable Mitch Lang had fallen for her?

Margaret Lang did have a face reminiscent of a Botticelli angel, which none of her children had been fortunate enough to inherit. But at that precise moment she hadn't looked so much angelic as frozen.

As a teenager Gillian had gone through a predictable period of curiosity about the father she didn't remember, and that curiosity had gone unsatisfied. Confronted by anything related to her ex-husband, Gillian's mother retreated behind an immovable mask and stayed there, impervious to questions, threats, or tears. Gillian might have been dropped by the stork, for all her mother had told her about her father.

Gillian ticked off the facts she knew, matching them to her stride along the path. Alec McLeod had been a gifted artist, a footloose Bohemian who would have fit more easily into Haight-Ashbury than rural Pennsylvania. He'd left his wife and baby daughter with her family while he went to spend the summer as artist-in-residence at Lake House. Then he'd run off before the end of the summer, and his wife and daughter had never heard from him again. That was the end of the story, until now.

The path led past a beach. Gillian paused for a moment, watching children splashing in the shallow water. A baby slept with the intense abandon of the very young, sprawled on a towel under a striped umbrella.

Perhaps a baby had been the breaking point for Gillian's father. Her birth had meant the end of his carefree, hand to mouth existence. He'd had to get an ordinary job and work at his art in his spare time. The artist-in-residence summer must have looked like a reprieve, like one last chance to live the life he wanted. Sometime during those weeks he'd come to a decision. He wouldn't go back.

Gillian didn't blame her mother for feeling bitter. She felt that way herself sometimes. To walk away from a wife and daughter without a word, that was hard to understand.

Her mother believed he was dead. That was easiest, maybe. Margaret had Mitch now, who adored her, and the three children they'd produced. Mitch always treated Gillian exactly the same as he treated the others. It certainly wasn't his fault she sometimes felt extra, the proverbial red-headed stepchild.

The trail started to climb, headed for the top of the cliff opposite the hotel. Gillian hadn't passed any cottages, or any other building for that matter. All she had seen were hemlocks, pines, and an occasional drift of pinkish white mountain laurel. Wherever the artist's cottage was, it wasn't this way. There'd be a good view from the top, though, so the hike wasn't a waste.

It was hot and still on the trail, and the air smelled of moss and pine. Her jeans stuck to her legs by the time the trail burst into the open at the top of the cliff.

Gillian's breath caught in her throat. The white cliff fell away in front of her, dropping to the lake below. Opposite her, Lake House nestled along the azure water, looking almost as if it floated on the lake. With its random turrets and balconies, it was a magic castle, like something out of the illustrated Brothers Grimm Gillian had as a child.

Only one thing hampered her view: Matt O'Donnell.

"Well, now." He paused, lifting his dark eyebrows. "I

didn't expect to see you up here. I thought you'd be hard at work, tracking down evidence of mismanagement."

Gillian bit her tongue to hold back an angry retort. One of them should try to maintain a professional attitude, and it clearly wasn't going to be Matt. "Brenda's getting an office ready for me. I thought I'd take a look around in the meantime."

"Assessing damages?"

Gillian took a firm hold on her temper. Maybe it was time to tell Matt where she stood. "Look, this would be easier if you'd just understand I'm not here to pass judgment on what went wrong."

The explosion she expected didn't come.

"You like to clear the air, don't you?" Matt's voice was surprisingly mild. The tension seemed to drain out of him. "Okay." He sat down on a flat slab of granite, patting the sun-warmed rock beside him. "Truce, then. Sit down, catch your breath."

Gillian sat down warily, not sure she believed this sudden turn-around. The rock under her was warm, almost welcoming.

Matt leaned back on his elbows, stretching his long legs along the rock. His faded denim jeans were taut over strongly muscled thighs. He'd rolled the sleeves of the rust and tan flannel shirt back to the elbow, and his arm rested against hers. Gillian wasn't sure whether the warmth she felt came from him or the rock.

Or both. Matt O'Donnell knew exactly the effect he had on women. Anybody this comfortable in his own skin had to.

His dark eyes were narrowed against the sun, sending a fine network of lines radiating from them. Where the sun touched his hair it was the color of ripe, glossy chestnuts. There was a cleft in his chin she hadn't noticed before, and his mouth . . . Gillian caught herself wondering how his mouth would taste.

No. This trip was business, not pleasure. She couldn't afford to be attracted to Matt O'Donnell, of all people. Aside from the business considerations, there was the little matter of her father.

Could Matt have been here when her father disappeared? The sudden thought jolted her. Thirty years ago Matt would have been about five. In all probability he'd been here then. Gillian frowned, biting her lip. How could she ask him? What could she say, that wouldn't rouse his suspicions and yank her hidden agenda out into the daylight?

"Hey." His finger touched her mouth, startling her. "Don't bite that pretty lip. Whatever the problem is, just spit it out, don't chew on it."

Gillian was surprised into laughter. "Is that Texas philosophy?"

That got her the first genuine smile she'd seen from him. The warmth spread to his eyes, fanning out in relaxing lines. "Guess it might be something the old man would say, at that."

"The old man?"

"My grandfather." He gave a warm chuckle. "Jared Young is as Texas as a Texas longhorn."

Gillian blinked. Jared Young? If Matt had an oil baron for a grandfather, why did he need help from Lockwood? "Isn't your grandfather interested in investing in Lake House?"

The smile vanished, and Matt's face tightened. Then he leaned closer, deliberately, until his face was only inches from hers. She inhaled the mingled male scent of musk and leather and felt his warmth everywhere they touched.

"Tell you what." He drawled the words out, his voice as rich as honey. "Why don't we save business for the office?" His fingers traced the line of her jaw, and Gillian felt a pulse hammer in her throat. "Outside the office, we can get better acquainted."

Gillian put her hand on his chest and felt hard muscle, alive to her touch. "I don't think that's a good idea." She pushed.

It was like pushing against the granite slab. He rolled back from her slowly, eyes questioning. "Because you're not attracted?"

"No. Because I have a job to do." The words were right, but the touch of his hand lingered on her lips like a kiss.

"Your job." Matt's fist clenched, as tight as that square, stubborn jaw. "It'll be over soon, one way or the other." He looked away from Gillian, down toward the hotel, which was sleeping like a cat in the sunlight. "Either Frederick will buy in, or he won't. If he doesn't, I'll sell to the highest bidder." His dark brows drew down, turning his face into a forbidding mask. "Sometimes I don't think I care that much either way."

"How can you think that?" Shock made Gillian say more than she should. "This place has been in your family for generations. Don't you feel any loyalty to it?"

Anger flared dangerously in his eyes. "Loyalty? I don't feel loyalty to this place. Why should I?" He caught her arm suddenly, his fingers like steel, turning her to face the lake. "Look down there. You know what happened there? Thirty years ago this summer my mother drowned in that lake. Every time I look at it that's what I think of. You tell me why I should have any loyalty to that."

3

"*I'm sorry.*" *Gillian's mind* raced dizzyingly. Thirty years ago? The same summer she lost her father, Matt lost his mother.

The vibrant creature of her dream whirled back into Gillian's thoughts. No, that image wasn't real. It was a product of her imagination. The real Clarice O'Donnell was probably totally different.

Matt turned away, his face shuttered. For an instant he reminded Gillian of her mother. "Forget it. I shouldn't have said it. I don't know why I did. It's not something I talk about."

His pain pierced Gillian's confusion. "I know it's tempting to keep something like that bottled up." Her own family was a sterling example of that. "But it doesn't work."

"Maybe not." Matt stared down at the lake, the lines in his face deepening. "My father did what he thought was best. Told me my mother had to go away, sent me off to Texas to visit my grandfather." His lips twisted.

"They all tried to protect me. They'd have been better off to tell me the truth."

"I know." Gillian stopped, not sure how much to say. She'd never expected to find this painful common ground between them. "My father deserted us when I was a baby. For years my mother pretended he'd never existed. I guess she figured I couldn't miss what I'd never had. She was wrong."

Matt turned, focusing on her as intently as if he saw her for the first time. His look probed past her skin to the person she hid inside.

"I guess you do know what I mean," he said slowly, as if he found it hard to admit.

Some elemental bond seemed to link them in that instant. She was acutely aware of each breath he took, of the slightest tremor in the muscles of his jaw. She could almost hear his heart beating. She had an overpowering desire to reach out and take his face between her hands.

"Sorry." Matt shoved himself off the rock in a single fluid movement. "I didn't mean to tell you all of that."

Before Gillian could think of a response he'd turned toward the trail.

"I have to get back."

She watched until his tall figure disappeared in the trees. Then she looked down at the lake again, shaken. Crystal clear, beautiful—it represented nothing but pain to Matt, and somehow his pain had moved her. Maybe it was safer to concentrate on what he'd said, rather than what she felt. If she could.

What did his mother's death have to do with her father's disappearance? Or was it just the long arm of coincidence?

Clarice Young had been an artist, like her father. Probably her interest had been the driving force behind the artist-in-residence program that brought Alec McLeod here that summer. Then he left, and she died, or the other way around.

Gillian flung herself off the rock and started for the trail. This did no good. There might be no connection at all between the two events. She hated working blind. She'd never try to come to conclusions on a business project with this little information.

She had to find someone who could tell her about that summer. Della? If only she could think of any excuse to ask those questions without seeming nosy.

By the time Gillian got back, Brenda had an office ready for her, a tiny room wedged between the gift shop and the library on the first floor. Gillian looked with affection at the computer on the desk. At least here she knew what she was doing. The current status and future prospects for Lake House could be reduced to neat rows of facts and figures. Unlike other mysteries, this one had a solution, given enough time.

Gillian worked steadily through the afternoon, her notes filling one sheet after another of a yellow legal-sized pad. Finally she pushed herself back from the desk and stretched, yawning. It was tedious work. So far no answers had emerged, just an unhappy picture of a dwindling clientele and increasing expenses.

She glanced at her watch. It was time to call it a day and change for dinner.

The green and rose room was welcoming after the tiny office. As she rummaged in the dresser drawer for a pair of pantyhose, Gillian's fingers brushed the envelope she'd put there. She pulled it out reluctantly, holding it for a moment before opening it.

The ruby and diamond ring fell into her palm, the

gems winking at her from their twisted gold setting. Gillian stared at it, as if the ring might tell her its secrets if she looked hard enough.

Mitch had given it to her just before she left at the end of that disastrous trip home.

"Your mother thought you should have this." He held the ring between his fingertips as if it were hot. "She won't talk about it, so there's no use asking her. I thought she'd thrown it away years ago."

Gillian slipped the ring on her finger. "Why would she want to get rid of it? It's lovely."

She looked up and saw the answer in Mitch's face. He never could tell a lie.

"It wasn't hers. It was in a suitcase your father left at the railroad station in Chicago. When he never came back to claim it, they sent it to her."

Gillian closed her hand over the ring. It fit her perfectly. Why had there been a woman's ring in her father's luggage? "She'd never seen it before?"

Mitch's face twisted in pain, showing Gillian for the first time what her mother's silence cost him. "Whoever it belonged to, or whoever he bought it for, she doesn't want to know. Anyway, you should have it. Maybe it'll help you find the answers you need."

Gillian stared at the ring, remembering the pain on Mitch's face. She hadn't realized. Maybe she'd been too involved in her own feelings to think about anybody else's. Poor Mitch. Did he feel he'd always come in second to that dashing young artist?

She dropped the ring back into the envelope and slipped it to the bottom of the drawer. She dressed slowly, her mind still on the mystery the ring represented.

The jeweler she'd taken it to hadn't been much help.

The ring was expensive and antique, a Florentine design. He'd finally deciphered the initials. R.C. to N.K. She didn't know anyone with those initials. Maybe, as Mitch said, the ring would help her find some answers. Or maybe it was just another loose end that would never be tied up.

Gillian could hear muted conversation and the clink of china as she walked down the hall toward the dining room. The day's newspapers, displayed on a rack by the door, screamed of the latest Washington political scandal. She paused momentarily to scan the headlines, then went into the dining room.

The few guests sat scattered sparsely, like small islands in a sea of round tables. At a table for two overlooking the valley, Gillian's mind returned to the newspapers outside the door, and she realized she'd been ignoring a source of information.

The local papers would have covered Clarice O'Donnell's death, if not her father's leaving. They might give her some facts to go on, nice solid facts, instead of a fog of fragmentary information and half-forgotten memories.

Only the fact that the newspaper office would be closed kept Gillian from deserting her dinner. Tomorrow she'd find some excuse to go into town and check the newspaper files.

"May I join you?" Henry Morrison stood with his hand gingerly on the chair opposite her, as if prepared to flee at a frown.

"Please." Gillian gave him a warm smile. According to Della, Henry Morrison had spent time at Lake House for years. He could have been here the summer her father was. Maybe he was the source of information she'd been looking for.

Questions would have to wait, though. Henry picked up the menu and studied it as seriously as if it were a proof sheet. Obviously he considered the ordering of dinner a grave matter. The single sheet of cream-colored paper with today's date listed four or five choices each of appetizers, soups, salads, entrees, and desserts.

"Lamb with rosemary." He tapped the menu with one finger. "You can't go wrong with that, although the chef also does a wonderful Chicken Kiev. And the salmon pâté would be my choice for appetizer."

"This is like being on a cruise ship," Gillian said. "If I eat this way every day, you'll have to roll me out of here at the end of my stay."

"A little thing like you? I don't believe it. Just go out and hike the trails everyday." Henry patted his flat stomach. "That's the ticket."

"Is that what you do?" How exactly was she going to introduce that particular summer into the conversation? "You certainly look fit."

He ducked his head, and she thought she saw a slight flush on his cheeks. "Metabolism," he murmured.

The waiter arrived, looking expectant. With a vague feeling of creating a bond between them, Gillian followed Henry's advice on the menu. A notice at the bottom caught her eye.

"Seasons at Lake House: An Illustrated Lecture by Henry Morrison. Nine O'clock, Lake Lounge," Gillian read aloud. "You're giving a lecture tonight?"

Henry's embarrassment deepened. "Just a talk, really. People are interested in my pictures, not in what I have to say. I do have quite a decent collection of slides of the House and the mountains at every season. Perhaps you'll come?"

That served her right, she told herself, as their appetizers slid in front of them. "I wouldn't miss it. These are all scenes, not portraits?"

Henry spread salmon on a cracker and popped it in his mouth, nodding.

"That's a change from your usual work, isn't it? I thought you mainly did portraits, like the photos of Clarice O'Donnell you were talking about earlier." That was not particularly graceful, but it did introduce Clarice's name. "Are any of them on display here?"

His blue eyes became opaque. "A few. In the Blue Lounge." He passed her the roll basket. "Now that I'm retired, I do what pleases me. And what about you? Is your job enjoyable, working for Frederick Lockwood?"

He'd certainly put up a No Trespassing sign. Gillian nodded. "I'm enjoying it so far. Working at the corporate level of a chain is different from the management jobs I've had in the past. I've usually been at resort hotels, something like Lake House."

She glanced around the half-empty dining room. "Is it always this quiet in the summer?" And were you here in the summer thirty years ago? No, she couldn't come right out and ask that.

"It varies. Were your other hotels places where the high season was summer?"

Telling him about the hotel in Palm Beach should only have taken them through the soup course, but prompted by Henry's questions, the subject lasted through dinner. Gillian began to see how Henry had achieved his photographic results. He effaced himself, becoming such an appreciative listener that you were betrayed into revealing more than you intended.

Eventually their plates were swept away, to be replaced by Peach Melba and coffee. "Anyway, I'd had enough of beach resorts for a while, so the opportunity to go with Lockwood came along at the right time."

Henry stirred sugar and cream into his coffee. "We do have a beach here, you know." His faded blue eyes twinkled. "Not quite the caliber of Palm Beach, but a beach nonetheless."

Gillian smiled, remembering the infant under the umbrella. "I saw it while I was out walking today. The children seemed to be enjoying it."

"I remember . . . " Henry paused. "You don't want to listen to me reminisce."

"Of course I do. You've listened very patiently to me, haven't you?"

He smiled. "But that was a pleasure." The smile softened into something half-sad. "You mentioned my portraits of Clarice O'Donnell earlier. I remember some studies I did at the beach here." His eyes looked at something far away. "Matt must have been about five at the time. What a handful he was. He ran in and out of the water, never still for a minute. He could swim like a fish, even at that age. No fear at all."

He was making it so easy, just when she'd given up expecting. "You were photographing them?" she asked softly, afraid of interrupting his train of thought.

"Actually Clarice was trying to sketch him. You knew she was an artist?"

Gillian nodded.

"I got some wonderful pictures of the two of them together, but the imp wouldn't hold still long enough for his mother to draw him. Clarice finally bribed him to sit still by letting him hold my camera. The little demon got sand in it. It was never the same afterward."

Henry's smile faded. "I don't know what happened to

that sketch. I hope Matt still has it. It must be one of the last ones she did of him. She died soon after, you know." His eyes filled with tears. "Drowned in the lake, the night of the Fourth of July."

A lump formed in Gillian's throat. "That's terribly sad."

"Yes. One doesn't forget, you know. I can still see that vibrant smile of hers. The scent of jasmine always reminds me."

Gillian thought of the jasmine she kept noticing. "If it was Clarice's perfume, it seems odd that it's such a signature scent around the hotel."

Henry stared at her, his face frozen in an odd expression she couldn't quite identify. "Signature scent? You've smelled jasmine here, at Lake House?"

A chill slid down her spine. "Yes, of course. I thought it was some sort of air freshener or . . . " Her words trailed away at the look in his eyes. Recognition, she thought. And fear. "You mean it's not?"

He shrugged in a way that was probably intended to be casual but wasn't. "Not that I know of, but I could be wrong." He glanced at his watch. "Heavens, look at the time. I have to organize my slides. Please excuse me."

He was gone before Gillian had time to nod, but not before she recognized his emotion. Fear. That's what she'd seen in him. Fear. Something cold touched the back of her neck.

She was not about to start believing in ghosts at this point in her life. The implication that there was something supernatural about the scent of jasmine was ridiculous. Henry didn't know everything about Lake House. He couldn't. The housekeeping staff had started using a new air freshener, or someone had overdosed on jasmine cologne. That must be the answer.

At least now she had a date. July 4th, thirty years ago, Clarice O'Donnell died. The newspapers might give her a little more, but she needed to know exactly when her father had left Lake House. Since her mother wouldn't talk about it, maybe she should write and ask her. It was worth a try, anyway. She'd jot a note to her mother before this lecture she'd obligated herself to attend.

The lecture was a bit on the dry side, but Henry's slides were superb, so it was well worth the hour spent. Afterward Gillian lingered in the library, reading a magazine and yawning. Finally she faced facts. She was putting off going to bed, half-afraid of another vivid dream.

That was silly. Gillian went up the staircase, trailing her hand along the smooth rail. She remembered this sensation from childhood, going reluctantly up the stairs, afraid of what she'd dream if she went to sleep. She couldn't remember what the scary dreams had been, but they were probably the usual childhood monsters. She did remember the yellow starfish night-light her mother had finally put in her room.

Grown-up Gillian didn't need a night-light. She switched the bedside lamp off without bothering to pull the shade. Moonlight traced its way into the room, touching her as she drifted to sleep.

The children's laughter reached her first. They seemed to be playing at the edge of the lake. Sunlight dazzled her eyes, so that she couldn't see clearly.

A red and white beach ball bounced among them and then, taken by the wind, bobbed out into the water. One little boy, braver than the rest, dashed in after it. He ducked under the surface, frightening Gillian, but then he came up grinning, water streaming from his dark hair. He flung the ball to the beach and came out after it, shaking himself like a wet puppy.

"Matt, it's too cold for that. Come over here and wrap up in the towel."

Clarice's emerald swimsuit matched her eyes, and she seemed younger with her hair tied back in a ponytail.

"Come on, sugar." The love in the woman's voice made Gillian's heart ache. Clarice wrapped the towel around Matt's sturdy body, hugging him and rubbing him dry at the same time. Their faces were close together, and the love that sparkled between them was so tangible she could almost touch it.

"Just sit still a little longer," Clarice coaxed. "Just a little longer. I'm almost finished. Then I'll put the picture in a shiny silver frame for you, and you'll have it always." A cloud crossed her face. "Always. It'll remind you of how much I love you."

Gillian felt the ache of tears in her throat. She wanted to speak up, wanted to tell Clarice . . . What? What could she say, even if Clarice could hear her? Nothing she could do or say would make a difference. The realization wrenched at her heart, and she tasted salty tears.

Gillian jolted awake with the sensation that someone had just called her name. She glanced at the clock. It was only six-thirty. She could go back to sleep for half an hour.

No, she couldn't. Some inner restlessness propelled her out of bed and drove her to the window. The restlessness danced along her nerves, prickling at her skin. It seemed to demand that she do something.

A lone jogger trotted along the lake path, his electric blue sweatshirt bouncing through the trees. That was what she needed, not an extra half hour of sleep but some fresh air to drive the dream away.

The memory she'd been holding away swept over her: Clarice, and the salty taste of tears.

"No," she said aloud. She wasn't going to start thinking about that again. She wasn't going to start imagining the scent of jasmine in the room. She'd get dressed and go for a walk.

Once she was dressed, Gillian started toward the path around the lake. Something seemed to stop her. *Not this way*, an inner voice prompted. Another path led into the woods, away from the lake, and instinct pushed her onto it.

She'd promised herself she'd explore some of the other trails, looking for the artist's cottage. Her subconscious must be reminding her of that.

The trail wound through fragrant pines, with the only sounds the soft thud of Gillian's steps and a bird song or two. She hadn't intended to jog, but she found her steps quickening, as if she were late for something. The early morning sunlight slanted through the trees, casting jagged shadows that reached toward her.

The trail grew steeper. It wound up the far side of the cliff opposite the lake, Gillian realized. She should have taken the level path around the lake if she wanted to jog, but something drove her feet on. Her breath came in little gasps, and her heart pounded in protest.

Some indefinable change in the bird song warned her that she wasn't alone. Ahead of her the trail wound sharply upward, threading in and out among a tumble of rocks. The hill itself was a jumbled rocky outcropping, as

if the giant hand that sliced the cliff face had tired and
dropped a careless handful of rocks here.

Someone headed toward her along the path. Gillian
glimpsed a white sweater through the trees. He came a
little closer, and she saw that it was Matt.

Her first feeling was embarrassment. With the miles
of trails to chose from, why did she keep running into
him? Almost immediately the embarrassment was swept
away by something stronger that flooded through her,
sending her feet hurrying forward. It was urgency.
Hurry, hurry. It pounded in her blood. *Hurry.*

The trail wound around huge boulders. Matt moved
out of sight, almost directly underneath the rocky outcropping. A flash of color yanked Gillian's attention to
the top of the hill.

Something or someone moved among the rocks. She
had an impression of movement almost too fast for her
eye to register just as Matt came back into her view.
Above him the cliff face seemed to quiver for an instant.
Gillian's warning scream tore at her throat as a torrent of
rock and loose earth plunged toward him.

She had a quick, vivid image of Matt's face, startled
and white, as he leaped, trying to get out of the way. For
an instant she thought he'd made it. Then something hit
him. He buckled as if he'd been shot, stumbling into the
river of moving rock. Almost in slow motion his body
rolled over and over down the hill, coming to rest still,
dead still, in a clutter of rocks and broken branches.

4

For just an instant Gillian froze. Then she raced toward Matt's crumpled body, her heart pounding frantically. Fragments of half-forgotten first aid lore flew through her mind.

He was breathing. She could see the rise and fall of his chest before she touched him. Relief flooded through her as she dropped to her knees beside him. Matt was breathing.

Gillian pressed her palm against his chest, immediately reassured by the warmth of his skin and the steady beat of his heart. One arm lay flung over his face, as if he'd tried to protect himself from the torrent of rock and brush. Cautiously she drew his arm down.

It was odd, to feel his fingers so slack in hers. In the brief twenty-four hours she'd known him, her impression of him had been one of vitality, energy, movement. His stillness frightened her.

Gillian pushed the thick, crisp hair back from his forehead. He wasn't bleeding, but a reddish-purple knot marred the tanned skin above his left eye. She slid her fingers through his hair, searching for any other injury, but found nothing. With the fringe of dark lashes against his cheeks and the even, steady flow of his breath, Matt could have been asleep, but he wasn't. He was unconscious, and she had to decide what to do.

She could run back to the lodge for help. It would take ten minutes, maybe fifteen to get there. Then she'd have to find someone, explain, and get back out here.

Gillian bit her lip, torn between going and staying. She hated not knowing what to do. It made her feel inept, incompetent. She put her hand against his cheek. If only he'd wake up, or someone would come down the trail.

She'd thought someone had been at the top of the outcropping. Gillian looked up, frowning. No one was there now. Maybe no one had been there at all.

The seconds ticked by. A bobwhite called nearby, reassured by her stillness. She should go for help, but something held her pinned to the spot, unwilling to leave him alone and defenseless.

Matt's eyelids flickered. Relief flooded through her, and Gillian patted his cheek. "Matt? Matt, can you hear me?"

His eyelids fluttered again, struggling open reluctantly. He stared at her—blankly at first, then with recognition, followed by wariness. He made an instinctive movement, as if to get up. Gillian pressed both palms against his chest.

"No, don't. You're hurt."

He made a sound that was half-grunt, half-agreement,

put a hand to his forehead and winced. His fingers explored the lump. "What happened?"

"A rock slide came down the hill. You were caught in it."

Gillian's voice had an embarrassing tendency to wobble as the scene replayed itself. She swallowed hard and forced some briskness into her tone. "I didn't want to leave you alone when you were out cold, but now I'll go and get help."

He caught her wrist as she moved, holding her motionless at his side. "No, wait a minute." His eyes closed, and the ugly bruise seemed to darken.

"You need help." Gillian tried to pull free, but his grip tightened. Fear flickered through her. Was he rational? Maybe that knock on the head had made him delirious. "You need help, Matt." She made her voice soothing, the way she would talk to her little sister. "Just let me go now, and I'll get somebody."

His eyes opened, and he glared at her in a way she found reassuring. "I'm not senile, damnit. Just dizzy." He reached for her with his other hand. "Help me up."

Against her better judgement, Gillian got both arms around him. She tugged, he pushed, and several agonizing minutes later Matt was sitting, his back against the rough trunk of a hemlock. He was pale and sweating, but something triumphant shone in his dark eyes.

"See? Good as new."

"Right." Gillian sat back on her heels. "You're fine. A week-old kitten could knock you over, but you're fine."

She thought he'd flare up at that, but he only grinned. "Guess you'll have to hold my hand then." He captured her fingers in a warm grip. "Protect me from any feisty kittens."

Gillian looked down at the hand encircling hers. "Maybe you're better than I thought."

Matt rested their clasped hands on his thigh. "Honey, I'm not going to give you the obvious answer to that." He closed his eyes, the brash confidence fading, and leaned back against the tree. "How did you happen to come out this way today?"

Did she imagine it, or did the muscles under her hand tense slightly as he asked the question?

"Just chance, that's all." He could probably hear the uncertainty in her voice. But she wasn't going to tell him, or anyone, about that sensation of being led—no, driven—here this morning. She didn't believe it herself.

"I was on my way up the path when I saw you above me. Then you were out of sight briefly." Her voice slowed as she replayed the scene in her mind. "I thought I saw someone above you on the hillside, just a quick impression of movement among the rocks. Then the rocks started to slide. I thought the whole cliff was coming down on you."

Matt watched her with a dark, intent look she couldn't interpret. Then he shrugged. "It was probably a deer. They're all over this mountain."

The image had been too quick and fragmentary for her to be certain, but she didn't think it had been a deer. Before she could argue the point Matt leaned forward, his arm going across her shoulders.

She looked up to find his face inches from hers, so close she could feel the warmth emanating from it. "What are you doing?" The words came out a little breathless.

Matt gave her a slow, sweet smile. "Several things come to mind." His breath caressed her cheek. "But I guess I'll settle for a boost to my feet. Think you can manage that?"

Gillian stiffened. "Better than you can right now. But I still think you should let me go for help."

He grasped her shoulder, sending warmth all the way down to her fingertips. "You're all the help I need. Ready?"

He'd probably try it without her if she didn't help him. She'd been right about that stubborn chin the first time she looked at him.

By the time Matt stood upright against the tree, they were both shaking. He closed his eyes and then, before she could react opened them again, frowning. He was angry at himself, probably, for betraying any weakness in front of her.

"Let's go," he said.

Exasperating, that was the word for his overabundance of male ego. "Maybe you ought to rest a minute first."

His arm weighed so heavily on her shoulders she nearly staggered. "I'm fine." The edge in his voice said he was ready for a fight. "If you don't want to help me, I'll make it myself."

Gillian slid her arm around his waist. She could hardly let him stumble his way down the mountain, however much he might deserve it.

After five minutes of staggering down the path, Gillian was sweating and breathless. What had happened to those joggers she'd seen earlier? They were all in having their breakfast, probably, by this time. She tripped, regained her balance, and then guided Matt to the nearest tree.

"You may be fine, but I need to rest a minute." She leaned over, hands on her thighs, trying to catch her breath.

"Sorry." Matt sounded as if the word were wrenched from him. When she looked at him, he managed a rueful smile. "I mean it. This isn't exactly the first impression I had in mind."

Something in his smile touched her. "I have news for you. It's way too late for first impressions," she said.

"That bad, was it?" Lines crinkled around his eyes. "I'd have to say my reaction to finding you at my breakfast table was . . . mixed."

"I could tell." Some of the barriers between them seemed to have crumpled along the path. "If we got off to a bad start, it was probably as much my fault as yours."

Matt raised an eyebrow, and she was struck again by his resemblance to his father. "Truce?"

They always seemed to be saying that.

She nodded. "Truce."

For a moment their eyes held. The silence stretched between them, promising something, she wasn't sure what. Matt seemed about to speak. Then he withdrew, the curtains coming down across his dark eyes. He was remembering, probably, who she was and why she was here.

Matt braced both hands against the tree trunk, pushing himself upright. "Why don't you go on back and have breakfast? I can make it the rest of the way on my own."

The barriers were back. Well, she could handle it as lightly as he could. "Sorry." She slid her arm around his waist again, feeling sleek muscles through the soft cotton of his sweater. "I don't want to get sued for negligence if they find you at the bottom of the hill. You'll just have to put up with my help a little longer."

He gripped her shoulder. "Look, I didn't mean . . ." His mouth tightened. "I've got a real gift for putting my foot in my mouth sometimes. Sorry."

The drawl had deepened. Was he aware of that, or was it some sort of unconscious defense mechanism?

"It's mighty nice of you to help me, ma'am." It was so Texan that all he needed was a Stetson and a gun belt. His eyes laughed, inviting her to laugh with him.

"You're welcome." She couldn't help returning the smile. "Just don't make a habit of landing on your head."

"It's probably hard enough to take it."

They went the rest of the way down the hill in a companionable silence. Matt seemed, with every step, to lean on her less heavily. She glanced at his face. The color was back under the tan. Maybe he was right about the hard head.

They'd nearly reached the lake path when Matt stopped, turning to face her, letting go of her support. "I'd better go the rest of the way by myself. It should cut down on the audience."

He didn't need to explain that to her. People in the hotel business tended to be paranoid where accidents were concerned. Accidents were bad for business.

She nodded toward the lump on his forehead. "How do you plan to explain that?"

"I walked into a door." He fingered the bruise. "Clumsy of me, wasn't it?"

Those moments when she hadn't known whether he was alive or dead swept back. "You should be more careful." It didn't come out as lightly as she intended. She reached toward him, almost involuntarily. "Matt, I really did see someone on the hill before the rocks fell. Maybe you should do something about it."

Matt's face tensed, withdrawing. "Put out a warning? That's all we'd need. The few guests we have would run over each other on their way out the door."

"But what if—"

"It was a deer. That's all." The aggressive edge had returned to his voice, and the momentary rapport between them disappeared. "This isn't New York City, you know. There aren't any muggers hiding behind the trees, hard as you might find that to believe."

Her temper rose at his tone. "What I find hard to believe is that you can ignore it."

"You're wrong," he said flatly, his eyes cold. "I appreciate your help, but you're wrong about this. Nobody was there. And nobody, especially not Lockwood, will thank you for saying anything else."

That certainly made it clear enough. Gillian took a step away from him. "You're the boss." She snapped the words. "I just hope I'm not around the next time a mountain decides to fall on you."

A wedge of cantaloupe and a cranberry muffin filled up the hollow spaces and took away the tendency Gillian's knees had to wobble. Breakfast did nothing, though, to diminish the mixture of empathy and irritation every brush with Matt engendered. His effect on her was complex, even without that surge of physical attraction she felt every time she got too close.

Lockwood certainly expected her to get along with Matt, even to spare his feelings as much as possible. And she needed his cooperation to do her job. She wouldn't gain it by quarreling with him at every opportunity.

Gillian stared out at the croquet lawn and, beyond it, the wooded mountainside. She could almost see Gibson girls in white shirtwaists and long skirts tapping colored balls through the wickets. The fact that two teenagers in shorts were actually playing didn't seem to disturb her image.

Granted, Matt was right not to draw any more attention to the rock slide than he could help. Anyone in the business would agree with that. But surely he should be concerned about the possibility that someone caused the rocks to fall.

Gillian frowned, running her finger along the rim of the cup. What was she saying? That someone deliberately set out to harm Matt? That didn't make sense. What possible reason could anyone have? The memory of Della O'Donnell's waspish comments slid uncomfortably into her mind. The woman was eccentric, to put it mildly. She was disappointed in her nephew, but that didn't mean she'd try to hurt him.

The accident had to be just that, an accident. Matt happened to be at the wrong place at the wrong time, and she happened to be there, too.

Was that coincidence? The memory she'd been holding at bay came surging back: the waking sensation that someone had called her name, the unexplained restlessness, forcing her out into the woods, the relentless sense of urgency that drove her along the path.

She was making too much of this. She hadn't slept well, and she'd awakened restless. There was certainly nothing supernatural about it. She didn't believe in such things.

"What happened to Matt?"

Gillian jerked as if someone had pinched her, and looked up into Della's dark eyes. They weren't vague now, but filled with a sort of malicious curiosity.

"I beg your pardon?"

Della slid into the chair across from her. The series of

silver bracelets on her wrist clattered against the table. "I saw you and Matt talking, out at the edge of the woods." Della nodded toward the view beyond the window. "When he came in I saw his head. What happened to him?"

"What did Matt say when you asked him?" Would he have used the bumping into a door story with Della? There seemed little point in putting on an act with her, but Matt might see a need she didn't.

Della shrugged. "Some nonsense about bumping into a door. I didn't believe it." She leaned forward, silver earrings swinging. "What really happened?"

"That's what he told me, too." That was true, at least. "You'd better ask him if you want to know anything more."

Della sat back in the chair. "You won't tell me. It doesn't matter. I'll find out. I always do. The house tells me things, you know."

"The house . . ."

"Lake House." Della fingered the twisted red thread of her necklace. "It tells me things, because I belong here."

Gillian felt a welcome rush of skepticism. Della was too strange to be true, with this mystical mumbo jumbo. She was putting it on. That dreamy facade masked a malicious shrewdness.

"That's fascinating." Gillian slid her chair back. "I'd love to hear about it, but I'm afraid I have to get to work."

In her room, Gillian changed to a skirt and jacket, then ran a brush through her hair. She should go over the registration procedures today, and then—

She stopped, staring. Dismayed, even frightened for an instant, she looked at the object that lay in the center of her pillow: the Florentine ring.

Gillian snatched it up, hand closing around the ring. The metal felt warm to the touch, as if someone else had been holding it. Or wearing it.

The whine of a vacuum cleaner, somewhere in the hall, intruded a welcome note of reality. Gillian clenched the ring so tightly it hurt her fingers. What was she imagining, that one of the resident ghosts had a passion for antique jewelry? She'd probably left it out herself, or maybe knocked it to the floor. The maid must have picked it up when she cleaned the room, and put it on the bed so Gillian would be sure to see it.

That was a nice, logical explanation, except for one thing. Where was the envelope the ring had been in? She distinctly remembered slipping the ring back into the envelope, and then sliding the envelope to the bottom of the drawer. Didn't she?

Gillian crossed swiftly to the dresser and jerked the drawer open. She slid her hands under a stack of lightweight sweaters. The envelope lay where she'd left it, flat and empty.

There had to be a logical explanation for everything. Gillian stared at the row of figures on her computer. They didn't jump off the screen and dance around the room. Rings didn't move themselves. Houses didn't talk. She was not letting Lake House drive her crazy.

Gillian stared down at the keyboard, unable to concentrate. She must have dropped the ring when she was putting it away. It could have landed, unnoticed, on the stack of sweaters and gotten brushed to the floor later. That must be what happened, and she'd thought about it enough.

She glanced at the clock. It was nearly four. If she intended to check the newspaper files in Claysburgh, she'd better leave now. She suppressed a flicker of guilt. No one expected her to punch a time clock, though. She could knock off work whenever she wanted, and if she waited until five the newspaper office might be closed.

Driving down the steep, winding lane off the mountain was a little more nerve-wracking than driving up it. Gillian steered down the middle of the narrow gravel road, hoping she wouldn't meet anyone coming up. She couldn't imagine how they got up and down in the winter. Maybe they just holed up and waited for spring.

She'd pass one more long horseshoe curve, as she recalled, before reaching the gatehouse. Gillian glanced at the sheer drop to the left, seeing the feathery tops of hemlocks and the unwelcoming gray boulders below.

Nausea, sudden and intense, struck her like a fist in the stomach. Her hands clenched the wheel convulsively as she felt cold sweat spring out on her forehead. Oh, Lord, she was going to be sick. She'd have to stop. She couldn't possibly go any further, as the road swam in front of her eyes. She had to stop but there was nowhere to pull off, nothing but steep rocks on one side and the fierce drop on the other.

Just as suddenly as it came, the nausea left. Gillian braked to a stop in the middle of the road, bending over the wheel. For a long moment she could only hang there, forehead resting against the hard plastic. Then she fumbled for the window handle, turned it, and felt the comforting rush of air against her face.

She was all right. Moving as shakily as a very old

woman, Gillian started the car again. She could stop when she got to the gatehouse and turn around. The nausea might come back at any instant. Maybe she was coming down with something.

By the time she reached the gatehouse, though, Gillian felt perfectly normal, not at all feverish. The nausea might never happened. She might as well continue on into town.

Smaller than she expected, Claysburgh boasted a winding main street lined with gingerbread-trimmed wooden buildings. She expected to find the newspaper office there, but instead it was on the edge of town, a long, low, modern plant.

Modern it might be, but files from thirty years ago were still kept on microfilm. The tiny room she was led to became stifling once she turned the machine on.

Gillian leaned over, feeling the heat from the lamp on her head, and narrowed her eyes to read the blurry print. She'd begin with the first of June and work her way forward, looking for any mention of Lake House or her father.

Lake House appeared from time to time, with accounts of special events, visitors of note, that sort of thing. But there was nothing about her father and nothing about the family.

She scrolled forward slowly, then stopped. Clarice O'Donnell smiled up at her from the front page, in an account of the upcoming one-woman show in New York. Even through the reporter's less than skillful prose, even from a distance of thirty years, Clarice's excitement came through. She'd been filled with confidence; it burst through the blurry print and seemed to flood the tiny, stifling room. All that joy, all that enthusiasm . . .

A week later she was dead. They ran the same picture

again, black-bordered this time. Clarice O'Donnell, wife, mother, artist, was dead at the age of twenty-nine, on the eve of artistic success.

Gillian leaned back, covering her eyes for a moment to rest them. She'd known, of course, what happened to Clarice, but she couldn't stop picturing her as alive and vital as she was in the dreams. Seeing the report of her death was like reading the obituary of someone she'd seen yesterday.

An inquest had followed the death. The newspaper report was cautious and understated, a monument to the influence of the O'Donnell family. The Lake House annual Fourth of July celebration had been under way, with a picnic, games, dancing, and eventually fireworks over the lake.

Sometime during the evening Clarice had left the party, apparently to go for a walk alone. No one saw her leave. Perhaps she wanted to find a better vantage point from which to watch the fireworks. When she didn't return by midnight, a search started. Her body was found in the lake the next day.

Gillian swallowed over the lump in her throat. She could picture the searchers, scouring the paths around the lake, flashlights bobbing through the trees. She could sense the gradual realization that there wasn't going to be a quick ending to the search. Clarice wasn't going to be discovered sitting on a log, nursing a sprained ankle.

Had Gillian's father been one of those searchers? Had he walked through the woods, swinging a light, calling Clarice's name? Or had he already left Lake House by then?

She scrolled forward, through accounts of the funeral, until she found a photograph. Robert O'Donnell's face stared bleakly at nothing. Only the shell of the man stood at the graveside, with nothing left inside. He held a child by the hand. Tears stung Gillian's eyes as she bent over, studying those blurred features.

Matt didn't understand. That came through in the photograph. He didn't understand. He looked up at his father with a question on his face, a question Robert O'Donnell had clearly been unable to answer.

Had there been any follow-up stories? Today, newspapers would probably beat the story to death, milking every heart-wrenching detail from the tragedy. Thirty years ago the Claysburgh paper, at least, had been more restrained. After the funeral, they'd apparently left the family alone.

Gillian flipped ahead quickly, toward the end of the reel, finding nothing about her father. Well, she hadn't really expected anything, had she? There was no mention of the young artist-in-residence at Lake House.

The only result of her excursion into the newspaper files was the burning in her throat that resulted from unshed tears. And she'd probably gained a few more vivid dreams to haunt her nights. Even from the safe distance of thirty years, the tragedy reached out to grab the heart.

Poor Matt. He'd probably never understood, at least not until he was much older.

Then another headline seemed to spring out at her. Gillian stopped, adjusting the focus with fingers that were suddenly cold and numb. *LAKE HOUSE OWNER DIES IN CRASH. Robert O'Donnell, proprietor of the famous Lake House resort, died late last night in a tragic accident, only six weeks after the death of his wife, Clarice. Mr. O'Donnell's car went out of control while descending the hotel's narrow mountain road, crashed, and burned. He was apparently killed instantly.*

Gillian turned the knob once more. A picture of the crash scene came into focus, almost in slow motion. She stared at exactly the point on the road where she'd been overcome by nausea.

5

Gillian fastened the butterfly pin at the neckline of her jade dress. Lake House expected its guests to dress for dinner. That had seemed charmingly out-of-date when she read it in the brochure. Now it was something comforting to hold on to. The ritual of changing and doing her makeup might help her avoid the things she didn't want to think about.

Unfortunately, it wasn't working. Nothing could keep her mind from returning, again and again, to the unbelievable truth. Robert O'Donnell had died on that curve. And when she drove down it unknowingly, thirty years later, she was overcome with a physical reaction so intense she had had to stop her car.

She hadn't known. That was certain, she hadn't known. The magazine article Della showed her had given her a comforting explanation for her first vivid dream. Henry's story might have accounted for the second one. But this . . .

She hadn't felt anything driving up the road, either time she'd done it. Was that because Robert hadn't died coming up the road, but going down? Could she really apply logic to a totally illogical set of circumstances?

Coincidence seemed the only explanation. It had to have been a coincidence. People could have strange physical reactions to all sorts of things. Some people broke out in hives at the scent of strawberry. It had to be something equally as reasonable, because if she couldn't explain it, she'd soon be as strange as Della, insisting the house talked to her.

Gillian picked up her key. She would go to dinner and forget all of this for a while. At some point, she'd have to drive down the road again, just to see what happened, but not now.

After dinner there was a showing of *An Affair to Remember* in the Lake Lounge. Gillian stood at the double doors for a moment, watching people file in. It was an older crowd, with a sprinkling of children and a few teenagers. That was evident wherever the guests gathered.

She had expected Lake House to appeal to affluent younger families. Instead the clientele appeared made up of people who'd been coming here for years. Where were the new guests? No resort could thrive without a steady stream of first-time guests.

The film was about to start, but Gillian was too restless for anything so sedentary. She turned to go and found Matt behind her.

The lump on his forehead had receded, turning shades of purple and blue. In the instant before he could speak, an elderly woman fluttered up to him.

"Mr. O'Donnell, whatever did you do to your head? Were you in an accident? It must hurt terribly." Her high-pitched voice caused most of the people in the lounge to look.

Matt's lips twitched in an unconvincing smile. "I'm just fine, Mrs. Eckland. Just fine." His drawl was intense. "It's all your fault. I looked at you in that pretty blue dress, and I walked right into a door."

She blushed and patted his cheek with her blue-veined hand. "The things you say." She turned to Gillian. "Now, don't you believe anything this one says to you, my dear. He'd as soon steal your heart as look at you." She fluttered on into the lounge.

Matt bent closer to Gillian, his smile turning rueful but genuine. "I don't know which of us came off worse that time. Any guesses?" There was laughter in his dark eyes. Apparently their brief quarrel that morning was forgotten.

"Well, you're a flirt and a heartbreaker, while I'm only gullible. I'd say you got the worst of it."

He winced. "Ouch. Let's get out of here before anybody else wants to ask me what happened. I'll give you the guided tour." He took her arm, turning her away from the lounge.

Warmth crept up her arm from his touch, and Gillian nodded. Matt was extending a peace offering. She'd be a fool not to take it. Maybe this time they could have a pleasant conversation, without the odd currents of emotion that kept bubbling up between them.

Establishing a cooperative relationship with Matt would make her job easier. Now, if only she could find a way to ignore her response to his touch, she might be able to get down to business.

Another little knot of elderly people moved toward them. Matt's grip tightened, urging her away. "Come on, before we get trapped again. I'll show you the first floor."

Gillian ran her hand along the satiny rail as they started up. The mahogany stairs were wide and shallow, and seemed worn smooth by generations of feet.

"I see you use British style. The first floor is actually the second floor."

"One of my ancestor's peculiarities." Matt stopped in front of the grandfather clock on the landing, nodding toward the portrait over the fireplace in the hall below. "That's Jeremiah O'Donnell. He emigrated in the 1800's, probably to escape the irate husband of one of his lady friends. He bought the mountaintop in 1857 and put up this center section, the old stone building, the next year."

"The rest of the place grew from that?"

He nodded, lines crinkling at the corners of his eyes. "Family tradition has it he bought the land with jewelry given him by the lady in question. Della denies that, but I think it's true. The old boy's got a wicked gleam in his eye."

So do you, Gillian thought. "I'll have to take a closer look at that portrait."

"Check out the old photographs. They're even better. You'll find them in the Archives Room." Matt led her up the rest of the flight.

"Archives Room? I didn't know you had such a thing."

"We've got everything." Matt opened a glass-paneled door. "If it's a monument to the past, it's here." He flicked a switch and the chandeliers came on, bathing the huge room in soft light. Matt flung out his hand, as if he introduced her. "A case in point: this is the Parlor."

It was the room she'd peered into briefly with Della. Every foot of the massive, high-ceilinged room seemed filled with objects in a conglomeration that ranged from unique to tacky. A museum-quality Ming vase held a bouquet of dusty peacock feathers. A ceramic cathedral stamped "Souvenir of York Minster" sat on a Duncan Phyfe table.

Gillian stared up at a life-size portrait of an Indian maiden above the fireplace. "It's overwhelming."

Matt leaned against the stone mantelpiece, arms folded across his chest, watching her with a sardonic look in his dark eyes. "Like it? We take bets on what people will say when they encounter the Parlor. My favorite is, 'Where did you get all this junk?'"

"It's not junk." Gillian ran her fingers over the elegantly simple Revere teapot. "Not all of it, anyway." The sugar and creamer next to the teapot were pottery, decorated with the Empire State Building and the Statue of Liberty, respectively. "Where did it all come from?"

"Every O'Donnell who ever went anywhere brought something back. Good, bad, or indifferent, it all ended up here. Believe me, some of my ancestors had terrible taste." He hefted a pewter model of Carnarvon Castle on his palm. "Della would have a fit if a single piece were moved. She says it's history."

Gillian turned slowly, trying to take it all in. There were three—no, four fireplaces in the room, and even they were probably insufficient to keep it warm. The two corners nearest the hall had alcoves built into them, elaborate affairs of mahogany with benches upholstered in burgundy velvet. Gillian walked toward the nearest, entranced. It was like something out of a seraglio.

"This must have been irresistible to a child."

"Every time I got in here, I'd pretend." Matt stroked the mahogany rail. "This was a pirate ship or a fort, most of the time."

Gillian wandered into the alcove, feeling as if she'd stepped into a fantasy. She sat down on one of the plush benches. "I can't imagine they turned you loose in here very often."

"Aunt Della chased me out whenever she found me." Matt sat down next to her, his arm brushing hers. "As I got older, I got better at evading her."

"But I thought . . ."

". . . that I deserted the place after my parents died?" Matt trailed his hand down her arm, circled her wrist, then clasped her hand, his palm warm against hers. Awareness tingled along her skin everywhere he touched.

"You did go to live with your grandfather. I guess I thought you rarely came back."

"You've been listening to Della too much. My grandfather sent me back every summer for a visit." His fingers tightened, and furrows etched themselves between his brows. For a moment he looked very like his father.

Gillian seemed to see fireworks against a black velvet sky. "I suppose another time of the year might have been better," she said. They had wandered into personal territory again. Where was the businesslike relationship she'd envisioned?

"Yes." It was brief, but at least she didn't have that sensation of barriers going up. He wasn't shutting her out.

Matt stared down at their clasped hands, giving Gillian the opportunity to study his face. A tiny, crescent-shaped scar marked the outer corner of his eyebrow, beneath the bruise. What had he done to get that? She was close enough to see a muscle twitch at his temple. She wanted to smooth away the frowning lines between his eyes with her fingertips.

He seemed to rouse himself from the dark memories. "Thanks for not telling Della about this morning."

"How did you know she asked me?"

He smiled. "I have my spies. Did she give you a hard time?"

"I can hold my own with her."

His fingers moved slowly along the back of her hand, setting up a warming tingle that spread, radiating from his touch.

"And with me?" The chocolate eyes darkened, challenging her. He toyed with the butterfly pin at her neckline, tracing the outline of its wings, then lay his fingers along her throat. He must feel her pulse, beating against his palm. Matt's face was inches from hers.

A pleasant, professional relationship, that was what she should have with Matt O'Donnell. This wasn't the way to get it. Reluctantly, Gillian drew back. "Maybe we'd better get on with the tour."

For a moment Matt didn't move. Then he turned away and got up. "What else would you like to see?"

Her skin felt cold where his hand had been. She stood up quickly, awkward and off-balance. She turned, at random, toward the nearest door. "What's in here?"

She opened the door on a long, narrow room which apparently ran along one side of the Parlor. Windows lined the opposite wall. They must give a wonderful view of the lake in the daytime, but now darkness pressed against the glass.

Gillian moved to the center of the room. She could glimpse the sparkle of stars through a skylight. Cabinets lined one wall, and splatters of paint covered the wide wooden floorboards. Gillian turned toward Matt.

He stood in the doorway, his hands braced against the frame on either side, as if he held himself back, unwilling or unable to enter.

"This was my mother's studio."

Gillian drew in a sharp breath. In her haste to put some space between them, she'd blundered into another error. "I'm sorry. I didn't mean to bring up unhappy memories."

Matt looked around, his eyes very dark. "I used to love coming here. She had a kid's easel and paints for me." His mouth twisted. "My father didn't like that. Painting wasn't suitable for a boy."

Gillian's heart contracted. The lost, questioning face from the funeral photograph slid into her mind. "You must have loved being with her."

"After she died, I kept coming back to this room. Looking for her, I guess. Remembering." His hands tightened against the door frame until the muscles stood out. He seemed to want to push the walls apart. "Now I hate it."

Gillian moved closer, wanting somehow to take the pain from his eyes.

She stopped. Something, maybe a trick of the light as it slanted in from the other room, altered his face. It drove deep, bitter furrows down his cheeks and turned a lock of thick, dark hair silvery.

"Grief." His voice was so soft she could hardly hear it. The Texas drawl had vanished. "Guilt. That's all I can feel here."

Fear shivered along Gillian's nerves. She wanted to be out of this room. The urge was so strong it was almost panic. It sent her across the floor in a few quick steps.

Matt still blocked the door with his body, big and somehow menacing.

"Matt?" She forced herself to put her hand on his arm. It was as solid and unmoving as iron. "Let's go. I'm sorry I opened the door."

He didn't move. Suddenly he released the door frame, and his hands closed painfully on her arms. Her breath caught as he pulled her against him. Their faces were so close she felt his breath against her lips. Passion, quick and sharp as summer lightning, sparked between them. She could almost feel his mouth on hers, his hands moving on her skin, the familiar shape of his body . . .

Panic surged along Gillian's veins. This wasn't right. This wasn't her.

"No!" She shoved Matt, the unexpected movement sending him staggering back a step or two into the Parlor. She darted past him, her heart pounding in her ears.

Three feet into the room the panic left, falling off her like a coat dropping from her shoulders. She felt weak and drained, and more than a little foolish, but her legs were still shaking and she wouldn't have gone back into that room for anything.

"I'm sorry." She couldn't look at him. Her numbed brain couldn't come up with any explanation or excuse that would make any sense. "Good night."

Matt watched her flee from the room. He drove his hand through his hair. What had just happened? This was crazy.

Anger ripped through him, and he swung his fist against the heavy upright post of the alcove. Damn it, what was going on?

He'd told himself it didn't pay to make an enemy of the person who controlled Lockwood's investment. He'd intended to mend a few fences with Gillian tonight. Instead he'd scared both her and himself.

He stared at the door into the studio, unable to take a step toward it. He used to love the place. When had it started—this feeling that he couldn't stand to be there? And why had he grabbed Gillian that way?

He was attracted to her, yes. All evening he'd wanted to taste that creamy skin and slide his hands down the long, sweet curve of her back. But in that moment in the studio he'd been out of control. He'd wanted her with a passion and a fury that didn't make sense. Worse, it still licked faintly at his veins, like the last flickering flames of a campfire, ready to spring to life again the instant tinder was added.

The sound of a step sent him pivoting toward the door. Brenda Corvo stood there. Desire turned to anger. How long had she been watching him?

"Well?" Why the devil couldn't the woman leave him alone for ten minutes at a time?

"I'm sorry to disturb you." Her smile said she wasn't sorry at all. More bad news, probably. That was her specialty. "Andre says the wrong cheese came in, and he can't possibly make tomorrow's quiche. He's threatening to quit."

Andre thrived on these little crises. If one didn't exist he'd create it, just to generate the proper level of excitement in his kitchen. Confident in his position as master chef, he refused to deal with an underling. Only Matt would do.

"All right." Matt flung a baffled, angry look at the dark studio, then slammed the door. "I'm coming."

❀   ❀   ❀

Gillian didn't slow down until she was in her room with the door locked. She leaned against it, breathing quickly. What had happened in Clarice's studio? One minute all she'd felt was sympathy for Matt, all the more poignant because she understood so much.

The next minute everything had changed. Gillian crossed the room, rubbing her arms to rub away the chill. A long shudder ran through her. She hadn't felt like herself. She'd almost seemed to tap into Clarice's feelings, as if they'd been left behind in the place that had been uniquely hers.

Gillian shivered again, and her gaze moved to the fireplace. Maybe a fire would drive away the shadows.

Laying the fire was a pleasantly soothing task, carrying her back to childhood camping trips with Mitch at her elbow, directing the placement of every stick.

Once the fire blazed she knelt in front of it, holding her hands toward the flames. The sense that she was shaking inside dissipated. She got up and moved the fire screen into position, then changed into her nightgown and robe.

Luckily she'd tucked a few paperbacks into her suitcase. She crawled into bed, propped the pillows behind her, and opened a new mystery novel. Going to sleep right now would be a mistake. She'd stay awake and read for a while to distract herself. She wouldn't go to sleep yet. The print seemed to blur on the page, growing dark and indistinct. . . .

Clarice stood in front of the easel, her brush moving furiously. Concentration emanated from her in waves, intense and complete. Gillian didn't think she'd ever seen anyone so totally possessed by what she was doing.

Light flooded in the windows of the studio, falling on Clarice. Gillian could see her clearly, even though the edges of the room receded into blurry shadows.

Clarice stepped back from the easel, frowning at the canvas through narrowed eyes. Facing her, Gillian couldn't see what was on the canvas, but the flash of triumph in Clarice's eyes said she was pleased.

She extended the brush toward the canvas again, the movement delicate and considering, as if she wasn't sure whether one more stroke might spoil something that was already perfect.

Suddenly the door swung open, slamming against the wall with a crash that sent Gillian's pulses racing. Robert surged into the room on a wave of anger so intense it seemed to charge the very air.

"What the hell are you doing?" Fury deepened the harsh lines of his face. "Don't you know where you were supposed to be this afternoon?"

Clarice stared at him, her emerald eyes wide, focusing slowly as she took in the dark suit and tie he wore. "The reception," she murmured. "Robert, I forgot."

"Forgot?" He took a step toward her, and Gillian's heart beat in her throat. "Forgot? The governor, two state senators, and the head of the tourism bureau were here at Lake House, and you forgot? How the devil do you think that made me look, not knowing where you were? It made me look like a fool!"

Clarice put the brush down, distress darkening her eyes. "Robert, I'm sorry."

"And for what?" Robert grabbed the easel, shook it as if he wished it were Clarice. The canvas toppled, and Clarice

snatched it. *"For some silly, stupid painting? When are you going to grow up, Clarice? This damn hobby of yours is interfering with our lives. With our business."*

Clarice set the canvas back on the easel, her eyes lingering on it as if it were more real than Robert was. *"Your business, don't you mean? This is my business. Not Lake House, and not . . ."*

"Not me?" He caught her by the shoulders, pulling her angrily against him. *"It's more important than Lake House, than me? Than this?"* His mouth closed savagely over hers.

Clarice didn't struggle, even for an instant. Her arms went around him fiercely, her mouth opening under his. He buried his face in her neck, then swung her easily up in his arms, laying her on the daybed, his body covering hers. His lips moved from her mouth to her eyes, down to her throat and the creamy skin of her breast. She clutched him frantically, returning kiss for kiss.

"Clarice." It was almost a groan. *"It's been so long. This is all I want."*

Clarice froze. It was as if she turned into a statue in his arms, a creature of marble instead of a warm, passionate woman.

"All you want." The words dropped from her mouth like individual pellets of ice. *"All you want is a woman in your bed and a hostess for Lake House. That's all."*

He drew back. *"Damn it, Clarice, you know that's not what I meant."*

She swung off the day bed in a quick movement, putting several feet between them. Gillian thought she struggled to maintain the icy control. *"I think it's exactly what you meant, Robert. Unfortunately, you seem to have picked the wrong woman."* She gave him a brilliant smile. "*You should have listened to all those people who advised you not to marry me.*"

"Maybe I should have." He flung himself off the day-bed, fury darkening his face. "If I had, maybe now I'd have a wife who cared more about me than a damn silly painting." With a quick, angry movement he snatched the canvas, lifted it over his head, and slammed it down, driving the post of the easel through the center of it. Before Clarice could move, he stormed from the room.

Clarice lifted one hand toward the canvas in an empty, futile gesture. Her eyes filled with tears, making them look as brilliant as twin emeralds. "Robert," she murmured. "It was the best thing I ever did."

She looked up then, staring across the room, tears spilling over. "It was the best thing I ever did," she said again.

With a shudder of pure terror, Gillian realized Clarice was talking to her.

6

Gillian huddled in the rocking chair by the fire, the bedspread wrapped around her. *A dream, it was only a dream.*

But she didn't believe that. That moment in which Clarice had spoken to her had been more real than most reality. If Clarice had touched her, if she'd felt that long-dead hand on hers, warm and alive, she wouldn't have been able to bear it. Shivering, Gillian poked the fire, sending a cluster of sparks flying. Sheer terror had wakened her.

Was she going crazy? She didn't think so, but how many explanations were there for this?

In a way, it would make sense if her dreams were about her father. She'd come here to find him. Instead, she was obsessed by two people she hadn't known existed just a few days before. *Obsessed.* Was that what it was—an obsession?

A fragment of memory slid into her mind. She'd been six or seven, awakened by the kind of dream that ended in screams and a cold sweat. Her mother and Mitch had soothed her, petted her, fed her warm milk, and finally left the room, satisfied that she was asleep, but she wasn't. She huddled under the covers, eyes open a slit, afraid to let herself relax.

Mitch and her mother paused outside the door. She could see them, dark figures against the light.

"It's getting worse." Her mother sounded frightened. "What are we going to do?"

Mitch put his arm around her. "We aren't going to panic, first off. She'll be fine."

"But what if she realizes?" It was a whisper. "What if she realizes she's dreaming true?"

"Don't say that!" Mitch's voice was as sharp as Gillian had ever heard it. "It's a coincidence, that's all. She needs to be distracted. We'll look into those gymnastics lessons she's been talking about."

"It's his fault." Her mother's voice faded as they moved away from her door. "He always claimed he knew things."

Gillian frowned at the fire, considering the memory. If she'd ever thought of that moment in the intervening years, she certainly hadn't attached any importance to it. Even at a time when her college friends embraced channeling and crystals, she'd been the scoffer. Because that was what she'd believed? Or because she was afraid of what she might find?

The fire burned low, so she tossed another log on, not wanting to give up its comforting light. Was that the answer? Did she possess some sort of—what, ESP? Some sixth sense she'd inherited from Alec McLeod that allowed her to pick up the vibrations left by people now dead? That was not a particularly happy conclusion, but maybe it was better than believing she was going crazy.

Reluctantly Gillian moved toward the bed. She didn't want to trust herself to sleep, but she wouldn't be able to function tomorrow unless she got some rest.

She curled into a protective ball against the chilled sheets. She would not dream again tonight. She wouldn't. Crazy or psychic, she would do the job she'd come here to do.

"There you have it." Ada Clemens, head of the Housekeeping Department, folded her massive arms over her equally massive bosom. "That's how my department runs." Her tone suggested that any criticism would be unacceptable.

"You certainly have everything at your fingertips, Mrs. Clemens." Gillian glanced over the charts which showed where every member of the housekeeping staff was at every minute of the day. She'd bet they were there, too. Mrs. Clemens was not a person to trifle with.

Mrs. Clemens acknowledged that compliment with the slightest inclination of her iron-gray head. She wouldn't be bought by cheap flattery. "I do my job." She looked with satisfaction around the tidy, utilitarian office. "And I don't interfere in other people's business." Her face darkened. "Not like some I could mention."

Was that a hint of dissension in the ranks? Curious, Gillian prodded a bit. "It's important, in a place like Lake House, that departments don't get in each other's way." She paused. Would Mrs. Clemens bite, or would discretion win out?

"There's some who have to learn that. Coming in here with a fancy degree and fancier clothes, trying to interfere with my department. I soon told her what's what." Her mouth clamped shut.

Brenda Corvo was obviously the culprit who'd tried to interfere with the Housekeeping Department. She should have had more sense. You didn't interfere with the Ada Clemenses of the world. You either accepted them or got rid of them.

"You've been here a long time." Gillian looked at the framed picture showing a much younger Ada Clemens, arrayed with her staff on the croquet lawn. Had it been long enough to provide answers to any of the questions that burned in Gillian's mind?

"Forty years."

"That's wonderful. Not many people stay with one institution that long. The O'Donnells certainly must appreciate your loyalty."

"Some do."

If the woman got any more sparing with her words, Gillian would have to start paying her by the syllable. How could she possibly get the conversation around to the period that interested her when the woman wouldn't chat?

"Matt—Mr. O'Donnell—told me that yours was one department he never had to worry about." That wasn't exactly true, although Matt hadn't indicated that he did worry about Housekeeping. In any event, it seemed the right thing to say. Mrs. Clemens' frostiness thawed into a genuine smile.

"Matt knows he doesn't have to worry about me. I've been here since before he was born."

"I suppose you knew him well when he was a little boy. Before he had to go away, I mean." Gillian hesitated, willing to be interrupted, but the woman just nodded. "That was tragic—to lose both his parents and then have to go so far away."

"He shouldn't have." The words burst past the woman's iron control. "He shouldn't have had to leave. If Della hadn't wanted him to go . . . " She stopped, obviously thinking she'd said too much.

"Della wanted him to go?" That wasn't the impression Della gave her. "I thought she wanted to keep him, but his grandfather insisted."

"That's what she says." Mrs. Clemens paused meaningfully. "But I think—"

The door swung open, and they both looked up, like two conspirators.

"There you are, Gillian." Della floated in, a tie-dyed scarf billowing behind her. She looked vaguely surprised at finding Mrs. Clemens in her own office. Or was that all an act? Had she heard what the woman was saying and decided to interrupt?

Mrs. Clemens rose. "It's time I checked on my staff." She marched to the door, then turned. "My files are open to you, Ms. Lang. No one can say I'm not cooperative."

Della looked at the retreating figure. Gillian had an impression of active dislike, quickly masked by Della's usual out-of-focus air.

"Silly woman." Della drifted around the desk, touching papers aimlessly. "Why would you be interested in anything she had to say?"

"It's my job to look into every department at Lake House." Gillian removed a cleaning schedule from Della's hand and returned it to the proper stack.

"Lake House isn't facts and figures." Della's hands fluttered. "It's atmosphere, tradition. You can't define it with a ledger sheet." She swung on Gillian, her voice suddenly vehement. "You should know that. Don't you?"

Gillian's pulse jumped. Della sounded as if she knew about her dreams. "I don't understand what you mean."

"Don't you?" Something dark and shrewd in Della's eyes seemed to fade. "I just thought . . . well, never mind." She swung round in a little pirouette, scarf flying. "You saw Clarice's studio last night. What did you think of it?"

"How did you know that?" Gillian's voice was sharp. If Della thought she could spy on her, she'd better think again.

"I just know. Did you feel Clarice in there? That's where she is, you know. That was the only place in all of Lake House she cared about—her studio."

"What do you mean?" Gillian hoped she sounded more in control than she felt. "Why should I feel her presence?"

"I thought you might. You seem interested in Clarice. But you shouldn't be. She was never really part of Lake House."

Gillian clutched her pen until it cut into her hand. "Why wasn't she part of Lake House?"

Della made random brush strokes in the air. "Her painting. That was all she cared about. Not Robert. Not Lake House." Della's voice was a terrible echo of Robert's voice, in Gillian's dream. "Robert knew that, and it just about killed him. Oh, he tried to stop it—to stop her painting from taking her away. But he couldn't."

"How did he try to stop her?" Her lips were almost too stiff to form the words.

"He smashed one of her paintings." In a dreadful parody, Della raised empty hands above her head and then swung them down. Gillian winced as she heard the rip of canvas and Clarice's anguished cry.

"No." Gillian shot to her feet, leaned across the desk. She had to challenge this. "He didn't."

"He did." Something flickered in Della's eyes. "You knew, didn't you?"

"What's going on?"

Neither of them had heard his footsteps. Gillian blinked. Matt had obviously just come from working out. He had a towel slung over one shoulder, and his tank top clung damply to his chest, defining every muscle. He looked from her to Della and back again, frowning. "What's wrong?"

"Nothing." Gillian's cheeks warmed. How much of that bizarre conversation had he overheard?

Matt's dark gaze cut to his aunt, and she shrugged. "I was just telling Gillian about the dance Friday night in the lounge. She's going to come, aren't you, Gillian?"

Apparently Della was no more anxious than she was to let Matt know the subject of their conversation.

"I don't think so."

"But you must." Della went to the door. "Matt is looking forward to dancing with you."

He held the door for her with mocking courtesy. "I'll make my own dates, Aunt Della. Thanks anyway."

Della drifted out, and Matt closed the door. He turned to Gillian, his dark eyebrows lifting. "How about it?"

She looked at him blankly, her mind still unable to adjust to the jolts it had received. "How about what?"

"The dance. You should come. You can't work all the time."

She had to concentrate on one thing, instead of skittering from one problem to another. She tried to smile.

"Mr. Lockwood didn't send me here to play. I have work to do."

He frowned. "Is that it? Or are you afraid what happened last night might happen again?"

Last night . . . how could he know about her dream? No, he had to be talking about that equally crazy moment in Clarice's studio.

"No, of course not," she said quickly, not sure whether that was true or not. She had an insane urge to blurt it all out to Matt, to tell him about her father, the dreams, everything. But how could she? He'd think she was crazy. Maybe she was.

"Look, Gillian, a blind man could see you're upset. If it's not about last night, what is it?" He came past the desk and lightly touched her elbow. Up close his very skin seemed to glow with vigor. Energy radiated from him in waves. He didn't fit into this tiny office. It was like trying to keep a panther in a closet.

"It's nothing." She remembered Clarice, trailing her palm down Robert's chest, across his stomach, and had to suppress the desire to do the same thing. She groped for something safe to tell him. "Della just . . . " She let that trail off, not sure she wanted to bring up what Della said.

Matt's face hardened, a muscle twitching in his jaw. "What did Della say? You might as well tell me."

The urge to speak flooded over her. *Tell him, tell him everything, and be done with it.*

"She knew we were in your mother's studio last night." It would be easier to think if his fingers weren't caressing the sensitive skin on the inside of her elbow, if he weren't close enough to sense the blood coursing through his veins.

"Sometimes I swear she's got a surveillance system set up." His words were light, but anger radiated from him, his fingers tightening against her skin.

"She started talking about your mother and father."

Matt didn't move. He just . . . withdrew. "Aunt Della talks too much. Don't pay any attention to her."

Gillian took a deep breath. She had to find the words to tell him. "The incident she told me about—it was familiar to me." She looked up, meeting his gaze. "I dreamed about it last night."

His eyes seemed to go opaque, as if masking his thoughts. He let go of her arm as if it were hot. "I don't want to talk about them."

Now that she'd started she couldn't stop. She wanted somebody—she wanted Matt—to know what she'd been going through. "It wasn't the first time." She said it quickly, because he was turning away. "Ever since I got here, I've been dreaming about them."

Matt's fists clenched until the muscles stood out on his forearms. Anger rippled along his skin. "You hear a tragic story, so you dream about it. Some people get off on sad stories. I didn't think you were one of them."

"I'm not!" This was turning out all wrong. She hadn't begun to make him understand.

"But then I don't know you very well." He went on as if she hadn't spoken. "So let's understand each other. I don't want to talk about my parents. And I don't like gossip." He turned, giving Gillian the urge to hurl something at his broad back.

"I wasn't gossiping. I just . . . "

"Have work to do," he finished for her. "You'd better get on with it. My family's private life has nothing to do with you."

*   *   *

By Friday, Gillian's anger had subsided to a low simmer. She hadn't seen Matt at all, which was probably just as well. Even better, she hadn't had a single dream. It was as if, having reduced her to a state of sheer panic, her subconscious or whatever it was had decided to behave.

She came back to her makeshift office after lunch to find that someone had put mail on her desk—a note from a friend, a memo from the office, and a letter from Mitch.

Gillian walked to the window and stared out at the lake, the envelope in her hand. A single canoe drifted slowly across azure water. Was it a good sign or a bad sign that the note was from Mitch?

She opened it and read news about her sister, the twins, the latest on Mitch's summer recreation program. And then what she'd been waiting for.

Your mother wasn't willing to write you about this, so guess it's up to me. As far as we know, Alec McLeod left Lake House sometime the week of the Fourth of July. A letter she sent him was returned with a note saying he'd left before his contract was up, leaving no address. Your mother and grandparents did their best, but they didn't have the money to spend on private investigators. When a suitcase of his turned up later at the train station in Chicago, she assumed he'd gone to California. He'd tried to talk her into going before, so she figured—Well, anyway, that's all I know. Guess it's not much. Good luck and remember we love you.

Gillian walked slowly back to the desk and sat down. The week of July fourth. That wasn't much help. If, as she supposed, the Artist-in-Residence program was

Clarice's idea, perhaps he hadn't felt like going on with it after her death. Or Robert might have wanted to be rid of the program, with its reminder of Clarice. Although if that were so, surely they'd have told her mother that.

She folded the letter, then realized there was something else in the envelope. The photograph was old, but still sharp and clear. Two people leaned against a battered van, its rust covered by painted rainbows.

Her mother wore an ankle-length dress. With her hair parted in the center and flowing over her shoulders, the effect was remarkably medieval.

Her father . . . He was so young. That was her first thought. The face beneath the soft, straggly beard hadn't yet lost the curves of youth. Certainly he was too young to be responsible for the baby he looked at with so much love, love so strong the picture seemed to shout with it.

Gillian blinked back tears, feeling an ache in her throat. She'd never pictured them so young. Certainly she'd never pictured the love. If that was how he felt, why on earth hadn't he taken them with him? She might have grown up on a commune in California, renamed Moonbeam or something like that.

Maybe she already knew the answer to that. Motherhood had effectively ended Margaret's brief counterculture fling. She'd reverted to the solid Pennsylvania German stock from which she'd sprung. Her parents had been only too happy to have their erring daughter and her baby back under their roof. They'd probably been relieved when Alec McLeod decided to disappear.

The office door swung open without a warning knock. Instinctively Gillian dropped the photograph in her lap.

Della stood in the doorway, her eyes moving from the envelope on the desk in front of her to Gillian's face. Had she seen the photograph?

"Is there something I can do for you?" Gillian prompted.

Della drifted across the room, eyes returning to the envelope. "I just wondered." Della leaned on the desk. If she was trying to read the return address she'd be disappointed, because the envelope lay facedown.

"You wondered?" Gillian slid her chair forward, effectively hiding the photo under the desk.

"I mean, I wanted to remind you of the dance tonight." Della's hands fluttered over Gillian's desk, plucking absently at the papers. Gillian put her palm down on the letter from Mitch.

"I don't think I feel like dancing, Della. Thanks anyway."

"Oh, but you must." Today Della wore an Indian shawl, and its fringe tickled Gillian's arm as she leaned forward. The faint odor of sandalwood enveloped her. "I'm sure Frederick expects a full report. Doesn't that include sampling all that Lake House has to offer?"

Gillian gritted her teeth. If it meant getting rid of Della, it might be worth dancing on the tabletop. "Fine." She switched her computer on. "If I finish my work, I'll see you there."

Three hours later, Gillian began to think she wouldn't be finished. Something was oddly skewed about the reservation figures. She worked out the percentages again. Why should the cancellation rate be this high? Any hotel routinely expected a certain number of cancellations for any given date, but for a resort hotel, those figures should be on the low side.

Frowning, Gillian printed out her results and carried the printout down the hall to Brenda Corvo's office.

Brenda was on the phone when Gillian looked in. A shadow of annoyance crossed her face, but she gestured Gillian to a chair. "Yes, I'll take care of it. I'm afraid I can't talk any longer just now."

Today the blouse Brenda wore under her Lake House blazer was a designer model Gillian herself had priced, but not bought, in Saks. Most of Brenda's salary must go on her back.

"Now, what can I help you with?" Brenda gave her the attentive look of the perfect assistant. "Is the office working out all right? No problems with the computer?"

"The office and computer are fine." Gillian handed her the printout. "This concerns me."

A frown ruffled Brenda's polished surface. Gillian thought she suppressed the urge to say, *So?* "I don't see a problem here."

"You don't think the ratio of cancellations to reservations is rather high?"

Brenda paused, then spread her hands. "Well, I could deny it, but of course you're right. It was clever of you to spot it."

Gillian took that compliment just as sincerely as Brenda meant it. "How do you account for this?"

"I'm afraid it's another of Matt's innovations. He decided to relax the deposit requirement, so naturally people feel much freer to cancel."

"I see." Gillian waited a moment to see if Brenda would add anything. "You feel that accounts for this figure?"

Brenda ran a perfectly manicured fingertip along the dark fringe of her bangs. "I suppose word-of-mouth might affect it, and the economy, of course."

Did Brenda really accept that as an explanation? If so, she wasn't quite the efficient little assistant manager she pretended to be. It might not occur to Matt to check the cancellation rate, but it should be second nature to Brenda.

"Anything else I can explain to you?" Brenda dropped the printout on her desk and folded her hands on it with the air of one who's satisfactorily disposed of a problem.

"No, I don't think I need to trouble you any more about it." Not when she could find out for herself.

Gillian started down the hall toward the reservations desk and then paused, looking at her watch. It was late to start something so time-consuming today. She could make a fresh start tomorrow on the whole reservation system.

There had to be a flaw somewhere to account for this, and a relaxed deposit policy didn't cut it. There simply shouldn't be that number of cancellations. Maybe confirmations weren't sent in a timely manner, or guests weren't given the accommodations they requested. This problem, at least, she should be able to unravel.

The music that spilled out of the Lake Lounge was a Big Band sound that probably appealed to the hotel's older guests. Gillian paused in the doorway. The wood-paneled lounge with its polished floor had been turned into a ballroom. A fire blazed in the huge fireplace, and the nondancers who were settled in comfortable chairs around it would probably have to be blasted out of their seats.

"What do you think of it?"

Gillian turned to see Henry Morrison hovering on the edge of the dance floor. He gestured with a punch cup toward the orchestra.

"Shades of Tommy Dorsey," Gillian said lightly as she joined him. "It's a good choice for this crowd."

"The old fogies, you mean." Henry's smile took any sting out of the words.

"Not at all. I like music you can dance to."

"Then I shouldn't miss my opportunity, should I?" He flushed slightly, fumbling with the cup before putting it on a nearby table. "Shall we?"

Henry's dancing, unlike his photography, was uninspired. Gillian kept her feet from under his with an effort and tried to think of something to talk about.

"Is the orchestra a local group?"

Henry nodded. "Lake House has been the impetus behind a number of local musical groups, summer theaters, that sort of thing. They knew they'd have an opportunity to perform here, you see." Regret crossed his face. "Not so much anymore, unfortunately."

"Have things really changed that much?"

"Sadly, yes." Henry backed into another couple, flushed, and murmured an apology. "At one time, programs went on all the time. Lake House even produced a weekly newspaper of sorts. Oh, just a couple of pages listing events, telling who won the tennis tournament, what the fishing was like, that sort of thing. Small potatoes, I suppose, but it was nice. Made people feel they belonged."

"It sounds like a great idea." Could Henry hear the excitement in her voice? "How long ago was that?"

"Oh, twenty or thirty years." He smiled diffidently.

"I've been coming here a long time, I'm afraid. Creature of habit."

So maybe that paper had been in existence thirty years ago this summer. Here was an unexpected opportunity, dropping into her lap.

"Do you know if any copies exist of things like program booklets or the newspaper? I'd be interested in seeing them."

"Fodder for your report?" Henry raised colorless eyebrows. She couldn't tell if he took offense at the idea.

"Not exactly. It doesn't really affect the current status of Lake House, but it would give me a clearer picture of where it's been."

"You're in luck, as it happens." Henry tried a pivot and tripped. "Sorry. What were we . . . oh, yes, the papers. Knowing how reluctant Della is to throw anything away, I suspect it's all neatly filed in the Archives Room."

Matt had mentioned something about that the night he showed her around, but subsequent events had driven it from her mind. "Thank you, Henry." She gave him a smile that made him blink. "I'll try that."

Henry stumbled again. "I'm afraid dancing isn't my forte."

"Why don't we just watch?"

"It might be safer." Henry led her to the edge of the dance floor.

Should she try to tell him he wasn't so bad? Maybe a change of subject would be better.

"How did your photographs turn out the other day? Or don't you have them back yet?"

"They're finished. I have a darkroom here, in the depths of the cellar. They turned out fairly well, although summer isn't my favorite time for photographing the mountains." His neutral face took on more animation than she'd seen yet tonight. "As a matter of fact . . . "

Gillian felt her eyes begin to glaze over as Henry expounded on the qualities of light to be found at different seasons. She turned slightly to watch the dancers as she nodded and smiled, and found herself focusing on a particular set of broad shoulders across the room.

As if he felt her gaze, Matt turned. A moment later he'd put down his glass and started across the room.

He should have blended into the sea of dark suits, but he didn't. His self-assured, confident walk cleaved a path through the crowd, arrowing straight toward her. Light from above burnished his chestnut hair, emphasizing that strong jaw. His shoulders filled out the dark jacket just as thoroughly as they did the flannel shirts he preferred. A flash of silver against dark called attention to the ornate longhorn belt buckle he wore, defiantly Western in this conventional crowd.

"Mind if I steal this lady for a dance?" Without waiting for Henry's answer, Matt put his hand on her waist and turned her onto the dance floor.

Gillian's steps matched his without the need for thought. He settled his hand a little more snugly at her waist, drawing her closer. His breath touched her face, sending tendrils of warmth through her. "Giving me the silent treatment?" he said softly.

"Why would I do that?" Every cell in her body wakened to the strength of his arm around her, the way his hand enclosed hers possessively.

"I seem to recall a few sharp words the last time we were together."

Did he expect an apology? Gillian looked at him warily. "We were both upset." That was as far as she'd go.

Whether he accepted it or not, she'd only tried to tell him the truth.

"Thanks to dear Aunt Della." Lines tightened around his mouth. "She seems to have a gift for it."

Agreeing would be tactless, even if true. How far did that malicious streak of Della's extend? "I suppose she meant well."

Matt looked about to disagree, then seemed to think the better of it. "Maybe."

The orchestra swung into a slow ballad, and he pulled her closer. Her breasts pressed against his chest, and the dense, nubbly texture of his suit penetrated her thin silk dress.

"Now, this is my kind of song," he whispered, the movement teasing her skin.

Warm honey flowed along her veins, slow and languorous. Her body moved with his almost without volition. They might have danced this way a hundred times before. The beat of the music worked its way into her pulse, maddeningly familiar. She'd heard it somewhere, recently.

"What is that song?" Her lips formed the words against the warmth of his cheek, almost as intimate as a kiss.

"'A Summer Place.' Appropriate, isn't it?" He hummed a line, and the echo reverberated in his chest.

"Very." Also appropriate for the era that haunted her days and nights. A little shiver worked its way down her spine. "A Summer Place" was the song she'd heard the first time she dreamed about Clarice.

Maybe Matt sensed something. He guided her toward the French doors at the end of the lounge. "Let's get some air."

The wooden deck stretched out over the lake, where moonlight placed a silver path across the surface, barely hinting at the icy depths moving beneath. Gillian walked to the railing under a row of Japanese lanterns and looked down at black water.

"I feel as if we're floating. What's holding the deck up?"

"Steel beams, along with the solid rock shelf the hotel sits on."

Matt joined her, and they leaned on the railing side by side, arms touching from elbow to shoulder, his suit sleeve rough against her bare skin.

"Everybody said it couldn't be done, but I figured it was worth a try."

"You built this?"

"Every O'Donnell who's ever lived here has added something. I didn't personally lay every board, but it was my design." A smile tugged at the corners of his mouth. "I drove the contractors crazy until they agreed to do it my way just to shut me up."

He turned, drawing her around with him, until their backs were against the rail. A breeze from the lake sent little shivers along her skin, and he pulled her into the warm circle of his arm.

"Take a look at it." He gestured toward the massive building, all angles and balconies and improbable turrets. "Every generation contributed something. My grandfather built those little gazebos you see along the trails."

Gillian had seen the open summer houses perched on every height, most of them just big enough for two facing benches. They had odd conical roofs, vaguely Eastern, like pointed caps. "Let me guess. He'd been on a trip to the Orient."

She felt Matt's chuckle. "Right. Everybody adds something," he repeated slowly. "Even me. I'm adding Lockwood Hotels, Inc. to the family name."

"Don't." She touched his smooth cheek, the urge stronger than her caution. "It's a different time, that's all. A different situation."

Matt put his hand over hers, then turned his face to press a kiss into her palm. The movement of his lips on her skin was intimate and tender, sending a shaft of excitement along her nerve endings.

"You've got a soft heart under that business-like exterior, Gillian Lang." His hands moved to her shoulders, then slid slowly, possessively, down her back, drawing her against him.

"I don't think I look especially businesslike tonight," she whispered. His touch did odd things to her breathing.

"No, you don't. I like you better this way." His fingers combed teasingly back through her hair, slid to the sensitive nape of her neck. "Let's forget about business for a minute or two." His lips brushed hers, featherlight. "Okay?"

Gillian pushed common sense aside. "Just for a minute or two," she repeated.

His mouth claimed hers lazily, as if they had all the time in the world. He laid a trail of moist, seductive kisses across her cheek, to her temple, the delicate skin of her eyelids. Gillian was drowning in something warm and sweet, and she never wanted to move again.

He came back to her mouth deliberately, his tongue tasting the contour of her lips. Gillian slid her hands under his coat, molding the fine cotton of his shirt to the warm hard muscles beneath. His heartbeat quickened— or was that hers? For an instant the image of Robert and

Clarice, locked in each other's arms, flickered across her mind like lightning across the summer sky. Disturbed, she drew back a fraction of an inch.

"Maybe . . ." she began, her mouth against his.

The door opened, spilling music and several people onto the deck. Matt released her calmly, unembarrassed, keeping one arm snugly around her.

"Time to circulate." He sounded as if he regretted it. "The owner's always on duty."

"I know." Maybe by the time she got inside, her heart rate would return to normal. The image of Robert and Clarice touched her mind again, chilling her. It didn't have anything to do with this.

Matt circulated. She circulated. Was it her fault their glances touched so frequently across the crowded floor? Each time it happened, her mind swung dizzily.

There were several very good arguments for not letting herself become involved with Matt. But they kept sliding away each time she looked at him.

First of all there was her job, not to mention his feelings about her job. She shouldn't kid herself that he'd forgotten that. But when he smiled at her, warm and secret from across the room, she wanted to forget.

There were too many things he didn't know, her rational self argued desperately. Her dreams, the secret about her father . . . the list was dauntingly long. Against it she could only stack the fact that no one had ever made her feel the way that Matt did.

The orchestra played a final number. People started for the doors. Gillian saw Matt turn, eyes searching the room for her. Pure panic enveloped her. If she didn't stop this now, when would she?

Brenda Corvo put her hand on Matt's arm, claiming

his attention. Gillian couldn't hear the words, but they seemed to be arguing about something. Matt, his face dark with anger, shook his head. Brenda persisted. Finally, looking furious, he followed her out.

Gillian went up to her room alone, feeling as if she'd gotten all the way to the top of the high dive and they'd closed the pool. She didn't have to make a decision after all. At least not now. She didn't have to wonder whether she'd have let Matt walk up to her room, unlock the door, go inside . . .

Two steps into the room, Gillian found a good reason to be glad Matt wasn't with her. In the middle of her pillow lay the Florentine ring, and the air was filled with the scent of jasmine.

7

Gillian stared at the ring, suppressing the urge to back out of the room. She wouldn't do that. Whatever happened, she wouldn't run away.

Cautiously, as if it might bite, she picked up the small gold circle. Again it felt warm to the touch. She didn't know whether to be relieved or not. Weren't ghostly presences supposed to be accompanied by bone-chilling cold? The ring was warm, the room was warm, and the smell of jasmine was overpowering.

She crossed to the balcony door, unlatched it, and threw it open. The breeze cooled her face, carrying the dark, mingled scents of the forest. The air should get rid of the jasmine, but it couldn't get rid of the cause.

If Matt had come into the room with her, would he have been able to smell the jasmine? Or was it something only Gillian herself could sense?

She stared out at the moonlight reflecting on dark

water. There were only two alternatives. Either she had been visited by a spirit, or someone was playing tricks on her. This wasn't a figment of her imagination, whatever else it was.

The repeated appearance of the Florentine ring had to mean something. Gillian held it up, so that the ceiling light sparkled from its stones. The fine, twisted gold filaments of the setting formed an intricate nest for the center stone, almost as intricate as the situation.

Had someone given this to Alec McLeod, or had he bought it for someone? She couldn't think of another conclusion. Was that someone connected with Lake House? That seemed to be the message behind the appearance of the ring now.

Gillian jerked her mind away from a conclusion she didn't want to consider. Quickly she went to the closet, pulled out her suitcase, and dropped the ring inside. She locked the suitcase and put its tiny key in her handbag. That would make it harder for a living person to play tricks on her. Whether ghosts were deterred by locks was another story.

Could it be Della's doing? It wasn't hard to picture her indulging in malicious tricks. In fact, this was just the sort of stunt that would appeal to her. Unfortunately, that assumed Della knew about the ring and understood its significance, which was unlikely, if not impossible.

At least, in any rational world, it would be impossible. Nothing that had happened to Gillian since she came to Lake House fit into a rational pattern.

She should concentrate on what she could do, instead of tormenting herself with questions that didn't have answers. Gillian forced her mind to focus on solid courses of action.

On the job front, she had to lock down the cause of that anomaly in the cancellation rate. And on her own personal agenda, she had to find the artist's cottage. She'd check out the Archives Room first thing in the morning. There had to be answers somewhere, and she was going to find them.

Gillian set the file drawer on the oak table and glanced around at ceiling-high shelves and rows of filing cabinets. Everything that had ever been printed about Lake House was stored in the Archives Room, which was surprisingly well-organized. Some of Della's scatter-brained exterior must be camouflage, if she was responsible for this.

The file drawer for the year Gillian wanted contained a little of everything: menus, newspaper clippings, advertisements, an earlier version of the trail map, and copies of *The Lake House Gazette*. Gillian spread one of the four-page newsletters out on the table.

The Gazette had been poor quality mimeographed copy thirty years ago. It wouldn't be easy to read, but a sense of excitement gripped Gillian nonetheless. At last she'd find some mention of Alec McLeod. If Lake House went to the trouble of having an Artist-in-Residence, they'd certainly publicize that fact.

She sorted through the copies. There wasn't much point in starting to read earlier than late May. Her father hadn't arrived at Lake House until the first of June.

The Lake House Gazette had been written entirely by Della O'Donnell. The woman clearly had more gifts than Gillian had thought at first. Della's devotion to Lake House shone through her sometimes awkward

prose. Gillian found descriptions of the flowering rhodo-
dendrons, sketches of new flower plantings, and lists of
upcoming events. There it was, in faded purplish ink:
Artist-in-Residence Arrives.

The article described the new program in less than
glowing terms. Gillian frowned. Was that an indication,
even then, of Della's dislike for Clarice's artistic inter-
ests? Maybe, since Della waxed eloquent over every
other cultural event at Lake House.

Gillian stacked the summer's worth of papers in front
of her and began to read. Since she didn't know what
she was looking for, other than any mention of her
father, she'd have to read them all.

Fifteen minutes later, she rested her gaze on the far
wall, frowning. *The Gazette* covered every event faith-
fully. It listed sketching walks, drawing classes, and an
exhibit of pen-and-ink drawings. Again and again, articles linked the names of Clarice O'Donnell and Alec
McLeod. Was she imagining it, or was there really a
malicious undertone to Della's reporting?

Gillian turned a page and found a sketch of the artist's
cottage. She stared at it, committing the design to memory. The tiny cottage had a porch across the front, decorated with intricate gingerbread trim. She hadn't seen
anything like that yet at Lake House, but when she did
see it, she knew she'd recognize it.

She picked up the July 1st issue with a sense of dread.
Enthusiasm for the upcoming celebration bubbled from
the pages. An outdoor picnic would go on all day, along
with a band concert, games and races for children and
adults, and dancing under the stars, all of it culminating
in a spectacular fireworks display over the lake.

Unknowing, the paper went on to list events for the

following week. They'd probably never taken place after the tragedy.

Gillian paused at the mention of a familiar name. Frederick Lockwood, local businessman, was one of the speakers for a seminar to be held that week. That shouldn't surprise her. Lockwood came from this area and had ties to Lake House. The phrase *local business-man* seemed a little slighting, but thirty years ago Lockwood Hotels, Inc., had been nothing more than a gleam in the man's eye.

A quiver ran along Gillian's nerves as she turned to the next issue. This would be the first issue to come out after Clarice's death. How would Della handle that?

It was dated July 22nd. Apparently it had taken that long to bring things back to some semblance of normality. Clarice was remembered in a touching, black-bordered biography, written by Henry Morrison. Henry's admiration for her gifts and his grief came through clearly.

Blinking back tears, Gillian turned the page. It was morbid for her to become so upset by a death, no matter how tragic, that had taken place thirty years ago.

Artist-in-Residence Program Ends. Startled, Gillian stared at the article for a moment before starting to read.

The Artist-in-Residence Program ended unexpectedly earlier this month with the departure from Lake House of artist Alec McLeod. Apparently upset over the death of Mrs. Robert O'Donnell, patron of the Residence Program, Mr. McLeod left Lake House in the early hours of July 5th, leaving behind a brief note of apology to the students he was disappointing. Anyone having unfinished work at the Artist's Cottage may collect it during the afternoon hours this week. Lake House apologizes for any inconvenience this has caused its guests.

Gillian flattened the paper under her fingers and read the piece again, as if that might make it easier to understand. Her father left Lake House in the early hours of July 5th, in other words, probably immediately after the discovery of Clarice's body. Why? Why would Clarice's death, however tragic, affect him so badly that he'd leave immediately? Hadn't he at least wanted to stay for the funeral?

She could think of few possible explanations, and she didn't like any of them. Had Robert, in his grief, turned on a person he suspected of having too close a relationship with his wife? Or had Alec's sorrow been so great he couldn't bear to stay? Either way, she was drawing closer and closer to a conclusion that she didn't want to face.

The computer on the reservations desk beeped obligingly and displayed the reservations for the month of February. From a few feet away, Fred Carsten, the clerk on duty, watched Gillian covertly, blue eyes round and curious.

A summer intern, Fred gained college credit by working at Lake House for a tiny stipend. He hadn't been here in February, so he couldn't tell her anything about reservations or cancellations.

Gillian frowned at the screen. She might not be any more knowledgeable than Fred was, in this case. In the good old days, before computers, every transaction would have left a paper trail. That would have given her something to go on. There seemed no way of telling, from the sparse information recorded on the computer, why there were so many cancellations.

She scrolled backward. A flood of reservations for the

winter sports season had come in early in January. That was just what she'd expect. The hotel should be full every weekend, with a respectable midweek crowd.

But when she flipped ahead to February, the actual numbers were far below expectation. Not only had people cancelled, in many cases they'd cancelled so late that it had been impossible to fill their rooms.

"Hard at work, I see." She looked up, startled, to find Matt leaning across the reservations desk. "Or have you decided to take over from Fred?"

"I wouldn't dream of it. Fred has to go back to school in the fall and justify his internship with all he's learned."

Fred, observing them, couldn't guess at the undercurrents beneath their casual conversation. Matt had to be remembering last night, just as she was.

Matt propped his elbow on the monitor, apparently planning to stay for a while. He glanced at Fred, who seemed to pick up an unspoken message.

"I'll . . . I'll just run these files down to Ms. Corvo's office now, if that's okay." He flushed, then quickly slid from behind his desk. "Back in a few minutes."

When he'd gone, Gillian shook her head. "You shouldn't chase the poor kid off that way. He's already scared to death of you."

"Won't hurt him to be a little in awe of the boss." Matt's eyes crinkled. "It's good for my ego."

"I'm not sure your ego needs any help."

He captured her right hand in his. "I enjoyed last night. I wanted to see you later, but Brenda had another emergency."

The way her pulse raced from the pressure of his palm against hers, maybe Brenda's emergency had been

a good thing. Gillian shouldn't become involved with
Matt O'Donnell. Unfortunately, her body didn't seem to
be listening to her brain.

"Something Brenda couldn't handle on her own?"
She tried to sound as if she cared about Brenda and her
problems, but it wasn't easy when Matt chose to rest
their clasped hands on his thigh.

A spasm of annoyance crossed Matt's face. "Brenda
has a bad sense of timing. Since we didn't get to finish
our conversation last night, how about this afternoon?"

"This afternoon?" Gillian wavered between yes and
no. She shouldn't. She wanted to.

"You haven't enjoyed one of Lake House's greatest
pleasures yet," he said in low voice.

It took some effort for her to achieve the right amount
of lightness. "What might that be?"

Matt's dark brows lifted. "Why, horseback riding, of
course. What did you think I meant?"

Gillian was saved the embarrassment of answering by
the swift click of heels as Brenda Corvo hurried into the
room. Her expression when she saw them together
nicely mixed surprise with deference. Somehow Gillian
didn't quite buy the surprise.

"Oh, I'm sorry, Matt. I didn't realize you and Ms.
Lang were working."

Matt let go of Gillian's hand and slid off the desk with
no impression of hurry. "I'm not working, just interrupting Ms. Lang's work. Was there something you wanted?"

"Fred mentioned that Ms. Lang was here." Brenda
allowed a shade of annoyance to enter her expression as
she looked at Gillian. "I thought I'd given you all the
information you needed about reservations."

Gillian's eyebrows went up at her tone. That sounded

like a challenge. She'd walked onto Brenda's turf, and Brenda didn't like it.

"I find it helps to work directly with the reservations desk. Do you have some objection?" If she did, she was going to have to voice it in front of Matt, and Gillian didn't think she'd do that.

Matt didn't give her the opportunity. "Brenda, I thought I made it clear Ms. Lang was to be given access to everything." His hand wasn't holding hers anymore. Instead it was curled into a fist. "She's to have everything she needs for her report to Mr. Lockwood, understand? Everything."

The harsh words were directed at Brenda, but the backlash of his anger hit Gillian. For a time, last night, he'd been able to forget why she was here. Now Brenda had managed to underscore that fact forcefully. Had she intended it? Gillian wasn't sure.

"Yes, of course, Matt," Brenda murmured. "I was only trying to help."

She'd helped, all right. Matt withdrew, clearly regretting he'd let down his guard with her. All in an instant, they were back on opposite sides of a chasm.

"I'll let you get back to work," he said curtly. Brenda followed him out the door, her lips curving in the slightest of smiles.

Brenda was certainly the busy creature, involving herself in every aspect of her employer's life. She had to have known that Gillian was here, and that Matt was, too. Last night her emergency had effectively stopped whatever might have happened between them, and she'd just managed to do the same thing again.

The annoying thing was that Gillian ought to be thankful. Brenda had put a businesslike barrier back between her and Matt, which was just what she'd been telling herself she should do. So why was she angry enough to want to call Brenda up on the computer screen and delete her?

An hour later, Gillian was ready to delete herself, if she could have. There had to be some way of figuring this out. Why wasn't she smart enough to see it?

"Are you ready?"

Gillian looked up, blinking in surprise at Matt. When he'd stalked out earlier, she'd assumed he wouldn't come back.

"Ready for what?"

"Riding." His glance flickered over her suit. "You'll have to change. You'll scare the horses if you go out dressed like that."

His attempt at a light touch didn't quite work, and he seemed to know it. Before Gillian could say anything, he shook his head.

"Sorry. Look, I was rude earlier. I apologize." He bit the words out, as if apologizing wasn't something he did well.

Gillian chose her words carefully. "I know this situation is difficult. Maybe it would be better if we kept it as businesslike as possible."

Amusement gleamed in his dark eyes. "You think you can do that?"

She tried not to smile back. "Well, I can try."

"I don't want to try. I want to go riding. With you." When she still hesitated he rolled her chair away from the desk. "You're working too hard. I want to talk to you, and I think better on horseback. Come on."

If Matt wanted to talk, that made it business, didn't it? That probably wasn't valid reasoning, but she'd go with it anyway.

"You win. I'll be ready in twenty minutes."

"Make it fifteen."

There didn't seem to be any doubt in his mind that she'd do just that. Maybe somebody ought to dent that confidence of his a little, but it wasn't going to be Gillian Lang.

Gillian let Matt take the lead as they started out the trail that wound past the tennis courts and the baseball field. She wasn't a bad rider, but she certainly wasn't in his league.

Matt settled into the saddle as if he'd been born to it. His body had a fluid grace, moving in tune with the big paint gelding. The horse danced nervously as a tennis ball hit the fence near him, and Matt controlled him with the slightest pressure of his long legs.

"Remind me never to let you ride behind me," Gillian said.

Matt drew his horse to the side so that she could come up next to him. He grinned. "Bouncing a little, are you?"

"Bouncing a lot," she admitted. "It's been a long time since I was on a horse."

He surveyed her critically. "Not bad. Carry your hands a little lower. Trixie doesn't need much guidance to do this trail."

"In other words, all I have to do is stay on. And listen."

He looked at her quizzically. "Listen?"

"You said you wanted to talk."

She was sorry she'd mentioned it when his face tightened. For a moment he looked very much like his father.

"I decided I owe you an explanation."

Gillian wasn't sure what to say. "It isn't necessary—"

"I think it is." He frowned, patting the curved neck of the pinto. "I've given you a hard time the last few days."

He had given her a hard time, but knowing what she did, she could understand.

"I don't much like going in with Lockwood, and that's the truth of it." He hesitated, and for a moment she thought he wasn't going to say anything else. Then he shook his head. "I don't like failing." He spat the word out. "Hell, I don't even like saying the word. That's what going in with Lockwood means. I failed."

She'd thought his brash confidence needed denting, but that had already happened, and she found she didn't like it. If only she could find something to say that would be both comforting and honest. Matt would know in an instant if she said anything she didn't really mean.

"I'm sorry," she said finally. It was the only thing she could think to say.

He stared at the trail ahead for a moment, his jaw tight, and then he nodded shortly. "Okay. Thanks."

They rode in silence for a few minutes, long enough for Gillian's guilt feelings to kick in. It hadn't been easy for Matt to admit that to her. He was being honest, at least. While she . . . she tried not to think of the long list of things she hadn't told him.

She'd tried, hadn't she, to tell him about her dreams? He hadn't wanted to hear it. What she hadn't said was the crucial piece. She hadn't told him who her father was. The weight of it seemed to ride along with her, though she honestly didn't know whether it would make a difference to him or not.

"Have a look." Matt reined his horse in, and she drew up beside him. Her breath caught in her throat.

"What is it?"

Ahead of them stretched an area the size of several football fields, completely filled with rocks and boulders, with scraggy bushes clinging to them precariously here and there.

"The boulder field." Matt nudged his horse forward. "A few eons ago, the glaciers withdrew. They carved out the lake and the cliffs. And they dropped this field full of boulders on their way."

Off to the left of the trail, the ground dropped down to the lake. A boat dock extended into the water, several rowboats tied to it. The trail itself wound through the boulder field, then entered the woods again on the other side.

"It's astonishing." The word didn't seem adequate. "Isn't it dangerous? I mean, if someone tried to walk on it?"

The horses moved along the trail, placidly indifferent to their surroundings. Gillian felt as if she'd been dropped onto an alien lunar plain.

"The rocks won't shift, if that's what you mean, not out in the center of the field. You just have to be careful not to trip and break an ankle, that's all."

"That's all?" she echoed, and Matt grinned.

"Relax. The horses know their way around." He nodded to something ahead of them. "There's the only area where we have to be concerned about rockfalls."

A rocky hill veered sharply upward at the end of the boulder field, its base a scree of loose stones. "That looks recent," Gillian said.

"Nothing's happened lately. The last fall was quite a few years ago."

The horses moved closer. There had been a building of some sort there, partially demolished by a rock slide.

"I'd intended to stabilize the whole area and put in

some cottages here." Matt's face tightened. "We'd done the preliminary plans before things got so tight."

In other words, the hotel's financial problems had forced him to abandon the project. How many other plans had Matt had to give up? He'd tried to tell her Lake House didn't mean much to him, but everything she saw told her just how much it did mean.

"What was here before?" Even as she asked the question, she knew the answer. She recognized the ginger-bread trim on the porch.

"Just a cottage," Matt said. Obviously it didn't mean anything to him. "It was used for different things. At one time it was fitted up as an artist's studio."

Gillian swallowed hard. "Can we go inside?"

He looked surprised. "Sure, if you want. It's safe enough. Just not worth repairing."

Matt dismounted, helped her down, and then tied the horses to what was left of the porch railing. Gillian started up the rickety steps, and he grabbed her arm.

"Careful. I wouldn't guarantee there's not a rotten board or two."

Gillian didn't answer. Some feeling she couldn't begin to describe forced her into the cottage. She had to go in. Something waited for her there, had been waiting, maybe for years. She put her hand on the sagging door, pushed it open, and stepped inside.

Sunlight poured through the broken skylight. Dust, cobwebs . . . No one had been here in years. Thirty years, maybe?

She took another step and a wave of emotion swept over her. It battered her, a fierce storm of grief, guilt, desire . . . above all, fear. Her own fear, so strong she battled to keep it under control.

"A mess, isn't it?" Matt kicked at the blackened logs in the fireplace. "I'd like to tear it down and build something decent here."

Couldn't he feel it? He stood there talking casually, oblivious. She tried to cling to his calm voice, but she couldn't. Something pushed her toward the fireplace, like hands shoving her urgently. Fear trickled along her veins, and her legs were so heavy she could barely move.

She stared down at the remains of a long dead fire. Matt's kick had dislodged something. A fragment of something that had once been white uncurled itself. It demanded that she pull it out.

"Careful," Matt said as she reached toward the fireplace. She stooped, warily touching the thing that called to her.

Canvas unrolled in her hand. The scorching along the edges didn't keep her from seeing what it was.

The painting was half-finished. Deep down, Gillian knew why it hadn't been completed. Because it couldn't be. Because its subject was gone. Dead.

Clarice's long hair swirled about her face, brushing the shoulders of an elaborate Renaissance gown. The gown wasn't finished, but the face was.

So were the hands. On one long elegant hand, Clarice O'Donnell wore the Florentine ring. Gillian didn't need to look at the scrawled *McLeod* in the corner to know who had painted Clarice wearing it.

"It's . . . my mother." Matt sounded winded, as if someone had struck him in the stomach. She'd feel sorry for his shock, but she couldn't cope with her own feelings.

She dropped the canvas, and it rolled back in on itself, hiding what it contained. Too late, that was all she could think. It was too late. She'd already seen it. Maybe, in some terrifying way, she'd known what she was going to find. She could only see one answer. Her father and Matt's mother had been lovers.

Rage, black and fierce, battered at her. Rage, then heart-wrenching grief. Then guilt, so strong it nearly pulled a sob from her.

Gillian stumbled to her feet. Didn't Matt feel it? The emotion swept through the ramshackle cottage, building like a tornado, and like a tornado would destroy everything. She had to get out of here. She had to!

8

Matt stared at Gillian. She was afraid; he could sense it. He wanted to reassure her, but the words eluded him. A sick tide of guilt surged over him. Before he could speak, Gillian bolted from the cottage.

"Gillian, wait!"

He burst through the door. She had stopped a few steps from the porch, gasping for breath, her whole body shaken by inaudible sobs.

"What is it?" He grasped her wrists, his heart pounding, and turned her to face him. "Why did you run?"

"The painting," she murmured. She stared at him, her pupils dark and dilated. Why did she react so strongly to this? He was the one who'd received the shock.

"My mother," he finally said. Pain twisted inside him, and he tried to speak through it. "I had no idea it was there. It must have been painted that last summer."

"Yes."

Gillian brushed back a lock of russet hair. Her hand was shaking. Why was she so upset? If anybody had a right to overreact to what they'd found, it was he.

"What's going on?" He gripped her shoulders so hard that she winced under the pressure of his hands. "Why are you so upset over it, Gillian? Why?"

She stared up at him, her eyes still wide with shock. For an instant longer anger controlled him. Then, before he knew what was happening, he pulled her against him, his mouth seeking hers.

She resisted briefly. Suddenly she came to life against him, her mouth eager, her arms going around him. She clutched him with frantic need.

Desire pounded in his blood. No, more than desire. Desire wasn't a strong enough word for this. Her lips, her body, her very breath was his. He'd found her, he held her at last, he'd never lose her again . . .

It was like the night in the studio. With a wrench that felt like cutting off his arm, he put her away from him. He was dizzy with longing, with need. Slowly, one breath after another, he regained control.

"Sorry. I didn't mean to do that."

Gillian took a cautious step away from him. She looked as shaken as he was. This was crazy. What the devil was happening between them?

"I'm sorry, too." She shook her head. "That was as much my fault as it was yours. I felt . . . "

She stopped, as if afraid to say any more.

"What? What did you feel?" He carefully didn't touch her, even though he wanted to force the words out of her. He didn't know what might happen if he touched her again.

She didn't answer.

"Look, Gillian, we have to talk. Why were you afraid?" Damn it, she had to explain. Somebody had to.

For a moment the emotion he'd felt in the cottage swept through him again. Guilt, intense, soul-searing guilt. Then it was gone. "Well?" he demanded.

Gillian moved to the mare, patting her absently, and Trixie rubbed her nose against Gillian's shirt. Maybe that contact with reality was what Gillian needed. When she looked at him again, the fear faded from those blue-gold eyes. In its place was caution mixed with a kind of rueful humor.

"I don't think you want to hear this."

Damn it, he couldn't scare her again, not if he wanted answers. He leaned against the porch post, trying to look more relaxed than he felt. "Try me."

"I did try, the other day." Her eyes darkened. "I tried to tell you about the dreams I've been having since I got here. You thought I was crazy." She gave a shaky laugh. "Sometimes I've thought so, too."

That again. He would cut her off short except for one thing. Something weird happened to him, too. Something that wasn't quite himself took over that night in the studio, and again just now.

"I don't think you're crazy. No more than I am, any-way." He sat down on the porch step, forcing himself to stretch his legs out, lean back, at least look accepting. "Okay. You've had dreams about my parents since you've been here. Maybe you're . . . " He groped for an explanation. ". . . sensitive to the atmosphere."

"You really think that's it?" There was doubt in her voice.

"I don't know," he said slowly. "But I've been places in the world where uncanny things happen."

The strain in her face ebbed at his words. He patted the step beside him, and she sat down warily. He couldn't blame her for that.

Gillian stared down at the ground. The sunlight, slanting across the boulder field, turned her hair to flame. He had the notion it would burn him if he touched it.

"I'd like to think it's nothing more than atmosphere," she said, the doubt still there.

Somehow he had to get her to relax enough to talk to him. They had to make some sense of this.

"Out in the desert, at night, I've felt things I couldn't explain, things I didn't want to talk about the next day. Maybe there wasn't any explanation. Maybe there are some things you just have to accept."

She looked up with a ghost of a smile. "I've never been very good at accepting things I can't explain."

"The perfect businesswoman," he said lightly. "Why don't you try telling me what you felt in there?" He reached for her hand, then stopped. No, that wasn't a good idea.

"I felt . . . I felt as if something made me find that piece of the painting. As if it had been waiting for me. I felt . . . " She shook her head. "A lot of emotion, and none of it mine. Guilt, mostly. It scared me."

Guilt. It hit him like a body blow. Guilt. He was vaguely aware of something else being left unsaid, and he didn't know whether to push her or not.

"That was pretty clear. You ran out of there as if a stampede was after you."

"That's about how it felt. I'm sorry." Her hands linked together, her knuckles white.

"You don't need to be sorry." There was something he had to say before she blamed herself any more. It wasn't going to come easy, but he owed it to her.

Her hands twisted. "But I've reminded you . . . "

"Don't," he said shortly. "Look, Gillian, maybe the guilt feelings you're picking up are mine."

"Yours?" She looked at him, startled. It was clear that hadn't occurred to her. "What do you have to feel guilty about?"

Now it was his turn to stare at his hands. He could feel that intense blue gaze on his face, and willed himself to stay expressionless. "I told you my mother drowned in the lake. I didn't tell you all of it."

She went very still, watching him. "What else is there?"

"That night, the night she died, she came to my room to tell me goodnight." He'd been angry that he had to go to bed before the fireworks. He'd planned to stay awake, somehow, so he could watch from the window. "She was upset, I could tell. She talked about how she might be going away. She told me goodnight, but it felt more like good-bye."

He heard the soft intake of Gillian's breath. "And you think . . . "

"I think she was telling me good-bye. Maybe what happened that night wasn't an accident. Maybe my mother killed herself."

Gillian put her key in the lock, then hesitated. If the ring was out again, it would be one blow too many. She forced herself to open the door.

The room was just as she left it, with her blazer slung across the chair. The ring was apparently still where it belonged, thank goodness. The things that had happened this afternoon were enough to contemplate.

Once he'd dropped that bombshell about his mother, Matt had withdrawn. He wanted her to accept what he said with no questions and no discussion. She could hardly blame him. If he really believed his mother had committed suicide that night, what a terrible blow for a five-year-old to handle!

And there was something more: the question of guilt. After bringing it up, Matt had clearly not wanted to pursue it. He felt guilty. He felt, with a reasoning she could understand only too clearly, that he was somehow to blame.

She knew that feeling. Maybe every child who lost a parent at an early age felt that. She certainly had. Even though she didn't have any memory of her father, she still felt guilty. Maybe, if it hadn't been for her, he wouldn't have left.

She walked to the window. The sun, low in the sky, cast dark shadows across the lake. Gillian shivered. Matt had said the Indians called it the bottomless lake. It never warmed up, even at the height of summer. The night Clarice died it must have been cold, dark, terrifying.

If she had killed herself, where did Alec McLeod fit in? When Gillian looked at the fragment of painting, out there in the cottage, she'd been sure the ring on Clarice's hand was the Florentine ring. Now, suddenly, she was assailed by doubt.

Even if her father had painted Clarice wearing the ring, did that necessarily mean that they had been lovers? She'd assumed all along that if she found the woman linked to the ring, she'd have found the answer. Now, she just wasn't sure. Or maybe she didn't want to be sure.

She still hadn't told Matt everything, not the details of the dreams, and certainly not who her father was. She didn't know what Matt might do if she told him that. It would shatter the fragile bond that had begun to grow between them, and she couldn't stand that thought.

If he knew, Matt might complain to Lockwood about her. She didn't like to think about Lockwood's reaction, if he knew his employee had been using an assignment to pursue something personal.

Gillian ran a hand through the tangles of her hair. She had to be sure about the ring in the painting, that was clear. After telling her about his mother, Matt had gone back into the cottage and come out with that piece of canvas, his face tight and expressionless. He'd carried it into his office when they got back. It was probably still there, and she needed another look at it. She had to be sure.

And she had to find someone to talk to about that summer. Della? She rejected that thought immediately. Della was too unpredictable, and she had too much at stake in this situation.

Henry Morrison was probably the only real choice. He'd been here that summer, and he'd already talked to her about it.

Fear had flickered on his face when she'd mentioned the scent of jasmine in the hotel. Did Henry see things or smell things here at Lake House, too? If so, he ought to be curious enough about her to talk.

She felt better with a clear objective in sight. No, two objectives: get another look at that painting, and talk to Henry Morrison. One or the other of those actions ought to give her something to go on.

°   °   °

Sitting with Henry at dinner would have been ideal, but he was already at another table when Gillian entered the dining room. The two elderly couples seemed determined to monopolize him. They settled in the library with him after dinner, still talking, while Gillian glanced idly at the books on the shelves and fumed.

Henry finally excused himself and strolled out into the hall. Gillian slid a wildflower book back onto the shelf and followed him. She caught up with him on the porch.

"Out for a walk?" She tried to sound as if bumping into him was a pleasant coincidence, and wasn't sure she succeeded. But it didn't really matter, as long as she could convince Henry to talk about that summer.

"I thought I'd walk through the flower gardens. Would you care to join me?"

Gillian nodded, falling into step beside him. How was she going to bring up such a difficult subject? Henry pulled out a pipe and made a production of getting it going. That gave her a few minutes to think.

Unfortunately, no brilliant ideas occurred to her. They walked around the corner of Lake House, where the path wound through dozens of rosebushes.

Henry waved the pipe. "This is why I take a walk every evening. It's my one vice, and I don't like to inflict it on others."

"Any excuse is a good one to come out on an evening like this." The setting sun traced a path of gold across the rippling lake, and the air was heavy with the scent of old-fashioned roses.

Henry stopped to pluck a pale pink one from the bushes that lined the path. He handed it to her and she took it carefully, inhaling the rich scent.

"The Audrey Hepburn rose," Henry said. "The gardeners try a few new varieties each year, although most of the beds are laid out as they have been for the last hundred years."

Enthusiasm warmed his usually neutral expression. Apparently Henry had another passion beside his photography that kept him at Lake House.

"I'm afraid I know very little about flowers," Gillian confessed. "My mother tried to make a gardener of me, but it didn't take."

It might break the ice with Henry to talk about something he loved, but her thimbleful of knowledge wasn't going to get her very far.

"You can't come here and not appreciate the gardens."

Henry led her under an arbor, gesturing with his pipe at the swaths of flower beds that spread out beyond it. They curved across the green lawn, a rich mosaic of color. Each bed was crowded with a single variety of flower, in a single color.

"Look at them. This may be the best example of Victorian bedding gardens in the East."

Gillian stopped. "These are begonias, I know that. I love the salmon color. Why are the beds all laid out with a single color?"

"Typical Victorian idea. Tame nature, make it behave itself." He looked as if he found that amusing. "The beds are shaped into geometric patterns, so that the whole effect is that of a tapestry, laid across the mountain. They were originally designed by Matt's great-grandfather. He had to have the soil brought up from the valley. Nothing would grow in the thin layer of soil over rock that was here originally."

"It's spectacular." Gillian identified periwinkles and pansies, as well as the brash orange of marigolds. Maybe she hadn't forgotten everything her mother taught her. Her mother would be pleased if she thought those hours in the garden hadn't gone to waste.

Henry guided her toward a round stone summerhouse, its peaked roof echoing the tiny gazebos that sprouted along the trails. "Let's sit and enjoy for a few minutes." He pointed to the green foliage that surrounded the base of the summerhouse as they went in. "Oregano, sweet basil, peppermint." He inhaled. "Wonderful aroma."

This was her chance. Gillian leaned back on the stone bench. If she could figure out how to bring up the subject, she had Henry all to herself. Unfortunately that was a big if.

"I hear you and Matt went riding this afternoon. Did he take you out the Laurel Trail?" Henry puffed on his pipe, and the smoke obscured his face.

"I don't know the name of the trail, but we went out past the boulder field. We stopped at the old artist's cottage."

Henry tensed slightly, but when he spoke his tone was calm. "That old place should have been torn down years ago. It's dangerous."

It had felt dangerous to Gillian, but not in the way Henry meant. She hadn't been afraid of any physical danger. She couldn't tell him that, but she'd have to tell him something if she expected to get him talking.

"Maybe it's a good thing it wasn't torn down. We found something there today."

Henry's hand gripped his pipe until the knuckles whitened. "Found something? What was it?" He didn't succeed in making the words sound casual.

"A fragment of an old painting, apparently of Matt's mother. Odd that it would survive so long, but I guess it was protected by the logs on top of it."

"I see." Henry made a production of knocking his pipe against the stone bench. Maybe it gave him an excuse not to look at her.

"It wasn't in very good shape, but I'm sure Matt will be glad to have it anyway. The canvas was signed *McLeod.* Do you know who that was?" Gillian held her breath.

For a long moment Henry didn't answer. She began to think he wouldn't, but then he cleared his throat.

"Alec McLeod. He was here that last summer, the summer Clarice died. The painting must have been done then."

"Was he a guest?"

"No. No, Alec McLeod wasn't a guest." Henry braced his hands on the edge of the stone seat, looking down. She couldn't see his face. "Clarice talked Robert into having an Artist-in-Residence that summer. The idea was that McLeod would encourage the amateur painters, give a few classes, do some painting of his own that would be exhibited here."

"And one of the paintings he did was of Matt's mother?"

Henry frowned. "I remember that there was talk of her sitting for him, but I didn't realize it actually happened. Clarice was so busy that summer. A major show of her own was scheduled for autumn." His voice roughened. "The gallery had it anyway, of course, but she wasn't there to see her triumph."

This was heading in the wrong direction, and Gillian wasn't sure how to bring it back except to be blunt.

"She must have found some time to sit, because the

painting was partially done. Matt has it in his office, if you want to see it." She paused, but he didn't add anything. "I'm afraid Matt was upset by the whole thing. He remembers that it was a difficult summer, even before his mother's death."

She couldn't bring herself to repeat what Matt had said about the possibility of suicide. That was a confidence she wouldn't share with anyone.

Henry shook his head. "I didn't realize Matt had picked up on that. I suppose children understand more than we think. Clarice was on the verge of success, and poor Robert couldn't seem to share it. All he could see was that her painting was taking her away. It made things very lonely for Clarice."

"She had you. You certainly understood her artistic gifts. And I suppose McLeod must have been someone she could talk to, as well." She was holding her breath. She let it out carefully, as if it might give her away.

Something pained crossed Henry's face. "Yes, she had me, much good as I was to her. I'd have done anything in the world for Clarice."

The words sounded like a benediction. Gillian looked at his averted face. It still wore the polite, well-bred mask, but she thought she saw what lay beneath.

"You were in love with her, weren't you?" Gillian wanted to call the question back as soon as it was out. She shouldn't intrude on his pain this way, no matter how desperately she wanted to know the truth.

To her surprise, Henry leaned back with a little half-smile. "Does it still show, after all this time? I suppose it does. Oh, it was never a secret."

"Robert knew?" Given Robert's jealousy, that was hard to believe.

Henry nodded. "Robert knew how I felt about Clarice. Perhaps he even thought it was amusing. He knew he didn't have anything to worry about from me."

Did Robert worry about Clarice and someone else? That was what she should ask, but before she could find the courage to get the words out, Henry stood up.

"Sometimes I think every man who met Clarice fell half in love with her. That's the kind of woman she was. And in the end . . . " He paused, shaking his head. "In the end, none of us could save her."

Gillian sat in her office, hands idle, staring out at the darkness. She'd come in here to work, but instead she kept replaying that conversation in her mind. Poor Henry. He'd loved Clarice, and apparently lost her twice, once to Robert and then again, finally, to death.

Why had Henry talked so openly to her? There were a dozen points in that conversation at which he could have cut her off, and as many opportunities for him to try and find out why she was interested. Did he guess? No, how could he? Maybe he just wanted to talk to someone about Clarice. Clearly he still loved her, after all this time.

Gillian put down the pad on which she'd been trying to organize some notes for her report. Nothing Henry said proved that her father and Clarice had been lovers. But he'd borne out her belief that Clarice had been desperately unhappy that summer. Caught between her artistic success and her husband's demands, she could have turned to someone else for comfort—someone who shared her dreams, someone who understood what drove an artist.

Maybe she was jumping to unwarranted conclusions. She'd been sure, since she saw the ring and learned it wasn't her mother's, that a woman had given it to her father. But that didn't prove anything. It didn't prove that Alec McLeod and Clarice O'Donnell were lovers. It certainly didn't prove that Clarice had committed suicide because of him.

Gillian shoved her chair back. She had to look at the painting again. If she was certain that the ring on Clarice's hand was the same ring found later in her father's things, she'd have at least one fact nailed down.

She couldn't ask Matt to let her see the painting again. What explanation could she possibly give? But he'd put it in his office, and the offices were seldom locked. Nothing prevented her from walking in and looking. Nothing, she thought as she switched off the light and closed the door behind her, except her own fear of finding out, or of being caught.

The hallway stretched, silent and empty, in front of her. Gillian strolled along, glancing at the photographs that lined the walls. It was after eleven. No one was around. There'd be no one to see her slip into Matt's office. She slowed as she reached the door, took another quick look down the hallway, and turned the knob.

As she'd expected, the office was unlocked and dark. That presented a problem she hadn't foreseen. She'd have to turn the light on and risk being seen by anyone passing on the outside. Maybe she'd better stay away from a life of crime. It didn't look as if she'd be very good at it.

Gillian switched on the light and crossed quickly to the desk. Sometimes you just had to take a chance.

Matt could have put the piece of canvas anywhere,

but she'd expect it to be in or near his desk. She pushed the swivel chair away from the desk. It creaked, setting her nerves jangling.

This had been Robert's desk. The thought slid insidiously into her mind as she touched the warm, smooth mahogany. He'd run his empire from here, all of it except the woman he loved and tried to control.

That wasn't just based on her dreams. Della had confirmed it, and Henry had added his impressions. He thought Robert feared losing Clarice to her success.

A wave of sadness swept over Gillian. If Robert loved Clarice, instead of just wanting to control her, he'd acted in exactly the wrong way. He'd forced Clarice into making a choice she probably hadn't wanted to make, and in doing so he lost her.

What was she doing, standing here thinking when someone might come in and find her at any moment? She yanked open a drawer. She had to find the canvas, look at it, and get out.

It wasn't in the top desk drawer. Feeling like a thief, Gillian slid open the second drawer. There it was.

Matt had wrapped the canvas with clean paper. She lifted it carefully onto the desk top and let it unroll. She intended to look only at the ring, but her eyes were drawn inexorably to the painted face.

Was it a trick of the light, that desolation she saw there? Clarice's emerald eyes were filled with sorrow, seeming to beg for understanding, for help. Gillian shook her head. No, she was seeing what she expected to see, that was all.

There wasn't any doubt. The ring on Clarice's hand and the ring in Gillian's suitcase upstairs were exactly alike. For an instant she toyed with the idea that there were two identical rings, but she knew that was ridiculous. The Florentine ring had been Clarice's.

Gillian let the canvas roll itself up again and slipped it back into the drawer. She'd come here to find the truth. She just hadn't expected it to weigh so heavily on her.

She slid the drawer closed, then rested her hand on the warm surface of the desk. There wasn't anything else to be found here. She should leave, before someone walked in on her.

Something moved slightly, in the corner of the room. Gillian looked up, trying to focus her eyes on the faintest shift in the air beyond the range of the lamp. The shadows in the corner seemed to draw together, thickening as she watched, almost as if someone stood there, lingering in the dark. A chill ran down her spine. Something was there, something . . .

The door swung open suddenly, and Brenda stood staring at her. The shadows, if they'd been anything more than her imagination, receded.

Brenda took a quick step into the room. "What are you doing here?"

Gillian's hand closed on a notepad that lay on the desk. "I was about to leave a note for Matt. Is anything wrong?" Her pulse slowly returned to normal.

"I suppose not." Brenda's expression said she didn't believe Gillian for a minute. "If you'd like to give it to me, I'll be glad to see that he gets it."

"No, thank you. I'll leave it on his desk when I'm finished." Gillian looked pointedly at the door. "You don't need to wait."

Brenda lingered in the doorway. Gillian stared at her, raising her eyebrows.

"Fine," Brenda snapped. She slammed the door.

Once Brenda was gone, Gillian scribbled a brief note. She had to. No doubt Brenda would report this late night visit to Matt at the first opportunity.

She half-expected Brenda to be waiting outside the door to watch her leave, but the hallway was empty. Gillian walked quickly toward the stairs. It was too empty, too lonely, and there were too many things she didn't want to think about, not now.

Maybe she wasn't alone after all. She could hear a thread of music, coming from the Lake Lounge. Someone was playing the piano.

She rounded the corner and stopped. Beyond the staircase, the double doors to the Lake Lounge stood open. The lounge was dark, and from the darkness came the tinkle of piano keys. "A Summer Place."

For a moment she stood there, her mind spinning. Then her thoughts crystallized into anger. Someone was playing a trick on her, probably the same someone who'd moved the ring around her room until she'd locked it away. This time she'd catch him or her.

Gillian had to step into the dark to reach the light switch. She touched the switch, and the lights blazed on. The music stopped abruptly. She could see the piano from where she stood. No one sat there, and the lid was closed.

But she wasn't alone. Figures moved, dancing just beyond her line of vision. As she swung to look they vanished, but she caught the faintest breath of jasmine in the air.

9

Gillian looked from her computer screen to the receipts that were spread across her desk. This didn't make sense. But then, maybe nothing would make sense this morning, after the sleepless night she'd had.

She'd run, actually run, all the way to her room from the lounge. Once inside she'd locked the door, but still felt frightened. What good was a locked door against the perils of her own mind, or her senses, or whatever it was that conjured up what she'd heard last night?

She couldn't say seen, not with any degree of certainty. She hadn't really seen anything, just that flicker from the corner of her eye. Somehow that sense of something lurking beyond the boundaries of vision had been more frightening than anything else.

For a long time she hadn't been able to sleep. She'd been afraid to. What might creep into her mind when she was helpless to stop it? Finally, sometime around three, she'd fallen into a heavy, dreamless sleep from which she'd had trouble rousing herself.

Now this oddity had cropped up to complicate matters. Frowning, Gillian went back through the purchase orders, back through the invoices, and back through the computer records. She'd done this three times, and each time she kept coming up with the same answer. She'd found a discrepancy in the food and beverage records.

Discrepancy? Was that the right word? This wasn't her area of expertise. She was management, not accounting. She knew enough to spot a problem, but not enough to tell whether it was a simple mistake in accounting procedures or something much more serious.

She went over the whole thing again, her head beginning to ache. Nothing changed. There was still a problem that had to be explained.

Finally, frustrated, she stuffed the records and her notes into a folder and slid the whole thing into a desk drawer. She could double check the records with Andre, the chef, but from what she'd seen of him, he wouldn't welcome such a discussion. And Matt certainly wouldn't thank her if she made his prized chef angry enough to quit.

No, this information had to go to Matt, and to Frederick Lockwood, of course, when she submitted her report. She frowned down at the desk. What would Lockwood make of this? She'd like to have something a little more definitive before she presented it to him. The only way to do that was to try and get to the bottom of it.

She slid her chair back. She had to talk to Matt about this. Maybe he would want to tackle Andre himself, and possibly bring in his accountant to look over the situation.

Matt wasn't in his office, and she finally tracked him

down in the Parlor. She paused in the hallway, looking in on a three-cornered discussion. He seemed to be refereeing a battle between Della and Brenda.

Gillian suppressed an urge to back quietly away. *Coward,* she told herself, and walked in on them.

Della's scarlet face expressed more feeling than Gillian had seen before. Something had certainly dissipated Della's usual vagueness.

"You've been told and told!" Della's voice rose as she glared at Brenda. "Nothing in this room is to be moved."

Brenda had gone icy with anger. She tapped a clipboard with one red nail, looking as if she'd prefer to use it on Della. "It's my job to make arrangements for the concert this week. We can't possibly have a world-famous pianist play in the midst of all this clutter."

Gillian winced. Clutter was definitely not the word to use.

"Clutter! This collection is priceless!" Della turned to Matt. "You tell her," she demanded. "Tell her you won't have things pulled about."

"There is a concert," Brenda said, emphasizing the last word. "We have to have space for seating."

"You can easily set the chairs around the things that are already here. There's no need to make a mess." Della grabbed Matt's arm. "Tell her!"

Matt detached himself from his aunt's grip with something approaching desperation. Gillian tried not to smile. If the man existed who wanted to intercede between two strong-minded women, Gillian had yet to meet him. At least this wasn't her battle.

Matt patted Della's shoulder. "I'm sure we can work this out. Brenda, why don't you let me discuss this with my aunt? You don't need to set up today, do you?"

"I suppose it can wait until tomorrow." Brenda's tone was grudging, and she slapped the clipboard against her hand. "But then I have to have a decision. We can't expect Theodore Banks to perform in such slipshod conditions." She stalked out of the room.

"Matt, you must—"

"In a minute, Aunt Della. I think Gillian wants to talk with me."

Before Gillian could speak, Della had pounced on her, grabbing Gillian's arm.

"Gillian will bear me out," she declared. "It would be criminal to haul things around in here. That Brenda would send a crew in and clear the room if she had her way."

"I'm sure she wouldn't . . . "

"Set up rows of folding chairs, I suppose," Della went on. "Try to make it look like a high school auditorium for Theo's visit."

"You certainly wouldn't want that," Gillian said, glancing at Matt.

He rolled his eyes, looking as if he'd rather face a stampeding herd than his aunt right now.

"Della, don't you think we might move just a few objects, in order to make more room for chairs? That wouldn't spoil the atmosphere, would it?"

Della obviously didn't want to admit that much. "I don't see why we have to move anything."

"Just a few of the more delicate pieces," Gillian put in. "You wouldn't want to risk their being damaged, would you?"

That thought clearly hadn't occurred to Della, and she wavered. "I suppose not. But no wholesale shifting things around, now."

"Nothing like that." Gillian glanced around for something to make the point. Her gaze fell on a dainty lacquer games table, set up with an antique board and tiles for mah-jongg. "This, for instance. You wouldn't want to lose any of these tiles, and it would fit perfectly over here, next to the Ming vase."

Gillian lifted the small table and carried it across the room. She didn't know why it wasn't next to the vase all the time. This setting provided a perfect corner for a quiet game, well shielded by an embroidered Oriental silk screen.

"There. Doesn't that look nice?" She glanced up to find the two of them looking at her with identical expressions of shock. "What is it? Is something wrong?"

Matt shook his head slowly, his gaze fixed on the table. "No, not really. The lacquer table used to be there, that's all. My mother liked it there."

"Clarice." Della spoke the name in little more than a whisper. She stared at Gillian with an odd expression that seemed to mix jealousy and anger, and perhaps even a little fear. She gripped the red necklace she wore. "Just like Clarice."

With a sudden swirl of her filmy dress, Della darted from the room. The air seemed to rustle, as if it welcomed her leaving.

"I'm sorry." Gillian stared down at the table, nerves prickling. Why had she moved it there? How had she known?

"It's just a coincidence," she said aloud. "It's the logical place for the table. Anyone would see that."

Matt took a long moment to reply. "Sure," he said at last. "Anyone would see that." He shrugged, as if loosening tight shoulder muscles, and Gillian had an urge to do the same. There was too much tension in the room.

She had to get the conversation away from the subject of Clarice. "So Theodore Banks is coming. I didn't realize that. Have you been advertising his concert?"

"It's not a money-making effort. Theo comes every summer, for a rest. He always does a performance while he's here, but we don't push it. After all, he is coming as a guest."

She couldn't seem to say the right thing. Or maybe he just regretted everything that had passed between them the day before. He was probably sorry he'd confided in her.

"Well, it's quite a coup, in any event," she said lightly. "I heard him once at Lincoln Center." She touched a key, and the sound echoed. "Is he an old friend?"

"He was a friend of my mother's," Matt said shortly. "Was there something you wanted to talk to me about?"

A friend of Clarice, she should have known. And Matt obviously didn't want to talk about that. He probably wasn't going to be any more enthusiastic about what she had to say.

"I've been going over the food and beverage operation yesterday and today. I found something I can't explain." She looked up, to meet resistance in Matt's face. No, he didn't want to hear this.

"What kind of something? Can't you just put it in your report to Frederick and leave me out of it?"

"I think it's something you should deal with. There's a discrepancy in the accounts. It might just be sloppy record keeping. I'm not a good enough accountant to tell." She took a deep breath. "I think we should bring in an independent auditor to go over the whole operation before the deal is finalized."

Matt's face seemed to freeze over. "I see," he said

slowly. "In other words, you think I'm ripping off my own hotel."

"No!" Why did he persist in interpreting everything she said the wrong way? "That's not what I mean at all. I don't think you're a thief. I think you're a victim."

Matt slammed the flat of his hand down on the piano, setting a vibration humming through the room. "You're wrong. Nobody here would . . ." He stopped.

"I don't know whether anyone here would try to cheat you or not," she said carefully. "They're your employees. You know them better than I do. All I can do is tell you what I'm finding. Something is out of kilter in the food and beverage accounts. And I'm not happy with the cancellation rate either, although I can't pin it down."

"You can't tell me anything but suspicions, is that it? And on the basis of your suspicions, I'm supposed to assume someone is cheating the hotel."

"I don't want you to assume anything." Gillian's temper rose in the face of his stubbornness. "I think you should have an expert look into the situation."

"I thought you were supposed to be the expert. Isn't that what Frederick pays you for?" That came out sounding like an insult, which was probably what he intended.

"My background is in management, not accounting, but even I can tell something's not right around here. For heaven's sake, Matt, you should be doing two or three times the business you're doing! I may not know all the answers, but at least I know to ask the questions."

Anger flickered in Matt's eyes, like summer lightning across a dark sky. "Meaning I'm too dumb to know what to ask?"

"Maybe meaning you don't want to ask! You keep

ignoring what's happening, as if it will go away if you don't look at it. Like the rock slide. You could have been killed, and when I tell you I saw someone on that hillside, you tell me it's my imagination. Well, I don't believe it!"

Something changed in his face at that. He knew something about that incident, something he hadn't told her. Gillian's anger suddenly seemed out of place. He knew something.

"What is it?" she said, hearing the apprehension in her words. "What aren't you telling me?"

Matt shook his head. "Nothing. If someone was on the hill that day, it can't have anything to do with the rest of this."

"Why?" She put her hand on his arm, wanting to shake the information out of him. His muscles were hard and tense, as if his whole body was determined to keep a secret. "You know something about that. What is it? What have you found out?"

He hesitated a moment longer, and then she felt the decision to tell her in the sudden relaxation of tension.

"Della," he said. "If anyone was on the hill that day, I'm sure it was Della."

"Della! You can't be serious. Why would your aunt want to hurt you?" Even as she asked, she realized she might already know the answer to that question.

Matt shrugged, his face grim. "Who knows what Della could do? You must have seen how unstable she is. Lake House has always been her home, and she's made no secret of how she feels about my running it."

"Even so, to do something so dangerous . . ." She wasn't sure why she was arguing. She'd thought all along it might be Della.

"She probably didn't think it would be that dangerous. She might have just wanted to scare me out of taking Lockwood in."

"It wouldn't."

"No, it wouldn't." He managed a smile and put his hand over hers. His tension penetrated her skin. "Della doesn't think things through. She could have acted on impulse and then regretted it. And you . . . " His fingers tightened. ". . . she probably scared you as much as me."

"Yes." She looked up at him. She couldn't say this without giving away too much of herself. "I don't want to see you get hurt."

His eyes were bleak. "That's wishing for the moon. This place gets me so crazy sometimes I'd like to burn the whole thing down."

"Don't." Impulsively she reached up to touch his face. His skin was cool and smooth under her fingers. "Don't feel so guilty. It's not your fault."

"Isn't it?" For a moment longer he was motionless, and then he brought her hand to his mouth, pressing a kiss against her palm as he'd done once before. She felt his warmth flow into her, and recognized the flicker of desire that sparked between them, needing very little to burst into flame.

Slowly Matt's arms went around her. He glanced toward the door into the studio, and something baffled and angry moved in his eyes.

The warmth seeped out of Gillian, leaving cold in its place. He didn't know. He didn't know whether, when he touched her, something else, *someone else,* was acting.

She took a careful step away from him, even though every separate cell in her body wanted to stay in the circle of his arms.

"Maybe we'd better save this for another time."

"Or another place," he said. The anger dissolved into a rueful look. "When I kiss a beautiful woman, I like to think I'm acting on my own feelings, not the remnants of somebody else's feelings, floating around in the atmosphere."

"Is that really what you think it is?"

"Damned if I know." He touched her hair, letting the strands wind through his fingers. "Let's just say my rational side has taken a beating in the last few days."

"I know what you mean." Relief surged through her. At least they were on the same side, for the moment. "I've always prided myself on being a sensible businesswoman. Lake House has had an odd effect on that."

He gave her a little push toward the door. "Let's get out of here. There's nothing sensible or rational about what I'm thinking of doing right now, and I'm not going to do it here." He gave her a look that brought a flush to her cheeks. "I think we both need some fresh air."

As it turned out, Matt was called to the phone as soon as they went downstairs. Gillian went for the fresh air alone.

She walked along the path that surrounded the lake. It was a fairly easy trail; she wasn't in any mood right now for anything challenging. She needed to think.

Would Matt take her advice about an audit? She just wasn't sure. Unless and until he did, she had no choice but to keep poking around on her own and hope she could turn up something.

When she reported to Lockwood, she'd have to tell him everything, but she could put that off for a while.

He didn't expect a report this soon. She'd like to give Matt a chance to clear up the situation himself. It wasn't being disloyal to her employer to let him do that.

At least Matt didn't think she was crazy. That was a step in the right direction. In a way, his admission that he felt something odd made her feel a little better. She wasn't the only person affected by Lake House.

Was it something in the atmosphere, as Matt said, that touched people who were sensitive to it? For the first time, Gillian found her sturdy rationality a disadvantage. Maggie, her college roommate, who'd hung crystals all over the room and consulted the Ouija board for every decision, would have an edge in a situation like this.

One of the trailside gazebos perched on a rock overlooking the lake. Gillian sat down, propping her feet on the opposite bench. The breeze lifted her hair from her neck and cooled her face. The woods were still, except for the persistent call of a bobwhite somewhere behind her. The lake made small murmuring sounds against the base of the rock. Peace flowed over her.

Gillian leaned back. The rough timber warmed her back, and the anxiety she'd felt drifted away. It was so peaceful, sitting here. She had a happy sense of anticipation, as if something good were about to happen. If all of Lake House made her feel this good, she'd come here all the time. She closed her eyes, tilting her face to the sunlight, inhaling the pine-scented air.

She wasn't sure how long she sat there before she realized someone was watching her. She opened her eyes. Henry Morrison stood on the trail a few feet away, camera in hand.

"I'm sorry to disturb you." He gestured with the camera. "Do you mind?"

"Of course not." She swallowed an absurd sense of disappointment at seeing Henry. Maybe she'd really been hoping Matt would follow her here.

Henry snapped several pictures, while Gillian tried not to feel self-conscious. It wasn't every day that a world-famous photographer took her picture, and she could imagine how she looked—windblown and hot.

Finally Henry stopped and sat down next to her. He leaned back, looking around with obvious enjoyment.

"I think you've found the prettiest spot at Lake House," he said. "Just look at that view."

Obediently, Gillian looked. Along the curve of the lake to her left, Lake House spread along its rock shelf, looking like a mythical castle suspended over the water. The white cliff soared upward from the lake on the opposite side, topped by wave after wave of green. She'd never noticed before how many shades of green there were in a single tree.

"It is beautiful." A peculiar lassitude held her spellbound.

Henry fiddled with his camera. "I've been most places in the world, and I've never found anything I liked better."

"This is so peaceful." Gillian rested her arm along the smooth birch log that formed the railing. "I could stay here forever."

A shadow crossed Henry's face. "That's what Clarice used to say. Whenever things got too much for her, she'd take a walk. Renewing herself, she called it. I've seen her sitting here, just as you are, more times than I can count."

"Anyone would love a spot like this." Gillian could hear the defensive note in her voice. Coincidence, again?

"Yes, of course." He looked faintly surprised, and then wary. He picked up his camera. "Well, if I'm going to walk around the lake and be back by teatime, I'd better go."

Gillian watched his slight, erect figure disappear into the trees. Henry didn't realize he'd just given her something else indigestible to chew on.

This had been Clarice's favorite spot. And when Gillian sat here, thirty years later, she felt flooded with well-being, as if some magic still lingered.

No, it was more than that. She'd been more than happy, in those moments before Henry interrupted her. That sense of eager anticipation, as if something pleasant were about to happen, was that her own feeling? Or was it Clarice's?

Gillian stared down at the crystal water, looking at the same view Clarice must have looked at, time after time. Clarice had sat here happily, all right. She'd been happy because she was waiting for something, or someone. Who had Clarice been waiting for? Gillian was afraid she might know the answer to that.

Teatime was one of Lake House's most charming customs. Exactly at four, every day, guests wandered into the Lake Lounge for a cup of tea, a crisp, paper-thin cookie, and some conversation about the day's activities.

Gillian paused in the doorway, glancing around the room. The usual elderly couples were already settled at their usual tables. People fell into habits very quickly here.

"Darjeeling, please."

Mrs. Clemens, from Housekeeping, was pouring today, and she acknowledged Gillian's request with a nod. The honor of pouring rotated among the senior female staff, and they seemed to take it very seriously. Mrs. Clemens might have been pouring for the Queen, for all the care she took.

The china cup was banded with gold and embossed with the initials *L. H.* Gillian balanced it in one hand and took a coconut macaroon with the other. After a few more days of eating like this, none of her clothes would fit.

A laugh punctuated the low hum of conversation. Gillian turned. Della sat in one of the window seats, her cup on a marble-topped table in front of her. And next to her . . . Gillian blinked. Next to her sat the last person she expected to see at Lake House today. Frederick Lockwood lifted his cup, looking as settled and comfortable as if he'd lived here always.

A knot of tension formed in Gillian's stomach, and she put her macaroon down, untasted. What was her boss doing here? He'd said he trusted her judgment and knew he could count on her to do a thorough assessment. Maybe that was not quite true.

His presence was odd, and more so that he was engaged in a tête-à-tête with Della O'Donnell. Della was opposed to the partnership with Lockwood, or at least she certainly gave that impression. Why were they so thick all of a sudden?

Gillian set her cup carefully on the table and took a deep breath. She'd have to go and talk to him. It would look very odd if she didn't. She'd told herself there was time—time for her to find out what was going on at Lake House, and time for Matt to come to grips with things. She could only hope Lockwood didn't intend to ask her for an opinion immediately.

Frederick Lockwood looked up at her approach, then rose courteously. With his thick white hair and his well-worn tweeds, he looked like a retired diplomat instead of a hotel magnate. Gillian wasn't fooled. The lion waited behind the polite mask.

"Gillian, you're looking well. Lake House must agree with you."

Gillian shook hands, suppressing a hysterical desire to laugh. Lockwood wouldn't sound so confident if he knew what she'd been going through here.

"It's a lovely place," she said, aware of Della's dark gaze focused intently on her. She'd give a lot, right now, to know what he and Della had been talking about.

"You're wondering why I'm here." Lockwood went right to the point. "Don't worry, I'm not going to interfere with your work. I'm staying at my home here for a few days, and I've just come over to catch up with some old friends." He patted Della's hand. "Miss O'Donnell and I go way back, don't we, Della?"

To Gillian's astonishment, Della actually simpered, her pale face flushing. "More years than we care to count," she said. She picked up Lockwood's cup. "Now I'll get you another cup of the Earl Grey you like so much."

Della trotted off, and Gillian found herself the uncomfortable focus of Lockwood's attention. "So tell me, Gillian," he said, smiling a little, "what do you have to report about Lake House?"

10

Gillian took a deep breath. Stammering wasn't an acceptable response to this question. She had to reassure Lockwood, and she had to buy herself time. The fact that she even had the thought told Gillian clearly that her loyalty to Lockwood Hotels was in doubt.

"I'm not prepared to present my full report yet. There's a great deal to look into if I'm to give you the sort of information you want."

"Oh, I'm not expecting a complete assessment now, just some preliminary impressions." He smiled. "Come now. You can at least tell me the first reaction you had to Lake House."

If she told him that, he'd be convinced she was crazy. "Lake House is lovely," she said firmly. "It really does seem suspended in time, doesn't it?"

Lockwood glanced around the lounge, an expression on his aristocratic face she couldn't interpret. "Suspended in time," he said slowly. "Yes, that's a good way of putting it. This afternoon tea might well be taking place fifty years ago, or thirty, or yesterday."

Gillian's spine tingled. Why had he mentioned thirty years ago? Maybe it was so much on her mind that she broadcast it to everyone she met.

"And what do you think of Matt O'Donnell?" Lockwood's pale blue eyes were intent, denying the casual tone of the question.

Another minefield opened in front of Gillian. She didn't want to talk about Matt with Lockwood. She glanced toward the nearest table, where two elderly couples sat sipping tea. "I'm not sure we should discuss this here, Mr. Lockwood."

His ice blue gaze rested on her face a moment longer, and then he shrugged. "Of course. I promised you time to do the assessment thoroughly, and now I'm rushing you. I certainly don't mean to do that. You must take all the time you need."

"Thank you, sir." She slid her chair back as Della approached, carrying a tray with a teapot and two cups. "If you'll excuse me . . ."

"Certainly."

Gillian turned away, but his voice reached her before she could take another step.

"We'll talk tomorrow, Gillian. I'll send the car for you at one o'clock. You'll bring me up to date then."

Gillian changed clothes slowly, her mind occupied with Lockwood's arrival. It could mean a lot of things, ranging from the simple fact that he was in the area for a few days to the scary thought that he was dissatisfied with her lack of progress. Or it could mean something else. With Frederick Lockwood, no one could tell.

She'd become too involved with things other than her job, that was the truth of the matter. Her father's disappearance, the tragedy of Clarice and Robert, above all the complex emotions Matt aroused in her . . . combined, they were more than she could handle.

She didn't need Frederick Lockwood to tell her it was inappropriate to become entangled with Matt O'Donnell. Her feelings could affect the validity of her report. In fact, they already had. She hung back, reluctant to talk freely to Lockwood, because she didn't want to make Matt sound like a fool.

If only she could stall Lockwood long enough for Matt to straighten out some of the difficulties. It didn't take a genius to figure out that the problems she'd uncovered would affect the bargaining positions of both Lockwood and Matt in this merger.

Della and Lockwood had sat with their heads together for nearly an hour, and Della, with her constant prying, was always a threat. Heaven only knew what she had told Lockwood. If Lockwood knew how involved she'd become, she'd be out of here before she could blink, and would consider herself lucky if she wasn't out of Lockwood Hotels altogether.

Panic rippled along Gillian's nerves. How had she gotten herself into this situation?

She worried at the whole mass of unanswered questions as she dressed for dinner. Unfortunately, she didn't seem to be coming up with any answers, just more questions.

Della hurried down the hall as she locked her door.

"Good, you're dressed." She grabbed Gillian's arm. "Come on, we're late."

Gillian pulled back. "What are we late for, Della?"

"Theo is here," Della said, as if that explained everything.

"Theodore Banks, the pianist? What does that have to do with me?"

Della tugged at her arm. "Matt has invited some people in for cocktails before dinner, to meet Theo. He wants you to come."

Gillian glanced down at her forest green knit dress. She wouldn't have chosen to wear it for a cocktail party, but Della obviously wouldn't give her time to change. Maybe these few minutes alone with Della were what she needed. Della might, given the chance, talk about her conversation with Frederick Lockwood.

She fell into step beside Della, who was considerably more dressed up than usual. Gillian looked closer. Della actually wore eye shadow, though inexpertly applied. Was this in honor of Theodore Banks? Or was Frederick Lockwood still here?

"I was surprised to see Mr. Lockwood here this afternoon." She hurried to keep up with Della's rapid pace. "He hadn't let me know he was coming."

Della shrugged. "Frederick turns up when he wants to. Not as often as he did when his brother was alive."

Brother? She didn't know Lockwood had a brother. "Did his brother live around here, too?"

"Too?" Della's voice went up, and she came to a stop in front of the Parlor. "Arthur owned Eagle's Nest to begin with." At Gillian's blank look, she repeated impatiently. "Eagle's Nest. Frederick's estate. Aren't you going there tomorrow?"

"I didn't know that was the name of it. It used to belong to his brother?"

"Everything used to belong to Arthur." They rounded the corner by the Parlor. Della sent a sidelong, suspicious glance in that direction. She was probably still worried about the mah-jongg table.

"Arthur owned the hotels?" she prompted.

"Only one hotel then. He was the older brother, you see. Dear Arthur." Della's face softened, and the years seemed to drop away. "We were very close, you know. We liked to go for long walks on the trails together."

This was a side of the situation Gillian had never guessed at. A girlhood romance between Della and Frederick's older brother? Maybe that was why she fluttered so over Frederick today. Stranger things had happened.

"What happened to Arthur?"

Della's eyes became misty. "He died. A long time ago."

"I'm sorry. I didn't know."

"We were all so close once." Della sighed. "Frederick was around a lot, too." A malicious look crept into her dark eyes. "Buzzing around Clarice like a bee round the honey jar. Just like all the men, except Arthur, of course."

Frederick Lockwood and Clarice? Gillian's mind reeled. Della couldn't be serious. How many more surprises did Lake House have in store for her?

Della stopped by the door to the family wing. She stared at Gillian as if she could see through her. "Oh, of course," she said. "You already know that, don't you? You know everything about Clarice."

Before Gillian could reply, Della had gone inside. Gillian had no choice but to follow her.

Gillian stopped inside the door. To her right, people stood in front of the blue-and-white Delft tiles of the fireplace. Opposite her, the French doors stood open to the balcony, and the lake sparkled in the setting sun. She turned slowly to the left.

Matt stood at the linen-covered table, head down, frowning. Gillian's heart gave an unpleasant lurch. This was too much like her dream. Instinct told her that nothing good would happen in this room tonight.

Then, in an instant, the frozen image splintered. Matt moved toward her, holding out a glass of white wine. The group in front of the fireplace shifted, then coalesced again in a slightly different grouping.

Henry was deep in conversation with a man she recognized as Theo Banks. The pianist was unmistakable, with that shock of golden hair falling over his high forehead and his strong, shapely hands gesturing widely. It was a characteristic movement, and she wondered whether he did it to draw attention to those gifted hands. Banks was getting a little old for the "Young Genius" label that had been attached to him thirty years ago, but his popularity never seemed to fade.

"Admiring our star attraction?" Matt stood beside her, so close the aroma of his musk aftershave touched her senses, bringing back memories of other moments. He handed her the wineglass, turning so that his body shielded her from the rest of the room. Their conversation was as private as it could be in a room full of people.

"He is the center of attention, isn't he?"

"Always." There was a wry note in Matt's voice. "I've known Theo since I was a kid, and I've never seen him when he wasn't performing."

Frederick Lockwood was deep in conversation with an elegant older woman she didn't recognize.

"I see Mr. Lockwood is still here." Gillian tried to keep her voice neutral and wondered whether, in such a small gathering, it was going to be possible to avoid him.

"Yes." Matt's face tightened, and she knew he didn't like the reminder. "He said he wanted to stay and speak to Theo. Frederick's leaving soon, though. Has a dinner engagement, he says."

With any luck Matt couldn't read the relief on her face. She had a respite, until tomorrow, at least. She didn't have to try and balance conflicting loyalties in the next ten minutes.

It was probably better if Lockwood didn't see her in intimate conversation with Matt. "Maybe we'd better join the others."

Matt's fingers stroked her wrist, the action hidden from the others by their bodies. "I'd rather talk to you." The words were deliberately provoking. "But you're right, we should circulate."

It would be his fault if her cheeks were red when she joined the cluster of people in front of the fireplace. Brenda had her hand on Henry's arm. He bent toward her courteously as she said something, soft-voiced, to him. Brenda looked up and saw Gillian, and an irritated expression crossed her face.

Brenda hadn't expected her and didn't like her presence. Maybe she'd anticipated being the only woman in this gathering of unique males: a concert pianist, a world-famous photographer, a hotel magnate. And Matt.

"Gillian, how nice." Henry took her hand and held it in both of his. He seemed tense. "I've located an interesting article on Victorian gardens that I wanted to show you. I'll drop it in your office, shall I?"

"I'll look forward to it." Henry obviously wanted to be rescued from Brenda, and Gillian didn't mind obliging him. "I meant to ask if you had any photographs of the gardens."

"Of course." Henry smiled, relaxing as they moved away from the others. "I'll be glad to show them to you."

"You're not boring this lovely lady with photography, are you, Henry?" Theo Banks swung toward them, his voice booming over everyone else's conversation. "Introduce me to this beautiful creature."

Gillian could almost feel Henry effacing himself behind that well-bred British expression. "Certainly, Theo. Gillian, may I present Theodore Banks? Theo, Miss Gillian Lang."

Gillian extended her hand and found it being extravagantly kissed. Up close, Theodore Banks's golden hair was streaked with gray, but he was as vibrant as a man thirty years younger. "Gillian, what a charming name. It suits you, my dear."

She could feel herself blushing. "Thank you. It's a pleasure to meet you."

"The pleasure is all mine." He still held her hand. "We haven't met here before?"

"No, but I had the privilege of hearing you play at Lincoln Center two years ago."

"The Tchaikovsky piece." Banks made a face. "Predictable, but that was what they wanted." He held Gillian out at arms length, surveying her. "Now this, this is a face more suited to Chopin. At my concert this week, I will play Chopin just for you."

"Careful, Theo."

Gillian hadn't noticed Della, standing behind Banks, until she spoke. Banks swung toward her, finally releasing Gillian's hand.

"Why do I need to be careful, Della, my sweet? You're not implying that I'm too old to compliment this gorgeous creature, are you?"

Della's smile was edged with malice. "You dedicated Chopin to Clarice, remember? You wouldn't want to mix her up with Gillian."

Theo Banks's volatile face darkened. "You have a nasty tongue in your head, Della. It could get you into trouble one of these days."

Instead of replying, Della gave them both her vague, unfocused smile and drifted off. Della had probably accomplished exactly what she intended to. But had that reminder of Clarice been aimed at her or at Theo Banks?

"That woman . . . " Banks began, then cut his words off abruptly. He gave Gillian the smile that graced his posters. "Let's not talk about her. Let's talk about you. How did you enjoy my concert at Lincoln Center?"

Gillian suppressed a smile. Even a conversation about someone else had to return to Theo Banks, obviously. The man had an ego the size of Manhattan, but he had a talent to match, so maybe that wasn't surprising.

"It was wonderful," she said honestly. "I've never heard the piece played better."

He beamed, but before he could expound on his performance that night, he was distracted by Frederick Lockwood's approach. Gillian smiled at her employer, then took advantage of their exchange of greetings to slip away. The last thing she wanted right now was to be trapped in a conversation with Lockwood.

She took a crab puff from the silver tray and surveyed the room. She could attach herself to any one of several conversation groups, but each one seemed to have dangers of its own. The French doors stood open to the balcony, and she slipped outside.

The sun had just disappeared behind the mountain, leaving a sky streaked with crimson and purple. Dusk settled in quickly here, with the peaks around the lake cutting off the light. The white cliff opposite the hotel shimmered in the gathering gloom. Gillian leaned her elbows on the railing, welcoming the fresh breeze from the lake on her face.

There were entirely too many crosscurrents of motives and emotion in that room behind her. She wasn't imagining that, and it wasn't just the effect of her dream. But they did connect to the dream, because all of them seemed to have their roots in what happened here thirty years ago.

Gillian clenched the wooden balcony railing. According to Della, every man who met Clarice fell half in love with her. Or had that been Henry's assessment? Henry certainly had. And if she read Della's remarks correctly, both Theo Banks and Frederick Lockwood had succumbed to Clarice's charms.

No wonder Robert had been jealous. Any one of them could have been Clarice's lover that summer, assuming she had one. If not for the evidence of the Florentine ring, Gillian could comfortably assume it had been one of the others, rather than her father. Unfortunately she couldn't ignore the ring, much as she'd like to.

Did she know for sure that Banks had been here that crucial summer? Maybe she was building too much on Della's remark about Chopin.

"Hiding out?" Banks's voice from behind startled her. She turned to find him standing in the doorway, or perhaps posed would be a better description. He paused for a moment before closing the door and joining her.

"Just enjoying the view." Gillian nodded toward the deepening shadows on the lake. "Perhaps you've been here enough that you're used to it, but I'm still captivated."

"I've always found Lake House the most restful place in the world. I hope Frederick's not planning any changes?" The lift at the end of the sentence made it a question. Apparently her mission and Lockwood's plans were not a secret any longer, if they ever had been.

"Mr. Lockwood hasn't discussed his plans with me," Gillian said. Bringing up that summer thirty years ago wasn't going to be easy.

"How discreet, my dear. I hope Frederick appreciates your loyalty."

Another sticky subject yawned ahead of her. "I'm sure he does. But I can understand why you don't want to see Lake House change. Matt tells me you've been coming here for a number of years. He said you were a friend of his mother's?" It was her turn to make a statement into a question.

"Friend?" Banks put a world of innuendo into the word. "I suppose you could say that. Clarice and I were very . . . close."

There was no mistaking the way his voice caressed the word. Banks was all but admitting that he and Clarice had been lovers.

Gillian was suddenly sick of the whole mess. But she had to say something.

"It must have been tragic for you when she died."

He nodded, shoving the tumbled lock of blond hair back from his forehead. "Tragic," he echoed. "We looked for her all that night, but somehow I knew instinctively that we weren't going to find her alive."

"How terrible," she murmured.

Theo Banks had even been here when Clarice died. Relief flooded through Gillian. It wasn't a happy ending, but at least she no longer had to think that her father had been the man in Clarice's life.

Banks put his hand on the railing next to Gillian, effectively pinning her into the corner of the balcony. She glanced up to find his speculative gaze drifting down her body.

"Now, why are we talking about such a depressing subject?" He smiled seductively. "When I'm alone with a lovely woman, I make it a policy never to bring up unhappy things. It spoils the mood."

There was no mistaking the gleam in his eyes, and Gillian groaned silently. Surely she wasn't going to have to fend off a pass. Theo Banks had a reputation as a womanizer, but she hoped even he wouldn't make a move on five minutes' acquaintance. Unfortunately that was exactly what he was doing. He touched her hair, then let his hand drop to her shoulder.

"Gorgeous hair," he murmured. "I've always fancied redheads."

Gillian tried to slide past him. "I think I'd better go in."

His hand came down, blocking her, and he leaned closer. "Not yet. We're just starting to get to know each other."

Gillian opened her mouth to respond. Suddenly something seemed to wash over her, enveloping her entirely. For an instant she couldn't catch her breath. She was suffocating, she couldn't . . .

Then a wave of exultation surged through her, vibrating into every cell in her body. She flung her head back, enjoying the sense of power. Imagine Theo, thinking she'd fall for his tired line.

"Stick to the piano, Theo." Her voice was husky, provocative. "It's the only instrument you'll have a chance to play around here."

Banks's entire body stiffened. He stared at Gillian, openmouthed with shock. Dislike battled fear in his eyes. "You . . . how did you . . . " He spun and practically bolted back into the room.

For an instant she stared after him, laughter bubbling irrepressibly. Then she sagged, stumbling against the railing, nearly falling, like a puppet whose strings have been cut.

Gillian clung to the railing, fear surging through her. *That hadn't been her. Someone had taunted Theo Banks with her voice, but it hadn't been her!*

She took a deep breath, then another, trying to control herself. She didn't want to believe it, but she had to. Those hadn't been her feelings, coming out when Theo Banks touched her. They'd been Clarice's.

Just as she assimilated that terrifying thought another hit her. Theo Banks had lied. He and Clarice had never been lovers. All she'd felt for him had been contempt.

So her brief moment of relief had been false. Her father wasn't off the hook at all. He might very well have been Clarice's lover. If he was, he probably bore a share of responsibility for her death.

Gillian had worked herself into a rare state of nerves by the next day. Her sleep had been troubled by fragments of dreams. They were not as detailed as the dreams she'd had earlier, but they were still upsetting.

She'd seen Clarice at the little gazebo, waiting for someone who didn't come. She'd had a quick glimpse of Clarice, posing for the portrait her father had started, wearing an elaborate Renaissance gown and a tragic expression. And she'd had flash after flash of the icy lake water, so that she woke feeling chilled in spite of the warm morning.

Now she had to go and see Frederick Lockwood. Gillian walked down the hallway to the entrance where she was to meet his limo, feeling as if she walked her last mile. Somehow she had to be honest with Lockwood while not giving away anything about her father, her strange affinity for Clarice, her feelings for Matt, and if she could help it, the problems she'd uncovered with Matt's management. This would not be easy. In fact, it was probably impossible.

Frederick Lockwood's estate, Eagle's Nest, was only a few miles, as the crow flies, from Lake House. Since she was not flying, the trip took longer than she'd expected. The driver sped down the narrow Lake House road to the gate house, wound along the valley floor, and then started up another narrow road which lead to the Lockwood estate which, like Lake House, had its own private mountainside.

Gillian expected to be impressed by Eagle's Nest, and she wasn't disappointed. The house sat on the edge of a cliff. In fact, it was cantilevered into the very mountain itself. It soared, all jutting angles and varying levels of wood beams, glass walls, and native stone. Its decidedly modern design was as much a contrast to Lake House as Gillian could possibly imagine.

Frederick Lockwood emerged from the front door to meet her. He was dressed casually, in slacks and an open-necked shirt, instead of his usual hand tailored Italian suit.

"Welcome to my home. What do you think of my view?" He gestured. "Is it the equal of Lake House?"

Gillian turned slowly, taking in a vista of mountain and sky. The longer she admired it, the longer it would be until she had to report. "It's spectacular. I don't know how you can tear yourself away to go to the city."

"It's difficult, of course." Lockwood smiled, looking with satisfaction at the house. "But the challenges are there, not here. This is a place to recharge my batteries." He pointed. "Look over there, on the next mountain. You can just see the topmost tower of Lake House."

Gillian glimpsed a bit of red roof above the trees. "I knew it was close, but I didn't realize how close. I could almost have walked over, couldn't I?"

Lockwood laughed. "Only if you're prepared to slog through thick woods and then climb a mountain. It could be done, but I don't think you'd like to try it."

"What is that?" The section of tumbled stone wall, nearly covered with Virginia creeper, looked oddly out of place in the midst of a carefully landscaped garden.

"That's a bit of a monument, I suppose." Lockwood took her arm, turning her toward the house. "My father built a hotel here, more years ago than I care to count. That little twenty-room inn was the beginning of Lockwood Hotels, Inc. Even though it was torn down long ago to make room for the house, I like to keep that section of wall to remind me." He smiled. "Sentimental, I suppose."

"Not at all," Gillian murmured, surprised at being shown so much of her employer's personal side.

She followed Lockwood into an elegant entryway, paved with Italian marble. They passed an immense living room, all soaring ceilings and mirrors, and went into an office.

Here the tone was function, not elegance. The comprehensive computer and communication setup indicated that Lockwood worked when he came here to, as he'd said, recharge his batteries. Of course the head of Lockwood Hotels couldn't afford to be out of touch.

"Please, sit down." His hand hovered over a bell on his desk. "Would you like something? Coffee, iced tea?"

"No, thank you, sir." Gillian smoothed her skirt nervously. Keyed up as she was, she might as well get this over with.

Lockwood sat behind the desk that was very similar to the one at corporate headquarters. He leaned back, steepling his fingers. She expected a grilling, but Lockwood seemed in no hurry to get underway.

"I'm glad you appreciate my house," he said. "I thought perhaps your tastes might have been blunted by an overdose of Victorianism in recent days."

"Not at all." Gillian glanced around the office. A compliment seemed in order, but what—Her gaze was caught by a painting of rugged cliffs that looked oddly familiar. "That's a lovely painting. Is the setting somewhere around here?"

"You have a good eye. That's the mountain you see from the far end of the lake, over at Lake House. If you've gone out Laurel Trail as far as the lookout point, you've seen that view. The cliffs are actually on my property, not O'Donnell land."

"Really?" Fascinated, Gillian got up and went closer. "It really is spectacular. I had no idea, seeing it from a distance, that the mountainside was that rugged."

"One of the most challenging climbs in the East," Lockwood said. "We're always fielding requests from climbers who want to try it, but we turn most of them down. Lawsuits, you know."

Gillian moved closer, trying to decide what it was that

fascinated her so about the painting. She usually didn't care much for landscapes, but something about this one seemed to draw her.

"I bought it for the subject matter," Lockwood continued, his voice casual, "but it really is fairly well done. It was painted by an artist who stayed at Lake House for a time. His name was Alec McLeod."

11

Luckily Gillian was standing with her back to Frederick Lockwood. She took a step closer to the painting, ostensibly admiring it, while she struggled to gain control of herself.

Her father's painting hung here in Lockwood's house. How ironic that was! If she told Lockwood, what would his reaction be?

She bit her lip, the tiny pain helping to clear her head. Lockwood must never know, not if she valued her job. Once even a little of the secret was spilled, the rest would be bound to come out. No, she couldn't risk that.

Desperately searching for something to say, she turned to face him. "Do you do any climbing yourself?"

"I did when I was a boy. My brother and I used to scramble all over these mountains. I've outgrown such dangerous pastimes, I'm afraid. Matt's father was an outstanding climber, you know."

"No, I didn't." A brief image of Robert, windblown atop a dangerous summit, flickered through her mind. "Matt doesn't climb, does he?"

Lockwood gave a short laugh. "I don't think they did much climbing on that cattle ranch of his grandfather's."

Gillian went back to her chair, surprised that her legs were so steady. At least she was safely off the subject of the painting. She could feel it lurking behind her back, as if ready to cry out at her. She had to get herself under control. Lockwood would begin talking about Lake House at any moment, and she had to be ready.

"I realize your report isn't prepared yet, Gillian, but I did want a chance to hear about how you're getting along. If I buy into Lake House, your findings will help me establish what management changes need to be made. So tell me what you think as of now."

Telling him what she thought was exactly what she couldn't do. Gillian took a deep breath. "Well, of course the place is unique, but you already know that. I've been looking into each separate department, trying to evaluate how well it's running and what its weaknesses are."

"And are you finding any weaknesses?" He sounded hopeful. It would put him in a better bargaining position if there were.

Gillian frowned. "The obvious problem is the fact that Lake House isn't running at anywhere near capacity. I've begun a separate section of my report dealing with that. I haven't had time, yet, to look into the advertising schedule or—"

The telephone on Lockwood's desk buzzed. He lifted a hand to stop her and picked up the receiver.

"Yes, I see. In a few minutes, then."

He turned to Gillian. "Please excuse me for a moment.

I have a call coming in from Singapore, and I'd like to take it upstairs. I'll be back shortly."

When he'd gone, Gillian let herself collapse into the leather chair. This situation had gotten impossible. How on earth could she justify not telling Lockwood about her suspicions? If he questioned her any further, she was going to have to tell him. And if she did, it put a weapon in his hands that he would use against Matt.

That was part of her assignment, of course. It was one of the reasons Lockwood sent her to Lake House, and she'd come prepared to find any edge she could for her employer. Unfortunately, she hadn't counted on becoming so involved with Matt O'Donnell.

Gillian got up, too jittery to sit still. The painting called to her, but she avoided looking at it. She couldn't cope with that right now. Somehow she had to block it out of her mind until she got through this interview.

She paced to the windows, away from the painting. A long library table sat in the curve formed by the wall of glass, and she glanced down at the papers that littered its surface.

Gillian frowned. That diagram looked familiar. She turned it and realized that what she looked at was a plan of Lake House. A plan of Lake House with a few changes made. She leaned over the table, studying it.

There was the existing hotel, as it stood now. And there, along the end of the lake, was a huge new addi-tion labeled *Conference Center*.

She lifted the plan, finding detailed architectural drawings underneath. Why on earth did Lockwood send her to Lake House in the first place? It looked as if he'd long since made up his mind to buy in, without even hearing her report.

Another thought, even more unpleasant, struck her. Did Matt know just what changes Frederick Lockwood had in mind for Lake House? If he didn't, how could she tell him? How could she not?

Footsteps on the Italian marble of the hall alerted her, and she hurried back to her chair before Lockwood entered the room. She steeled herself for the next round of questions, but Lockwood picked up a briefcase instead of sitting back down.

"We'll have to postpone the rest of our discussion," he said, his mind obviously elsewhere. "Something's come up, and I must leave almost immediately. The driver is waiting to take you back to Lake House."

"Yes, of course, sir." Maybe she didn't sound as relieved as she felt. She'd reached the door when Lockwood spoke again.

"Just keep on as you are, please, Gillian. Assuming the deal does go through, I'll want you to stay at Lake House until everything is finalized, and perhaps even longer. I'll be in touch."

Thus dismissed, Gillian scurried out of the room, half afraid that if she hesitated, he'd call her back.

All the way to Lake House she stared out the window, her mind running wildly. Her shock at seeing the painting was so great it was a wonder she hadn't fallen apart right in front of Lockwood. A cold sweat broke out on her forehead, in spite of the comfortable temperature of the car's luxurious interior.

This reaction was ridiculous. It wasn't as if she hadn't seen her father's work before. One of his paintings hung in the bedroom of her apartment. Why had she taken the sight of that painting so badly? Just because it hung in Lockwood's house?

The line of coincidence did seem to be stretching rather fine. And yet, she supposed it was natural enough, given the circumstances. She already knew Lockwood had been around that summer when her father was here. Of course he'd be interested in a painting of his property.

If she hadn't been so shaken to see the painting, she could have asked Lockwood about it casually. That might have netted her some information. Instead she'd panicked, and as a result come away with nothing.

Well, not quite nothing. At least the immediate demand to tell Lockwood what she knew about the situation at Lake House was gone. She had a little time before she had to do something she didn't want to do.

Maybe, in this breathing space, she could find the answer to what was going on at Lake House. Once it was out in the open, neither side would have a bargaining advantage. If Matt was too stubborn to help himself, she'd do it for him.

Gillian was not quite so optimistic later, sitting at her computer. If she'd taken one more accounting class back in college, she might have been able to solve the riddle of the food service records. She almost welcomed the tap on the door that interrupted her fruitless search for answers.

Fred, the young intern, poked his head in. "Hi, Ms. Lang, can I talk to you for a minute?"

"Sure." She swung away from the computer. "What's up?"

He gave her a grin that made him look childlike. Someday he'd be glad of the youthful halo of blond curls and round face, but he probably didn't feel that way now.

"I'm looking for something to do. I've been assigned to housekeeping the last couple of days, you know?"

Gillian nodded. Interns often moved from department to department, much as she was doing. "Having problems with Mrs. Clemens?"

He blushed. "Well, not to say problems. She just won't let me do anything. Or look at anything. She guards her schedule like it's the crown jewels."

"That's Mrs. Clemens, all right. But I'm afraid there's not much I can do about it."

"Oh, no, I didn't expect you to do anything. I just wondered if there was any way I could help with your report. Mrs. Clemens keeps chasing me out of her office, and I'm tired of trying to look busy."

Gillian struggled briefly with the ethics of stealing an intern from housekeeping. She didn't suppose Matt would have any objection, and Ada Clemens would probably be delighted to have him out of her hair.

"Well, sure, I guess you can help." She pulled out the file she'd amassed on housekeeping. "In fact, you can organize the housekeeping data. That way you'll get a look at the operation secondhand, at least."

Fred took the folder and pulled a chair up to the small table under the window. "Okay, great. That'll give me something to say in the internship seminar when I get back to school."

"I'm sure you'll find plenty to contribute," she said sympathetically. "Working at Lake House has to be good experience, even if Mrs. Clemens won't let you get a look in."

"Yeah, it has been. I'm from Boston, you know? All this wilderness kind of had me spooked at first, but now I really like it."

"I know what you mean." She smiled back at him. He was a nice kid, even if he did have a tendency to stammer every time Matt spoke to him. Apparently she didn't intimidate him in the same way. "How did you get interested in hotel management, anyway? Is it in the family?"

"Sort of. My dad has a grocery wholesale business. From the time I was about six I went with him on deliveries to the big hotels. Just got fascinated, I guess. I never really thought of doing anything else."

A grocery wholesaler, right under her nose, when she'd been wondering how to get to the bottom of this problem with the food service. It had to be fate.

"You know, Fred, there's something that would be a bigger help to me than that housekeeping file, with your background."

He looked up, all eagerness. "Sure, whatever."

"Have a look at this."

As he peered over her shoulder, Gillian called up the records, spreading out the invoices and the comparisons she'd made. "Take some time to look at these and tell me what you make of it."

She leaned back in her chair as Fred stared from record to record, a trace of excitement growing on his cherubic face. Finally he looked at her.

"I think something funny's going on." He frowned. "Or maybe somebody's just really bad at entering the accounts. I suppose it could be that."

Fred had arrived at the same impasse she had. "Do you know any way of telling, short of a full audit?"

He shrugged. "I'm not sure. It seems almost too obvious to be fraud, doesn't it? If I were trying to pad the wholesale orders, I'd do a better job of it than this."

"Remind me never to put you in a position to do that."

She swung back in her chair. "There must be some way of finding out."

Fred frowned at the records. "We could check these against the original handwritten records. I happen to know that Andre won't touch a computer. Every record of his is done by hand, and then put on the system by one of the waitresses."

Gillian raised an eyebrow, and he blushed. So one of the waitresses had been keeping Fred occupied.

"I'm not going to ask how you know that. Now tell me how I can get my hands on Andre's records."

"You can't," he said, grinning and unrepentant. "Not unless you want Andre to come after you with a carving knife. But I start work in his department tomorrow. You want me to see what I can find?"

"I don't want to get you into trouble."

"No trouble." Anticipation lit his round blue eyes. "I'm just a lowly intern. Nobody will think twice about my snooping around. I'll see what I can find, okay?"

"Okay. But Fred, be careful, will you?"

He flashed her a smile. "No problem."

Maybe Fred's artless enthusiasm was contagious. By the time she went to her room after dinner, Gillian had thought of two other approaches she couldn't wait to try on the cancellation problem. In fact, she might get in several more hours of work tonight if she went back to the office now. A knock on the door interrupted that thought.

Gillian's heart bumped into overdrive when she found Matt standing in the hall. He leaned against the door jamb, a smile lurking in his dark eyes.

"Hi." It would probably be better if she didn't look

quite so glad to see him, but she suspected it was impossible to hide.

"Hi yourself." His voice was a low, liquid drawl. "I got to thinking we haven't been able to finish a conversation in the last couple days. You noticed that?"

Here was the moment she'd tried to prepare for the night they'd danced. Judging by the way the blood rushed to her cheeks, she wasn't any more ready now. She took a deep breath and nodded. "Why don't you come in? Maybe we can do something about that."

The room seemed drastically smaller with Matt in it. Or maybe it was just the way the air was charged when he gave her that dangerous, seductive look.

"First Brenda, then Della." He moved closer, then ran his finger along the line of her cheek with slow deliberation. Her skin warmed everywhere he touched. "I think they're conspiring to keep us apart."

"They're not doing much of a job of it right now." Her voice came out husky and breathless. Dear Lord, if he had this much effect on her in thirty seconds, she was lost for sure.

"I told them I was going to work out." He stroked the line of her collarbone, the curve of her shoulder, and her bones weakened. "Let them try and find me in the men's locker room."

"You really think a little thing like that would stop your Aunt Della?" If he continued that slow, intent touching a moment longer, her legs were going to buckle.

"I think it might—" He broke off, his gaze sharpening on something behind her. "What's that?"

The sudden change in his voice was like a dash of cold water in her face. She turned, but Matt beat her to the small object that lay on her pillow.

The Florentine ring. It had reappeared again, and from a locked suitcase this time. Gillian's heart sank. How on earth was she going to explain this? What could she say?

She could almost see the process going on in Matt's head: first disbelief, then suspicion, then anger. "This is the ring my mother wore in the painting. Where did you get it?" He fired the question at her, the air between them sizzling with anger, instead of desire.

She could try to convince him, as she'd tried to convince herself, that it was just a similar ring, but she knew it wouldn't do any good.

"Matt, I . . . " The words wouldn't come.

He covered the space between them in two furious strides and thrust the ring in her face. "Where did you get it, Gillian? What's going on?"

Her throat thickened as she tried to speak. "I'm sorry. I should have told you before. I just couldn't."

"Told me what?" He looked as if he wanted nothing so much as to shake the truth out of her, but he didn't touch her.

"The artist who painted that portrait. Alec McLeod. He was my father." It was out. She should have been relieved, but she wasn't.

Matt stared at her, his dark brows drawing down in a way that made him look very like that portrait of Robert. "Alec McLeod was your father," he repeated. "Why have you been lying about it? Damn it, I don't care—" He stopped abruptly, fingers tightening on the ring. "That doesn't explain where you got this ring. If it was my mother's, what the hell are you doing with it?"

Her heart pounded so fiercely she could barely speak. She had to explain. "It was found in my father's luggage, after he left Lake House that summer."

"Found?" The word was sharp. "What do you mean, found? What happened to him?"

Matt didn't know this part of the story. Someone here must have known about Alec McLeod's disappearance, but they probably wouldn't have told a child.

"My father left here after your mother's death," she said carefully, as if the words were breakable. "He deserted us, and we never heard from him again."

Matt's rigid expression softened slightly. "I'm sorry. But that doesn't explain how you got the ring."

"Later, one of my father's suitcases turned up in a Lost Luggage department in Chicago. They couldn't find him, so it was turned over to my mother. The ring was in it."

"Was it his?"

That was the crux of the matter, and they both knew it. Gillian shook her head slowly. "My mother had never seen it before."

"I see." Matt turned away, and she couldn't read anything in the rigid set of his shoulders. "Why did you come here?" he asked.

"I hoped . . . I hoped I might find out something about why he left." It sounded so futile. "I didn't know how people would react if they knew, so I didn't tell anyone."

"React?" He swung back to face her, and there was no doubt now about what he felt. Fury. He looked as if he'd like to strangle her. "How do you think people react when they find out you've been lying all along?"

She was helpless in the path of his fury, worse because she deserved it. And yet, how could she have told him? "I didn't lie, not about everything," she said desperately. "I just didn't tell you who my father was. Everything else happened exactly as I told you."

"You expect me to believe that? All that talk about

your dreams, about the feelings you had here, that was all an act. You were using that garbage to try and find out about your father!"

"No!" His fury seemed to be pounding into Gillian's head. "I didn't! It was true, all of it. Matt, you have to believe me."

She put out her hand, and he recoiled as if her touch would burn him. "Nice try, Gillian." He tossed her the ring, and she let it drop to the floor. "For some strange reason I don't believe a word you say. You'd better get packed. You'll be leaving in the morning."

Before she could say anything, he slammed his way out of the room.

For a long moment she stood there, staring numbly at the door. Then she bent, picking up the ring that was the cause of this. With a quick movement, she threw it violently against the wall. It bounced to the bed and lay there, sparkling in the light.

Matt. She sank down on the bed, pain settling deep inside her. Maybe she hadn't realized until this moment how much he'd begun to mean to her. Now she knew it, when it was too late. He'd never believe her now. He'd never even want to speak to her again.

She reached out and picked up the ring. If she accepted the unacceptable, if the ring really did keep appearing as a result of some sort of ghostly intervention, then the spirits obviously didn't want her to succeed. Because Matt was going to force her to leave, and she'd never know what happened that summer.

The ring warmed, heat emanating from it. She clenched it as the room began to waver around her. Panic flooded through her, and she forced it down. If there was something else to see, she had to see it before it was too late.

The green and rose walls wavered, becoming insub-
stantial, replaced by something rougher and darker.
Light poured into the room from somewhere above her.
The light pooled in the center of the room. Then she
saw them.

Her father stood at an easel, brush in hand. He wasn't
looking at the half-finished painting, though. His gaze
was fixed beyond it, on the person posed in the chair.

Clarice wore a green velvet Renaissance gown. Her
thick black hair was drawn back on top, accentuating her
high, clear forehead. Her hands rested formally on the
arms of the chair, and the Florentine ring sparkled on
her finger. It was an elegant pose, perfect except for one
thing.

Clarice's emerald eyes were bright with tears. She
cried silently, the tears rolling down her cheeks as if
they'd never stop. Her body didn't shake with sobs; her
control was too perfect for that. The tears simply flowed,
quietly, with such despair that it hurt to watch.

The image faded suddenly, and in an instant it was
gone. Gillian was left with the ache of unshed tears in
her throat and a fierce need that drove her to her feet.
She had to go to the cottage. Now. She had to.

She changed quickly into jeans and a sweater, then
found the small flashlight in the desk drawer. It was
stupid, maybe even dangerous to go out there this late.
But she was going to do it. She didn't know why, but she
knew what she had to do. Something waited for her
there. If she didn't go now, the chance would disappear
forever.

Dusk was already drawing in by the time she reached
the trail. She went quickly past the tennis courts, not
bothering to switch her flashlight on there. When she

reached the woods it was full dark, and she flipped the light on.

This had been a pleasant ride on horseback, in the daytime. At night, the world narrowed to the round yellow glow of her flashlight. She expected to be afraid, but she wasn't. Maybe it was a measure of how far she'd come that her lack of fear didn't even seem odd to her.

She wasn't afraid, because someone was with her.

The presence walked steadily beside her. It pushed her along the trail, making her surefooted even in the dark. She sensed protection, as if nothing in the woods tonight could harm her.

The trail wound past the eerie, jumbled rocks of the boulder field. Pale light, crossing the field, cast bizarre shadows that came and went as clouds rushed by the moon.

Gillian hurried up the steps and into the cottage. In the faint light of her flashlight it looked different. The dust and debris of thirty years of neglect seemed to fade. The crumbling walls grew more solid. This must have been how it looked when her father was here.

Her breath caught. She could smell the oil paints. Here, in this deserted ruin, she could smell the paints her father had used thirty years ago.

The aroma was strongest near the fireplace. Gillian followed it, hardly knowing why, only sensing that this was where she had to go. She stopped, several feet in front of the hearth. A shaft of moonlight pierced the room, falling on the floor at her feet. It picked out one particular wide, uneven board, with a knothole that looked like a handle.

Why hadn't they noticed it when they were here in the daytime? Gillian stooped, running her hand along the rough edges of the board. She didn't remember even looking at the floor then, but now it fairly shouted at her.

Without any hesitation, she slipped her finger into the knothole and lifted. The board swung up easily, betraying a long cavity beneath. And in the cavity . . .

Gillian probed, first with the flashlight, and then with her hand. Her fingers touched something smooth and cool. She pulled it out, into the feeble light.

It was a long, cylindrical bundle of dark plastic. She untied the string that held it fast, already knowing what she was going to find. It was a painting, of course. A rolled-up painting.

The canvas crackled as she began to unroll it. Maybe she should wait until she got it back to her room, but she had to have a glimpse of it, at least.

She unrolled an inch or two. Sky and trees, a portion of rock. Not in her father's representational style, though. This had a light, swirling feeling that was somehow graceful and airy. Before she could put a name to it, a flood of emotion swept over her.

Danger! The word fairly shrieked along her nerve endings. Danger, maybe even evil, approaching her, threatening her. *Get out, get out, get out!* The warning pounded into her brain so loudly she was sure she'd actually heard it spoken.

Gillian turned, rising. The beam of her flashlight swung around the room, then stopped at the far corner. Smoke, gray wispy smoke, filled the corner. The cottage was on fire!

Even as she thought the words, Gillian knew she was wrong. No fire had even behaved that way. The smoke swirled around, like a tornado forming in front of her eyes. It thickened, darkened, coalesced, turning into a dark, spiraling mass the size of a man. As Gillian watched, terrified, it seemed to make an effort to shape itself. The smoke twisted and turned, writhing into the form of a human being.

A scream burst from Gillian's lips. Clutching the roll of canvas like a shield against her breast, she turned and fled.

12

Gillian hit the porch running, bolted off it, stumbled and nearly fell. She staggered to her feet and raced for the path, her blood pounding in her head. She had to get away; she had to!

She hadn't run more than a few feet when something struck her a glancing blow. Shoulder stinging, she swung around, terrified of what she'd see. But it wasn't the eerie figure from the cottage. This was all too clearly a flesh-and-blood menace—a man, in dark clothing, some sort of dark hood covering his head and face.

He threw himself at her, and Gillian staggered out of reach. Instinct sent her bolting sideways, away from the rush of his feet as he charged at her again. He stumbled. Seizing the momentary advantage, Gillian darted away from him, straight out into the boulder field.

Moonlight carved a pale pathway for her, lighting some of the rocks, casting others into shadow. Unable to stop and think, Gillian raced across the rocks. The blood pounded in her ears, so loud she couldn't hear his pursuing footsteps. *Danger.* Where was that sense of protection she'd felt earlier? It was gone. All she could feel now was the overwhelming sense of danger.

The rocks at the edge of the field were large and smooth, and she ran over them, hardly pausing long enough to see where her next step was. Suddenly a drop emerged in front of her and she stopped, teetering wildly on the edge of a hole. She leaped over it, dropping to her knees as she landed on the other side.

Where was he? If he was right behind her . . . Gillian strained her eyes, panting, trying to see. The moon had disappeared behind a bank of clouds, giving her a few moments of darkness. She had to take advantage of it. If she couldn't see him, then he couldn't see her either.

The rattle of rocks, a sense of movement, disturbed the air off to her right. She took a deep breath and held it. He wasn't far behind her, probably not more than fifteen feet at the most. She couldn't stay here, or she'd be a sitting duck when the moon came out from behind the clouds. And she didn't dare turn the flashlight on, or he'd be on her in an instant.

Quickly, before she could lose her nerve, Gillian moved, feeling in front of her with her foot at each step, praying she wouldn't hit the rubble of loose stones and give herself away. Five steps, six, seven; she was widening the space between them, wasn't she?

She took another step, her foot hit a hole, and she landed on her knees, palms stinging as she caught herself. Cold, hard rock bruised her hands. Her breath stilled in her throat. He'd hear her. He'd know which direction to come. Even as she thought it, the clouds parted, sending a pale shaft of moonlight back across the boulder field.

Gillian's heart stopped. He was there, not more than a few feet from her. Instinctively she huddled into the shadow cast by the rock that loomed over her. *The shadow of a mighty rock.* The old hymn line sprang into her mind.

He'd turn. When he did he'd see her. How could he help it? If she screamed . . . Gillian bit her lip. If she screamed, he'd be on her long before anyone could hear and come to her rescue.

Like a rabbit, freezing in view of the fox, she held her breath, not daring even to bat an eyelash. He was turning, she could see the slight movement. From this angle his dark figure was silhouetted against the paler gray of the night sky. He turned in her direction, he'd see her, she—

But he went past. He hadn't seen her. Gillian let out a long, shaky breath. She couldn't move, not until he did. The instant she moved, he'd see her, and he was too close. She had to have a head start before she tried to run again.

He moved, off at an angle, away from her. She could still breathe. She raised her head, very slowly. Could she make it back to the path?

Then he was there, almost on top of her! Gillian nearly screamed, and realized in an instant that she was wrong. The menacing shadow was just that, a shadow, cast by the branches of a scraggly bush that clung to bare rock.

Where was he? She lifted her head a little more, straining her eyes to see the smallest movement, her ears to hear the slightest sound. She didn't dare make a move until she knew where he was.

She saw him now, a dark shadow against darker shadows. He loomed between her and the path from the cottage. She didn't dare go back that way.

For a brief moment that smoky form she'd seen in the cottage filled her mind, chilling her blood. She wouldn't go back that way, even if she could. The thought of confronting that thing again . . . even the masked figure seemed preferable. At least she could fight bone and muscle. She didn't know how to fight smoke and spirit.

The thought of a fight sent her hands groping in search of something, anything, that she could use as a weapon. She still held the flashlight, but it was too light. The rolled-up painting . . . it was gone. She must have dropped it in that first headlong rush across the rocks.

No time to worry about that now. Maybe, in daylight, if she survived the night, she could come back and look for it. If . . .

He was far enough away now that she could barely see him. She had to move. She didn't dare stay here, waiting for him to come back. She had to try and get across the boulder field to the path. Once she reached the tennis courts there'd be lights, maybe even people still out. There, she'd be safe. But first she had to get there.

She rose to her feet cautiously, wary of even the slightest movement. Crouching so she didn't provide him with an outline against the paler rock, she crept in the direction she hoped the path was. She angled across the field, praying she could strike the path and know what it was in the dark. Would she? Or would she just stumble across it, wandering endlessly through these rocks until he caught her?

Gillian dared to lift her head. There! Surely that gleam was moonlight hitting the lake. A wave of thankfulness surged through her. She'd moved the right direction, at least. As long as she went toward the lake, she headed for the path.

Cautiously, silently, she crept from rock to rock. The journey took on an insane pattern. Creep along, feeling ahead of her, until she reached the edge of a boulder. Reach, straining her eyes, trying to make out the form of the next one. One misstep could cost her a broken ankle, or worse.

She stopped to listen. Where was he? Had he given up? Maybe she fled with no one pursuing.

No, there he was. Her heart pumped harder. He was heading this way again, coming faster. Because he'd seen her? She wasn't sure, but she had to move.

Another step or two and she knew. He came straight toward her, with none of the casting around or tentative movements he'd shown before. He'd seen her. There was no time now to creep and hide in shadows. She had to run for it, trusting to luck that she could reach the path and bolt to safety before he was on her.

Gillian took a shaky breath, gripped the flashlight a little tighter, and ran, straight toward that gleam she hoped was the lake. She heard the rush of footsteps and knew he was after her.

She stumbled, heart thumping frantically, regained her balance, rushed on. If she tripped here . . . she couldn't, that was all. She couldn't fall, because then he'd catch her.

She bolted on, feeling the large rocks change under her feet to something smaller. Her shoes slid on the scree of loose pebbles, nearly bringing her down. Arms waving for balance, she managed to keep running. She knew where she was now. The loose pebbles meant that she'd nearly reached the path.

Even as she thought that, she felt solid earth beneath her feet, and had an insane desire to fall to the ground and cling to it. She couldn't stop yet. She wasn't safe yet. She had to keep running until she reached the lights.

The path under her feet led her on. Gillian raced along it. She could see the pale ribbon of the path even in the dense blackness of the woods. She couldn't stop and think about how odd that was. She couldn't do anything but run and run, not knowing how close behind her he was.

She bolted out of the last patch of woods, seeing lighted tennis courts ahead of her and beyond, the myriad lights of Lake House. She was almost there. A few more agonizing breaths, a few more steps . . .

A dark figure shot out from the shadows beside the path, and a hand caught her arm, jerking her around. Gillian swung out wildly with the flashlight, gasping a breath to scream.

Then she sagged in relief. It was Matt.

"What is it? Gillian, what's wrong?" He gripped her tightly, his hands the only thing that kept her from falling.

"Someone chased me." She gasped the words. "Back there, at the boulder field."

"That's crazy! No one would do that." His grip shifted to her hands, and she winced involuntarily as he touched her scraped palms.

Matt turned her hands up, looking at them searchingly in the dim light, and swore softly.

"I'm all right," she murmured, realizing it was true. She was safe.

"Go over there to the tennis court, under the light." Matt gave her a push. "Wait for me there."

"Where are you going?"

"To see what frightened you." His face grim in the shadows, he started back the path at a run.

Legs shaking, Gillian stumbled to the tennis court and huddled against the fence, under the light. Even these lights weren't bright enough for her. She longed to be in the midst of a crowd. But Matt had said to wait, and she'd wait.

It had been fifteen long minutes by her watch when she saw Matt's tall figure emerge from the trees. A little tremor ran down her spine as he approached. After their last exchange, she hardly expected him to believe her.

"Did you find anything?"

"Nothing." The strong planes of his face were tense. "What the devil were you doing out here this late, anyway? You probably ran into a deer or a fox, wandering around in the woods at night by yourself."

"It was no fox! I know a man when I see one. He was as close to me as you are now." She rubbed her shoulder. "He hit me with something, and then I ran. I managed to lose him in the boulder field."

"That's crazy!" Matt's anger was out of proportion, and fear flickered through her. "You're making it up; you're lying to me!"

"No!" Her anger rose to match his, anger combined with something else. If she could make him this angry, didn't it mean he still cared for her?

"Dammit, who were you with? Tell me! Who were you meeting out there?"

She tossed her head, sending her hair back across her shoulders. "Robert . . . " She stopped, stunned. It was Matt, wasn't it? He was Matt and she was—She looked up into his face, seeing the lock of white hair falling over the lines of his forehead.

He grabbed her, his face contorted with rage. "Tell me who he is!" He shook her. "Tell me!"

For an instant they stared at each other. Then Matt recoiled as if he'd been shot, staggering back a step or two.

A tremor ran through Gillian. Matt. It was Matt. She was herself. But for a moment she'd seen someone else. And he had, too. He couldn't dismiss it, not this time.

"You saw it, too," she whispered. She caught his arm, her strength coming back. "It wasn't just me that time. You saw something."

Matt wiped his face, then drove his hand through his hair. "You . . . for a minute I thought I saw my mother."

She wasn't crazy. Or at least, if she was crazy, so was Matt. "That's what I've been trying to tell you. It's not my imagination, and it's not a lie."

"I don't get it. Damned if I know what's happening, but we can't talk about it here. Let's get back to the House and do something about your hands."

They walked back to Lake House in silence. Gillian wasn't going to talk about it where anyone else could hear, and she needed a few minutes to regroup anyway. Her mind refused to function. Maybe her rational senses had just taken too much of a battering lately. They were shutting down.

Gillian stopped when she realized Matt was leading her toward the family quarters. "Wait a minute. Where are we going?"

"My rooms." He frowned. "We need privacy for this conversation."

"I don't want to talk about it with Della."

He looked blank for a moment. "Did you think Della shared the family quarters with me? Lord, no. That would be too much to take. She has her own suite." He took her arm. "Come on. You'd better wash the dirt out of those scrapes."

Matt walked through the living room so fast she didn't have time for the reaction the room usually gave her. He led the way into a bathroom. Gillian stopped and blinked when he switched the light on.

She'd thought her bathroom was the ultimate in Victorian. This room . . . marble tile under her feet, cut velvet paper on the walls, light fixtures that dripped crystal pendants. The tub, with its mahogany surround, was big enough for two. She felt her cheeks grow warm at the image that presented, and turned quickly to the sink.

"I know." Matt turned the tap on. "It looks like a Victorian bordello. I did manage to get a shower installed, but the plumbers had to put it in around the corner. It's inconvenient, but at least I've got one."

While he talked, Matt held her hands under the stream of warm water, cleaning the scrapes with a soft washcloth. His hands were surprisingly gentle, given how angry he'd been a few moments before.

He was so close she could see the curve of his eyelashes and the hairline scar on his cheekbone. She stared, mesmerized. Fine wrinkles radiated from the corners of his eyes, as if he'd spent too much time staring into the sun.

He glanced up and caught her watching him. "What?"

She felt the heat in her face. "Nothing. I can do that." She tried to pull her hands away as Matt enveloped them in a towel, but he held them firmly.

"You're still shaky. Better let me."

He dried her hands, then turned the palms up, bending his head to look at them closely. "Doesn't look too bad," he murmured. He looked up, his face close enough that she could feel his warm, moist breath against her cheek.

Matt's eyes darkened, the pupils dilating. His fingers moved from her palms to her wrists, her pulse pounding against his skin. After a long, charged moment he released her.

"I'll get something for those scrapes."

He turned to rummage through the medicine cabinet, and Gillian sagged against the sink. It was all just too much. She couldn't think, couldn't reason anymore.

"Antibiotic cream." He handed her a tube but he didn't offer to put it on. Maybe he didn't want to touch her again. "Come in the living room when you're done."

A few minutes later, they were settled at opposite ends of the long couch. Matt must think he should keep a little space between them. She shivered. After what happened on the trail, she didn't blame him.

"Tell me." Matt's grim expression didn't inspire confidence. "All of it. I want to hear everything you claim happened to you."

Claim. "And then you'll tell me I'm either lying or crazy."

His fists clenched. "I can't make any promises. But if you're crazy, it must be catching."

That was all the reassurance she was going to get. Her heart sank at the thought of how unlikely it all sounded.

"You know who my father was. Is." She stopped. "We don't know whether he's alive or dead. My mother thinks he's dead. Maybe it's easier for her that way."

"You told me he disappeared after he left Lake House. Now tell me why you came. What did you think you'd find after all this time?" Faint anger flickered through the words.

"Nothing. I didn't really believe I'd find anything. When Lockwood sent me here, I hoped I could learn something about that last summer. I guess the truth is, I wanted to know why he never came back." She tried, and failed, to smile. "Isn't that the perennial quest of the deserted child? To find out why?"

Matt stared down, as if fascinated by the pattern of the worn Oriental rug. He might have been thinking about his own parents. Suicide was a form of desertion, too.

"Maybe so," he said finally. "Why didn't you tell me to begin with? It didn't matter to me who your father was."

"I might have, except that by the time I met you, I'd had the first dream." She took a deep breath and tried to put it rationally. "Look, I know the dreams sound crazy, but they were so real. I saw this room in my dream, before I'd ever been in it. I saw your parents, quarreling. When I walked in here that first morning, I thought I'd pass out."

He frowned, the lines carving themselves deeply into his face so that he looked like Robert. "There could be a hundred explanations for that. You might have seen pictures, you might be interpreting the dreams on the basis of what you found out later. . . . "

"Don't you think I've told myself that?" She couldn't help the frustration in her voice. He was going to go over all the arguments she'd already had with herself. "Everything that happened to me, the dreams, the illness I felt when I passed the place where your father died, everything could be explained somehow, I suppose. But how do you explain what happened to both of us tonight?"

"That's the problem, isn't it?" Matt leaned forward, elbows on his knees. "That night we were in my mother's studio, I felt something. And the first time outside the cottage. It almost felt as if . . . well, as if I weren't myself. And you weren't you." He sounded furious at admitting it.

Gillian shivered. "I know. I've felt it, too. But tonight it wasn't just feeling. It was seeing."

Matt stood up and paced to the fireplace. He swung to face her. "Collective imagination? Mass hysteria?"

"I was close to hysteria." She managed a smile. At least he was thinking about it now, instead of just reacting angrily. "I don't think you were."

"No." He came back, frowning, and sat down closer to her. His anger faded as he zeroed in on the problem. "Tell me exactly what happened tonight."

She took a deep breath. None of it would sound credible, but she didn't have any choice but to tell him. It was the only way they'd ever get to the bottom of this.

"After you left, I was upset." That was putting it mildly. "I picked up the ring, and I saw . . . " She stopped, phrasing the sentence carefully in her head before she spoke. "I saw my father, working on that portrait of your mother. I had an overwhelming feeling that I had to go back to the cottage, that there was something still there for me to find."

"You went to the cottage. I suppose you figured tonight was the only chance you'd have."

She nodded. "Since you're kicking me out in the morning, it had to be tonight."

"Sorry." His jaw tightened, and he bit out the word. "I lost my temper."

"I understand why. The only surprising thing was that you let me stay until morning. Anyway, I went to the cottage. All I can say is that I seemed to be led there. I know that sounds hokey and ridiculous, but that's how it felt. And after I got there, I did find something, another painting, wrapped up and hidden under a floorboard."

Matt stepped toward her. "You didn't have a painting when you came barreling out of the woods."

"I guess I dropped it when I ran. I'd forgotten all about it. Maybe if we go and look—"

"Not tonight. We'll look for it in the morning. Now tell me about the man you said chased you."

"I'd just picked up the painting." This was the unbelievable part. Matt would never buy this, but she had to tell him. "I had an overwhelming sense of danger. I looked across the room, and in the corner . . . " She stopped and swallowed hard. It was almost impossible to talk about this and keep her voice from shaking. "In the corner I saw a column of gray smoke. While I watched, it seemed to be turning into a figure." Her hands were shaking to match her voice, and Matt took them in a firm grip.

"What did you do?" His voice was surprisingly gentle.

"I ran. I ran out of the cottage and when I got outside, I nearly ran into the man coming toward me." She shook her head. "I guess, in a way, that thing that I saw did me a favor. If I hadn't run when I did, the man would have trapped me there."

She couldn't stop the shudder that ran through her. Matt put his arm around her shoulders and drew her against him.

"It's okay now. You're safe." Some reservation in his voice told her the barrier was still there between them. He'd just put it aside for the moment.

"Am I?" Her voice shook, and it made her angry. Why was this happening to her? "Am I safe, Matt? Or am I going crazy?"

His arm tightened, the solid bulk of him against her was reassuring. This, at least, was real. "Like I said, if you're going crazy, then I am, too." His drawl was very much in evidence. "So let's work from the premise that neither of us is crazy. And if we're not, what does it all mean?"

His calm, matter-of-fact tone gave her confidence. She wasn't alone in this any longer.

"I wish I knew. Ghosts? ESP? Possession?" She made a face. "All of it sounds equally nuts. I wouldn't believe a word of it if it hadn't happened to me."

"Let's take the simplest explanation. For some reason, you're . . . susceptible to what happened here thirty years ago." Matt looked at her as if he'd had a sudden thought. "That is right, isn't it? Just that summer? You haven't run into my great-grandfather roaming the halls, or anything, have you?"

"From what you said about him, I'd be more likely to find him in my bedroom. No, I haven't seen or felt anything that doesn't relate to that one summer. But does that mean I'm just reliving it, like some . . . some video recorder, playing scenes over and over again? Or is there some purpose to it all?"

Matt shook his head. "Damned if I know. Maybe it has something to do with that ring." He paused, and she felt him stiffen as the thought hit him. "You think you know what that ring means, don't you?" He swung to face her. "You think your father and my mother were lovers."

13

For a long moment Gillian couldn't speak. How would this affect her relationship with Matt? She honestly didn't know.

"I'm not sure," she said finally. "When my stepfather gave me the ring, he obviously thought my father had gotten it from a woman. And then when I saw it in the painting . . ."

Matt's face hardened. "I knew my mother was involved with someone that summer. I just never knew who."

"You knew?" She couldn't keep the astonishment from her voice. "But you were only five!"

"People never think kids know anything." The muscles in his jaw worked. "I didn't put it together, not then. But I heard my parents arguing at night, after they thought I was asleep. It wasn't until later that I remembered the words my father used, and then I understood."

Gillian swallowed hard. "We can't be sure. Probably even your father wasn't sure. He knew something was wrong, and he thought that was it."

"Are you saying that because you know, or because you dreamed it?"

"How can I tell?" She got up and paced across the room, unable to be still any longer. "It's all mixed up in my head. I can't separate what people have told me from my dreams. It all seems so real to me."

"And how does the attack on you tonight fit into anything?" Matt drove his hands through his hair in exasperation. "You're not claiming that was a ghost, are you?"

"I'm not claiming anything. I'm saying that someone was out there and chased me." She rubbed her shoulder. "I've got the bruises to prove it."

"Sorry." He came to her and put his hand on her shoulder. For the first time that night he seemed to see her without anger simmering underneath. "How bad is it?"

She moved the muscles under his palm. "Tight. Sore. But I guess I'll live."

He began to massage her shoulder in slow, gentle circles. "Better?"

"Wonderful," she murmured.

"You've had a bad time of it. I'm sorry. I didn't mean to make things worse for you. But this is all pretty hard to take."

He slid his hand into the open neck of her shirt, so that his fingers rested against bare skin as he kneaded her tight muscles. Slow, seductive warmth radiated from his touch.

She had to think, keep control so she wouldn't dissolve into a puddle at the nearness of him. "Maybe . . .

maybe we're looking at two different things. Two different patterns. First there are the things that relate to that summer, things we've both experienced."

"That's one pattern." Matt drew her a little closer, his right hand tracing its way down her back while he continued that slow, tactile massage with his left. "What's the other?"

His mouth was so close to her cheek that the question sent warmth feathering against her skin. Yes, the anger was going, dissolving in the heat they generated whenever they touched.

"The attack on me. The rock slide you were caught in. The irregularities I've found in the accounts and the reservations."

For a moment his hand slowed, and she knew she'd distracted him. "Sabotage?" His eyebrows lifted. "Not only do we have ghosts, we have sabotage?"

"Well, something's going on," she said defensively. "I thought tomorrow I'd try . . . " She stopped. "I guess I won't be here tomorrow to try anything."

"Gillian." He cupped her face in his hands, his palms rough and warm against her cheeks. "Look, I'm sorry. I don't want you to leave. For a lot of reasons, most of which don't have anything to do with either ghosts or the hotel. But I don't want to put you in danger, either."

She put her hand over his. "I won't leave, not unless you kick me out. I have to know what's going on, or I'll spend the rest of my life wondering."

"So. We fight it out together, whatever it is?"

Gillian nodded. "Whatever it is."

His thumbs caressed the line of her jaw, sending heat coiling through her. "You're one tough lady, you know that? That's what I thought the first time I saw you."

Her body swayed against him, and she tried to keep her tone light. "The first time you saw me, you wanted to be rid of me, as I recall."

"Oh, no." His fingers slid around to the back of her neck, painting dizzying circles on her skin. "The first time I saw you I wanted to do this."

His lips came down on hers slowly. As soon as they touched the fire sparked, racing along her skin, pulsing through her nerves. She slid her arms around him, feeling the hard muscles against her palms as if the fabric of his shirt weren't there. His quick, indrawn breath told her the effect she had on him. At least she wasn't the only one feeling this way.

"You are so beautiful." He traced her lower lip lightly with his tongue, then took her mouth again, harder this time. The pressure of his lips and the force of his hands as they slid down to the curve of her hips demanded a response.

She was drowning in sensations, in the taste and feel and smell of him. She pressed closer, her breasts tightening against his chest, running her hands up his back and then down again. Each separate movement seemed to call forth a response from him. Each response brought an answering sensation from her.

She wanted nothing more than this. Maybe she'd been created for this particular man, for this particular storm of feeling that took possession of her.

"Matt."

He drew back. She felt the change run through him and wanted to deny it. He pulled his mouth away slowly, so slowly, as if it were the hardest thing he'd ever done. Her lips felt chilled. Her body ached to be close again.

"This isn't such a good idea." The anger flickered in

his eyes again. Not at her, this time. She clung to that. Not at her. "Damn." The word came out in an explosion of breath against her skin. "How can we do this?" He held her away from him, his fingers biting into her skin. "Damn it, Gillian, I want to make love to you right now. But . . . "

"I know." She shivered, remembering the moment when she hadn't known whether it was Matt or Robert who held her.

He glared at her, baffled and angry. "Maybe we better think about this in broad daylight. Because if you keep on looking at me that way we aren't going to be thinking at all. And when I finally get you in my bed I'd like to be sure it's you."

In her room, Gillian stared at the bruise that marked her shoulder. That was real. So much was happening that wasn't, it was almost a relief to deal with something physical. She slipped her nightgown over her head.

Who had the attacker been? She and Matt were so distracted by everything that went on between them that they hadn't discussed that question enough. Tomorrow they should meet in some nice, public place where they wouldn't be tempted to touch each other.

She couldn't ignore what was happening between them. She'd never felt this way about anyone before, and she didn't want to believe it was just the echoes of a love affair that had ended thirty years ago.

She crawled into bed, every muscle in her body aching. Surely tonight she was too tired to dream.

❀   ❀   ❀

Clarice stepped from the bathtub, drying herself quickly with the terry cloth bath sheet, then wrapping it around her. She was going to be late for dinner, and Robert would be upset again.

She wound another towel around her wet hair. That was nothing new, was it? Robert was upset about everything, these days.

She hurried out of the bathroom, leaving damp bare footprints on the rug, and ran right into Robert. He caught her arms to steady her, frowning.

"You're not ready yet? Where have you been?"

"Alec wanted me to pose for him this afternoon."

Robert's face tightened. "Alec." He said the name with distaste. "And naturally, you felt that was important."

"He is a talented artist, darling," she said lightly. "I think I ought to encourage him."

"How, exactly, do you encourage him, Clarice?" He pulled her against him, and she felt the heat of his body through the wet towel. "The way you used to encourage me?"

She pushed down the pain at his words. "He's hardly more than a boy. You can't think I'd be interested in him." She let her arms slide around him. "Not when I have you."

For a moment she thought he'd push her away, and then his hands pulled her tight against him. His mouth found hers, demanding, angry, hungering for her.

Clarice's lips parted under the force of his kiss, and the familiar heat swept through her. He loosened the towel, and it dropped to the floor. Her body imprinted wet patches against his clothes, and he didn't seem to care.

Robert lifted her in his arms and carried her to the bed, shoving the spread back with an impatient gesture.

*He lowered her to the sheets, his lips clinging to hers
while he yanked impatiently at his clothes. And then his
body was on hers, hard and sweet, and everything was
just like it used to be.*

Gillian sat bolt upright in bed, her cheeks hot, her whole
body aching with need. No, this was crazy. This time she
didn't just see Clarice. This time she actually seemed to
tap into the woman's thoughts and feelings, to experience every sensation Clarice felt.

Pulling her knees up, Gillian wrapped her arms
around them and rocked herself back and forth, as she
had when she was a child. This couldn't go on much
longer. It couldn't. If she wasn't already crazy, she soon
would be. Nobody could survive living two separate
lives, both of them in emotional turmoil.

Turmoil, that was exactly what she felt in Clarice.
Gillian ran her fingers into her hair, massaging the tight
skin at her temples. What was she saying? She'd been
assuming, all along, that Clarice's marriage was disinte-
grating, and that she had another lover. And yet the feelings Clarice had experienced for Robert in the dream
seemed so strong.

Was that how it had been? Or was this dream a product of Gillian's own feelings? Maybe she was imposing
her feelings for Matt on the dream. If so, she was in
more trouble than she'd thought.

By the next afternoon, Gillian had managed to shove all
the emotional considerations to the back of her mind.
Concentrate on work, that was what she had to do. It

had always succeeded for her in the past, and it would this time. Maybe it helped that Matt had been tied up in meetings all day, so she hadn't seen him except for a quick exchange in the hallway earlier.

She thought briefly of checking on Fred, and then dismissed the idea. If he came up with anything on the food service discrepancy that would be a bonus, but she couldn't count on it.

Gillian looked down at the printouts she'd run of the reservations and cancellations, starting in January of this year. There had to be an answer to this problem somewhere. She spread the printouts across her desk, shoving the telephone out of the way. Then she stopped, staring at the phone.

An idea suddenly entered her mind. Lake House had an eight hundred number for reservations. If she checked the telephone records against the reservations, she might at least see whether someone had been careless in recording them.

It was a simple matter to call up the information she needed on the system. It was not so simple to wade through all the data, looking for the matches she needed.

An hour later, Gillian leaned back in her chair, pressing the palms of her hands against her eyes. Was she misreading this, or was she right? In something like seventy percent of the cancellations she'd checked back to the original reservation, there was no call billed to the eight hundred account for that reservation.

She must be getting punchy. Gillian went back through the files again, and came up with the same answer. Most of the reservations that had later been cancelled were not made to the toll-free number. The percentage was even higher than she'd first thought. What, exactly, did that mean?

Not everyone who called to make a reservation called the eight hundred number, of course, but surely most people did. How could coincidence possibly account for that large a percentage?

It couldn't, that was all. It just couldn't. Maybe she was missing something, but the only explanation that occurred to Gillian was a very unpleasant one.

Someone with access to the computer system could have logged in fake reservations, blocking a number of rooms for the prime winter sports season. Then, when it was too late to book other guests, that same person could have cancelled the phony reservations.

As a plan, it was both ingenious and simple, and unless you were looking for it, you'd never find it. The question was, who?

Who had access, first of all? Almost anyone who worked for the hotel, so that didn't narrow it down much. Gillian frowned. What about a computer hacker, coming in from outside the system? Certainly she'd heard of such incidents, but it seemed a little far-fetched to her.

Gillian's mind edged toward a possibility she didn't want to consider. Matt thought Della was unbalanced, to put it politely, and she'd shown considerable antagonism toward him. Would Della be likely to come up with something this sophisticated? She didn't have anything to gain by it, as far as Gillian could see. If Lake House went under, Della stood to lose her home.

There was someone else who didn't think much of Matt, but the same argument that applied to Della applied to Brenda. If Lake House went under, she'd lose her job.

Gillian could think of one other possible culprit. Frederick Lockwood could, she supposed, be involved in this sort of underhanded maneuver. She didn't have any illusions about what he might do where business was concerned, but she really didn't see him stabbing the son of an old friend in the back. Besides, what did he have to gain? He'd be damaging a business that he planned to become a partner in, and it would be his money that would have to repair the damages.

Gillian folded the printouts and stuffed them into a manila envelope. This wasn't something she should leave in the unlocked office for anyone to find.

The telephone rang as she debated where to put the envelope.

"Hi." Matt's voice was warm in her ear. "Working hard?"

"Sort of. I spent half the morning retracing my steps last night."

She didn't want to mention the boulder field, but Matt would know what she meant.

"Anything?"

"Nothing."

The disappointment was tough to swallow. She'd been so sure she'd find the rolled-up canvas lying where she dropped it. She'd scoured the area, to find absolutely nothing. The one thing she hadn't done was go back into the cottage again. She couldn't make herself do that, even in broad daylight.

"So your . . . visitor must have taken it."

"I guess so." At least he wasn't implying that it had been a figment of her imagination. "I've found some other things I'd like to talk over with you." She stopped. She couldn't discuss this on the telephone, either.

"Guess there's a few subjects I'd like to talk to you about, too." His Texas drawl was very much in evidence. "What say we get out of here for the evening? Dinner in town?"

"Sounds great." A wave of relief swept over Gillian. It would be good to get away from the complications Lake House represented, even if it was just for an evening.

Matt picked up the menu and looked over it at Gillian. She'd been quiet all the way down in the car, but now that they were comfortably settled in the little Mexican restaurant he'd discovered, she seemed to be picking up.

They both needed to get away from Lake House for a while. Maybe away from it he could figure out what it was he felt for her. He sure couldn't trust his feelings there.

"Leave it to a Texan to find the only Mexican restaurant in the area," she said.

Her coppery hair glowed like flame in the candlelight, and she brushed it back across her shoulder with one hand. The silky blue of her dress brought out the brilliance of her eyes, and the way it clung to her breasts— well, maybe he'd better not think about that.

"Now, I never said it was Tex-Mex," he cautioned. "That would be too much to expect. But it's not bad, for a Northern version of Mexican. You might want to try the chimichangas, if you like those. That's what I had the last time I was here. When I go home . . ." He stopped. He wasn't sure he wanted to talk about how much he'd longed, lately, to see sky that wasn't hemmed in by mountains.

Gillian's blue-gold eyes held a question. "You're thinking about leaving, aren't you?"

He toyed with the silverware, balancing a spoon atop the fork. "It's been in my mind," he admitted. "I'm not sure how long I'll be able to hack it once Lockwood comes in. Maybe we'll put a manager in, and I can go back to doing something I do well." He could hear the slight trace of bitterness in his voice, and knew Gillian heard it, too. But damn it, she must know how he felt about it by now.

"I'd hate to see you do that." She put the menu down. "Don't you think—"

The waitress came up then, to take their order, and that got them safely off the subject of his plans. By the time the woman left, came back with margaritas, and left again, he was determined that he'd keep off the touchy subject of his feelings about Lake House.

He lifted his glass to her. "Here's to unraveling mysteries."

Gillian clinked her glass with his. "I'll drink to that," she said fervently.

Her tone reminded him that she had just as much need to find answers as he did. They'd been avoiding the subject of her father and his mother, because it was just too damn painful, but it had to be in her mind, as it was in his.

"You said on the phone that you had something to tell me. Find any answers today?"

"I think so." She turned her glass slowly on the bright print tablecloth. "I tried looking at the cancellation problem from a different angle, and something popped up." She reached into her oversize leather bag and pulled out a manila envelope. "Take a look at this."

He spread out what looked like copies of the reservations, followed by telephone records, moving the candle in the center of the table to make room. "What am I looking at?"

Gillian reached across to tap highlighted items with her finger. "These are the reservations that were made back in January for the winter sports season, the ones that were later cancelled." She touched the telephone records. "Now, here's a list of calls to the toll-free number for the same period." She frowned, and for a moment she looked uncertain. "Maybe you'd better look at them yourself, and see if you see what I do."

He pored over the records, moving the candle to give him a better light. At first he didn't get what she was driving at, but then a pattern started to emerge. He looked up to find her watching him intently.

"Don't look so worried." He reached across the table to touch her lips, startling her and himself. He'd promised himself he wasn't going to do that, hadn't he? But he couldn't seem to be in the same room with her without wanting to touch her.

"I can't help it." He thought the color mounted in her cheeks, but he couldn't be sure. "I have to know. Am I imagining things?"

"Not if what you see is the fact that most of the reservations that were cancelled didn't come in to the eight hundred number." He frowned, hating to admit he didn't understand the system. It looked as if he should have put himself through that intern program young Fred was in, before he'd ever tried to run a place like Lake House. "What does it mean?"

Gillian hesitated, and then spoke. "I think it means that someone with access to the system made phony reservations. That way the rooms would be marked as booked. Then, when it was too late to fill the rooms, that same person cancelled them."

"I see." He looked down at the sheets spread in front of him, groping for another explanation. There didn't seem to be any. "Who?"

"I don't know." Gillian didn't meet his eyes, and he knew she must have some suspicion she didn't want to name. "It could be anyone with access to the computers. Or even somebody hacking into the system from outside, but I don't think that's likely."

"Della." He dropped the name in a dispassionate voice. He'd known for years that his aunt didn't like him, although he'd never known why. That was her right, he supposed.

But it wasn't her right to sabotage his running of Lake House. A slow anger started to burn through him.

The worried look hadn't left Gillian's face. "Not necessarily. It could be lots of people. I just can't think of very many reasons why someone would do it. You don't happen to have a handy competitor we could blame it on, do you?"

"Not unless the winter sports trade is a lot more cutthroat than I thought it was," he said. "Somehow I don't picture the local ski lodges setting out to sabotage my season. We don't necessarily attract the same crowd."

Her blue eyes were troubled. "I shouldn't say this, but what about Frederick Lockwood? You know him better than I do. Would he do something like this?"

"If this dates back to January, Frederick's the one person it can't be. He didn't come to me, you know, I went to him."

The memory of that moment was as humiliating now as it had been then. Some things were just too big to swallow, and going hat in hand to Lockwood had been one of them.

"I didn't go to him until March. And he only made the offer as a favor to an old friend. He made it clear Lake House wasn't the expansion he was looking for, but he felt he had to bail me out."

Gillian looked sorry she'd brought it up. "I'm sure it's not just that."

Their food arrived then, and he was thankful for the interruption.

"Look, let's not talk about it now," he said when their dinner was served. "There might be lots of possibilities. Tomorrow I'll have a little talk with Aunt Della. Just sound her out and see what she says."

It was time, he decided. Time to bring this antagonism of Della's out in the open and deal with it. But it shouldn't involve Gillian. He had no right to put her in a situation like that.

After dinner they drove down by the river. Matt parked the car where they could watch its slow, steady roll. On the other side, across the valley, he could pick out the mountain on which Lake House sat. He couldn't see the hotel from here, but he knew where it was. He just wished he knew what was going to happen to it.

Gillian shifted slightly, leaning forward to look at the river. "It's beautiful. This whole area is lovely. I'm going to have to readjust when I go back to the city."

"But you're going to stay until this is cleared up, remember?"

She sighed. "What if it's never cleared up? I'd like to believe we're going to find some rational explanation for everything that's happened, but I can't." She sounded a little desperate.

"I'll tell you what." He reached across to touch her hair where it curled on the nape of her neck. "Why don't we give it a rest for tonight? I think we both deserve to think of something else for a while."

She turned toward him. "Like what?"

He pressed his palm against the side of her face. Her flesh warmed to his skin. "Like this."

As he leaned across to seek her mouth, a little voice in his brain reminded him that he wasn't going to do this. Too bad. He had to kiss her, at least once. But he had a feeling once wasn't going to be enough.

Her lips met his a little tentatively, as if she had doubts about the wisdom of this, too. Her mouth was warm and sweet, and tasted slightly of margaritas. He deepened the kiss, telling himself he shouldn't, and felt her response in her quickened breath and the way she turned into his embrace.

Lord, she tasted good. He wanted her, and he knew, right now, this minute, that it didn't have anything to do with anyone else. This was Matt and Gillian, finding each other and knowing that something good was going to happen between them.

But was it? He drew back, reluctantly. Was something good going to happen, if the only place they could make love without ghostly company was in a parked car?

"The gear shift is putting several dents in my anatomy," he murmured, his lips against her smooth, soft cheek.

She ran her fingers along his jaw, her touch feathererlight, but enough to make him want to feel her body against his. "Maybe we're a little old for making out in a parked car," she murmured. There was a hint of laughter in her voice. "Do you get the feeling this is the only safe place we can touch each other?"

"Something like that." He tasted her lips again, very lightly, because what he wanted to do had no lightness in it at all. He slid back under the wheel. "Maybe we'd better go home. This is only going to frustrate the hell out of me."

She pulled the seat belt around her. "Tell me about it. My room isn't equipped with a cold shower, remember?"

On the way back, he took the road up the mountain slowly, because that was the only sensible thing to do at night. Beside him, he could feel Gillian tense as they got closer to Lake House. Well, he couldn't blame her for that. He felt that way himself. Too many problems, too many unanswered questions waited there.

She gasped suddenly, as if something had struck her. Then she lurched forward, clutching the dashboard with one hand, straining toward the windshield as she stared out.

"Gillian, what is it? What's wrong?" He hit the brake and reached for her with one hand.

She grabbed his arm. "Don't you see it?" Her voice was shrill. "Hurry! Maybe we can help them!"

"Help who?" He was frightened by the white, terrified face she turned toward him. "Gillian, there's nothing out there."

"There!" She pointed toward the black hillside. "Don't you see it? Don't you see the fire?"

14

Bright orange flames blazed against the night sky. Gillian could feel the heat from here. Why wasn't Matt racing toward it? Maybe they could help, maybe . . .

She swung toward him and read the truth in his face. He didn't see it. The fire didn't exist.

"Don't you see it?" She heard the desperation in her own voice. "Matt, don't you?"

He shook his head slowly, his eyes very dark. "There's nothing there, Gillian. Nothing. I promise."

She still saw it, bright orange flames against black sky. Then they faded. In a matter of seconds the fire flickered out, with not even a glow left. The dark mountainside loomed above her, untouched.

Gillian sagged against the seat, her breath rasping in her throat. It had been so real. "I saw it," she said. "I'm not crazy. I saw it."

"I believe you." Matt took her hands, holding them

firmly in his. "I know you saw it." He stared grimly out the windshield. "You were looking at the place where my father's car went off the mountain."

Tears thickened her throat, making it hard to speak. "I'm sorry. Matt, I'm sorry."

"It's not your fault." His grip tightened. "I know this isn't easy for you."

He didn't mention how hard it was on him, but she felt it as he put her hands carefully away from him and started the car. The distance grew between them, and she couldn't blame him for it. How else could he protect himself from the painful memories she brought to life? "We can try and find out who's sabotaging your operation." Gillian tried to keep the pain from her voice. "But I can't begin to guess how we tackle this. I don't think watching *Ghostbusters* once qualifies me."

The faint light from the dashboard cast shadows on Matt's face. "I don't know either." He frowned, and she could tell that he, too, made an effort to speak normally, as if he tried to forget that they were talking about his parents. "Are we dealing with ghosts, rather than . . . I don't know, maybe remnants of memories that we're tapping into?"

Gillian rubbed her arms, cold in spite of the warm night. "What I saw in the artist's cottage wasn't any remnant, believe me. It was there, and it was real." She tried to smile. "Or maybe that's a contradiction in terms." A thought hit her, and she gasped with the realization. "That thing I saw, whatever it was . . . it was male."

"Why do you say that?" Matt's voice was sharp.

"I don't know why. I just know that's what I felt." She swallowed hard, not wanting to say what she had to. "Do you think . . . "

"That it was my father?" Matt completed the question

for her, and his face twisted. "I feel as if I've strayed into a production of *Hamlet*."

She clenched her fists in frustration. "What does it mean? If it was a ghost or a spirit or whatever, why is it here?"

"Don't they say that ghosts stay around because they have unfinished business?" Matt pulled the car into his parking space and shut it off, but made no effort to get out.

Ghosts. Were they really sitting here discussing ghosts? "I've heard that, I think. Are you saying that your parents want something from us? That that's why this is happening?"

Matt pounded his fist on the steering wheel in an explosion of frustration. "Damn it, there has to be some purpose in this. I refuse to believe that we're going through this for no reason except some sort of cosmic fluke."

"I know. But I don't know what we can do about it except . . . well, let it happen. See where it leads."

"Right now it seems to be leading to the conclusion that your father and my mother had an affair." Matt's face was grim. "I don't see that we can do anything about that. If it's true, I'd rather not have known."

Gillian stared at the lights of Lake House. The night she arrived, the hotel seemed to lurk over her, about to fall. "That isn't the kind of truth I was looking for about my father, either. But what other conclusion can we come to? It has to be significant that this only started when I came here."

"Somehow . . . " Matt spoke slowly, as if feeling his way. "Somehow I feel like there's something we have to do. Something more we have to find out. But how?"

That was the question. How could they find out anything now about something that happened thirty years ago? Only someone who'd gone through it might know something.

"Henry was here that summer. Have you ever talked to him about it?"

Matt shook his head. "He's always closemouthed with me about my parents. Maybe he'd talk to you."

"Why would he talk to me? He doesn't even know who I am."

"You'll have to tell him, I guess. See what you can get out of him."

Gillian nodded slowly. "I'll try. At this point, I'd try anything."

"I'll tackle Aunt Della." Something grim and almost frightening darkened his eyes. "It's time she leveled with me."

She wanted to say something reassuring, but she couldn't find any words. She'd like to think Matt was right and a resolution existed to all this, but she wasn't sure she could.

Fred caught Gillian the next morning as she headed into her office.

"Ms. Lang, hi. Got a minute?" His blue eyes sparkled, and the mop of curly blond hair was more unruly than usual.

"Sure, come in."

Gillian closed the office door, shutting out the row of photographs in the hall that seemed to watch them. Fred's air of suppressed excitement said he'd come up with something, so they'd better have some privacy.

"I've got it!" Fred pulled a sheaf of papers from a canvas gym bag. "At least, I've got something."

"Tell me." She leaned against her desk. Was she finally going to have some hard facts to go on?

Fred shoved a stack of invoices into her hands. "Luckily Andre never gets rid of anything. I was able to find the original invoices for some of the orders that looked suspicious. Turned out the wholesalers were people my dad knows."

He hesitated, and Gillian wanted to shake the words out of him.

"Well?"

"We were wrong. Nobody's been cheating the hotel. The bills that were actually paid match the original invoices to the penny."

Gillian sank down in her chair. She'd been wrong. It had seemed so obvious, but she'd been wrong. How many other things was she wrong about?

She leafed through the invoices, checking them against the bills paid. Fred was right.

"Well, that's a relief." She tried to put some enthusiasm in her voice. "I wasn't looking forward to accusing anyone of skimming. Especially not . . . " Her voice trailed off as a figure on one of the invoices caught her eye. She'd noticed it particularly because of the date, February fourteenth, Valentine's Day. Frowning, she switched on the computer, calling up the record.

Fred came to look over her shoulder. "Did I miss something?"

"I don't know." Slowly she paged through the records until she found that particular figure, that particular date.

Fred let out a low whistle. "That's weird. The computer records don't match the actual payment. How can that be?"

"A mistake?" Gillian reached for the stack of invoices. "Let's check some of the others."

Painstakingly, they worked their way through the invoices, comparing the actual payments to the computer records. At least a quarter of them were wrong.

Gillian stopped, finally, looking up at Fred.

"You said Andre had one of the waitresses enter the data on the computer?"

He nodded, and alarm leaped into his eyes. "Hey, I didn't mean to get anybody in trouble."

"It's okay, I wasn't blaming her. She might have made a mistake transferring the amounts, but I don't think that's what happened."

Fred watched as she highlighted the errors. "You think somebody doctored the files so that it looks like Andre's skimming?"

"I think so. I don't know how I'd ever prove it, but I think so."

"Weird. I mean, nobody got anything by doing it."

"No," Gillian said slowly. Nobody got anything. But there were entirely too many funny things going on for it to be a coincidence. "Look, can I keep these?"

"Sure, they're just photocopies. Anything else you want me to look for?"

His round blue eyes shone with eagerness. Fred obviously enjoyed playing double agent. She probably shouldn't have involved him.

"Not just now, Fred, but you were great. I'll let you know if there's anything else you can do."

"Hey, anytime."

When he'd gone, Gillian sat there, lost in thought. What did anyone have to gain by making it look as if a theft was taking place?

Someone might have a grudge against Andre, but this was an oblique way of getting back at him. If she hadn't been doing the evaluation, the discrepancy might never have turned up. As it was, she might easily have missed it.

She gathered up the copies, stuffing them into a folder. It was yet another thing she didn't want to leave in the unlocked office. She'd take it to her room before lunch. She could lock it in her suitcase, and hope that whoever or whatever moved the ring around would leave the papers alone.

Late that afternoon, Gillian sat in the little gazebo overlooking the lake. She should go in and get ready for dinner, but the spot held her. In spite of Henry's comments about it being one of Clarice's favorite places, she couldn't stop herself from coming back.

Tranquility, complete tranquility. She needed a little of that after the day she'd put in.

She leaned forward, hands on her knees, stretching her tired back. She'd spent the rest of the day working on her report for Lockwood. It had begun to seem unimportant stacked against everything else that was happening, but it was her job. Lockwood could show up again at any time. He'd expect her to have the report ready.

She'd just be verifying what he already knew. Lake House was an excellent property, suffering from management mistakes and some underhanded practices whose author she couldn't name. Yet. She still had hope she'd find out who was behind the problems, but proof—well, that was another story.

She might have suspicions, but suspicions wouldn't stack up against the black and white columns of profit and loss. And Matt . . . what would Matt do once the partnership deal went through? Depending on the percentage of ownership he sold to Lockwood, he probably would have the right to stay, but he obviously didn't want to.

Unless something happened, Matt would sign the deal and take off again, for Texas or the North Sea or wherever. He'd always carry with him that sense of failure.

And she'd go on with whatever assignment Lockwood Hotels had for her, wondering why she'd been so eager to find out the truth about her father, when it proved so depressing.

If her father and Clarice had been lovers, it explained why he left so abruptly. Once his life was shattered, there probably seemed no other course left open to him.

She could think that quite logically, and all the while underneath she heard a little girl crying. *Why didn't he love me enough to come back? Why?*

A movement drew her attention to the trail. Matt emerged from the woods, walking quickly, and came to stand at the opening to the gazebo. He braced his hands against the railing, looking as if he'd like to push the whole thing over.

"Has something happened?" A little tremor moved down her spine. She wasn't ready for any more bad news.

Matt's jaw clenched, looking ready for an explosion. "Nothing I want to talk about." He spun around and grabbed her hand. "Walk with me. I need to move."

He led her onto the trail that circled the lake, moving away from the House. His taut expression barely covered the anger bubbling ferociously underneath. Something had happened, obviously, and just as obviously he didn't want to talk about it.

The trail wound down to the fringes of the boulder field. Its pitted surface mocked her. She'd had enough of that spot, first fleeing across it in the dark and then going over the same territory inch by inch in the daylight, in a futile search for the rolled-up canvas.

That painting had to have meant something, or else why had she been guided to it? Now they'd never know. The whole episode was one more failure, one more unanswered question.

When they reached the dock, Matt stopped. "Let's sit a while."

The wooden planks were warm under them. Gillian deliberately turned her back on the boulder field, staring out across the lake. Matt was so close that she could touch him, but he looked miles away.

"Do you want to talk about it?"

"No!" The word exploded. His mouth clamped shut. Then he shook his head. "Sorry. I shouldn't take it out on you. I talked to Della."

"I see." It hadn't been a pleasant talk, obviously.

"She denies everything. She would. So that leaves us with nothing."

Something still simmered under those tense muscles, something he didn't want to tell her. Maybe Matt had second thoughts about trusting her.

"I got somewhere today." At least she had something positive to tell him. "With Fred's help, I figured out what was going on with the food service records." She frowned. "I think I did, anyway."

Matt turned toward her, resting his hand on her wrist. He seemed to make an effort to push aside whatever put that dark look on his face. "Tell me. I could stand some good news."

"Fred got his hands on the original invoices and made photocopies. Maybe it's better not to inquire too closely how he did that."

Matt's expression lightened, some of the tension dissipating. "Probably not. What did this enterprising kid find?"

"As far as we could tell from the invoices, nobody has actually been doing anything wrong. The errors cropped up in the computer records, making it appear there was a discrepancy."

Matt frowned. His fingers caressed her wrist lightly, almost unconsciously. "You mean it was deliberate?"

"I don't know. I think so, and Fred does, too. There's no way to prove it. Apparently Andre despises computers, so he forces whichever of the waitresses can do it to enter the information. It could have been entered wrong. But it could have been changed, later."

"By someone who has access to the computers. Again."

"Yes." This news wasn't cheering him up as much as she'd hoped.

"It all seems so pointless." He grabbed a pebble from the dock and threw it into the water. It landed with a plop, disturbing the shimmering surface of the lake. "What did anyone have to gain by this?"

Gillian shrugged. "Confusion. That's all I can see. It just . . . confuses things."

"It hasn't been hard to confuse me, that's for sure." Matt stared across the lake. Something dark still moved under his expression, like the underground springs bubbling under the smooth, clear water. "If I could do it all over again, I'd bring in an outside consultant before I took over this place. Or maybe I'd never have come at all."

"You had to, didn't you? I mean, Lake House does belong to you."

"Does it?" A muscle twitched in his jaw. "I'm not so sure I belong here. My grandfather never wanted me to come. He thought I ought to sell the damned place outright. Maybe he was right."

She could understand that. Jared Young had lost his daughter to Lake House. He hadn't wanted to lose his grandson, too.

"If you'd never come here . . . " she paused, not sure it was wise to finish that thought.

"If I hadn't come, neither would you. We'd never have met. We'd never have found out a hell of a lot of things we'd rather not know." Something dark and angry moved in his face. "Maybe that would have been better for both of us."

She swallowed hard. Would it have been better never to know? If she hadn't come here she wouldn't have found out about her father's affair. She also wouldn't have known that someone like Matt existed in the world. Was that a fair trade, given all the pain this was going to bring her?

"I can't pretend this has been pleasant." She felt her way, trying to define things she hadn't said yet, even to herself. "Before I came here I thought I knew who I was, what kind of person I was. I was wrong." Her fingers tightened on the rough boards under her hands. "I've found out a lot of things that hurt, but maybe they're part of who I am. Maybe I needed to know that. Maybe that's why I ended up here."

"Some kind of cosmic plan?" His words were bitter. "Seems uselessly painful to me. What good did it do to find out—" He stopped abruptly.

There was more here than she knew, more than they'd talked about. Something else was going on.

"What is it?" Apprehension edged along her nerves. She gripped his arm. "Matt, what is it?"

For an instant he stared down at her hand. Then his mouth twisted, and he pulled her hard against him. Need, pain, grief ricocheted from his body to hers, and then all of it was swamped by desire. Fierce, hungry, it tore through her, leaving her melting and breathless.

Matt groaned, turning to lower her body to the dock. Rough, warm planks pressed into her back. Matt's body was equally warm and hard against her. She clung to him, urging him closer, unable to think or reason, only to feel. Matt, the warm sun, the water lapping against the dock . . .

Suddenly fear jolted through her, mindless, over-whelming fear. She couldn't breathe! Someone held her down, hands pressing on her, pushing her. Water closed over her face, cold and black. Black as the sky, pierced by explosions of light. She struggled against the hands, trying to break free. She could swim for it if only she could break free of the hands. But she couldn't. They held her mercilessly, she couldn't breathe, she was going to die . . .

"Gillian!" Matt shook her, both hands on her shoulders, his face white with shock. "Gillian, snap out of it! Come on, it's all right, you're safe."

She sucked in a deep breath, then another. Air. She was all right. She wasn't under the water. . . . She looked around, confused. It wasn't night, it was day. She was safe.

The remnants of fear fell away, as if she shed something that didn't belong to her. She grasped Matt's hand, gripping it tightly. "What happened?" she asked.

"You tell me." Shock and anger battled in his eyes. "You went crazy, struggling, fighting me. You acted like I was trying to kill you. What the hell was going on?"

She went cold at his words, fear pouring over her in waves. "That was it. That was what happened. Clarice . . ."

He gripped her hands painfully. "Clarice what?"

"She . . . for a minute I was her. Under the water, feeling it close over my face." Terror made the words shake. "Someone was there, holding me down. Someone's hands on my shoulders, holding me under the water. I couldn't breathe, I . . ."

She stopped. No matter what she felt, she shouldn't be saying this to Matt. It was his mother.

His face had turned into a rigid mask. He swallowed hard, the muscles in his throat working. "You felt that." He wasn't questioning her. It was a statement of fact.

"I shouldn't have said it, not to you. Matt, I'm sorry. I shouldn't have said it."

"You had to." Harsh pain filled his eyes. "You just confirmed what Della told me this afternoon. She believes that my mother didn't die by accident, or suicide. She believes my father killed her."

15

Gillian stared at him, shock exploding in her mind. Dear heaven, no wonder he looked so strained when he found her this afternoon. She touched his arm, finding it hard as granite.

"Matt, no. She can't have told you that. It can't be."

"Why can't it?" He shook off her hand, his face tight and angry. "Because you'd like a happy ending to this? There isn't going to be one, Gillian. You just felt what happened. Damn it, you of all people should believe it! You felt his hands holding her under the water."

"No!" Her mind scrambled for some other explanation. There had to be one. She couldn't accept the idea that Robert and Clarice's stormy relationship had ended that way. "I didn't see a face. I don't know who it was."

"Who else could it have been? Who else had a reason? Face it, Gillian. All this craziness has been pointing to one conclusion. Your father and my mother had an affair, and my father found out about it. And he killed her."

"You don't know that. There might be some other explanation."

He wasn't listening to her. His face had taken on a dull, sick look. "That accounts for the feeling I get sometimes." His voice was low and flat. "Despair. Guilt. That's what I feel. That's probably what he felt."

Gillian caught at his arms, wanting to erase that dreadful expression from his eyes. "Matt . . . "

He looked at her coldly. "Don't you understand? That's why he sent me away. He couldn't stand to look at me, knowing what he'd done."

"You don't know that," she repeated stubbornly. She tightened her grip.

With a sudden movement, Matt knocked her hands away. "Leave it alone, Gillian. You've done enough."

Anger surged through her, fierce and sharp, and it relieved the pain. "So that's it?" she demanded. "You've decided you know the truth, and you're just giving up?"

"I'm not giving up, I'm accepting reality. Maybe you ought to do the same."

Gillian scrambled to her feet. "Fine, you do what you want to do. Accept it. I won't! I'm going to do something about it!"

Propelled by anger, Gillian hurried back along the trail toward the House, but eventually the feeling began to dissipate. Doubts crept in, replacing it. What if Matt was right? A logical explanation for everything they'd experienced, that's what she'd wanted to find. Suppose this was it?

She couldn't accept that, she just couldn't. Every fiber of her being rebelled at the thought. Not Robert. He wouldn't have done that. No matter how angry he'd been, he wouldn't have held the woman he loved under the water until she was dead. He couldn't have.

She hadn't known him, though. Her vivid dreams convinced her she did, but she didn't. She based her opinion on the feelings she had from her dreams. How reliable a guide was that?

For a moment her determination wavered, but then the feeling flooded back. There had to be another explanation. If Matt wouldn't do anything, then she would. She'd confront Della and demand the truth.

She found Della in the Parlor, supervising the arrangement of chairs for Theo's concert. Brenda looked as if she could have done with a little less supervision. For once she seemed glad to see Gillian, as soon as she realized Gillian wanted to take Della away.

"You go ahead, Miss O'Donnell. I understand exactly how you want it, and we'll set it up just that way." Brenda's smile was strained. "Don't worry about a thing."

Della looked doubtful, but finally she nodded. "All right, but see that you don't move anything unless you check with me first."

She followed Gillian out of the Parlor. Gillian led her to the sitting room opposite, where they could close the door and have a little privacy. A bank of windows looked out on the valley. The view, no matter how spectacular, couldn't distract Gillian. Her stomach turned over.

She had to make Della tell her the truth. Somehow she had to find something to refute the terrible assertion that Robert had killed Clarice.

Della swung to face her, the skirt of her Indian print dress flaring out. Again she wore that odd necklace of red thread, and from somewhere a snippet of information popped into Gillian's mind. A charm, that's what it was. Some cultures believed that the bit of twisted red thread protected the wearer from spirits.

"Well?" Della said. "I really shouldn't stay away. I don't know what that woman might do if I'm not there to supervise."

She hadn't thought about how to approach Della on this delicate subject. Maybe, with Della, no subtlety was necessary. Della delighted in saying outrageous things to other people. Now she'd know how it felt.

"You told Matt you believed his father killed his mother," Gillian said bluntly. "I want to know why."

For a moment Della stared at her. Then she tossed her head, sending her turquoise earrings dancing. "So Matt told you." A speculative gleam came into her eyes. "I don't see what business it is of yours."

Several possible answers occurred to her, most of which she didn't want to tell Della. "It's my business because Matt told me about it. He's very upset."

"I see." The speculation became certainty. "So it's like that, is it? I'm not sure Frederick will appreciate his employee becoming involved with Matt."

Was Della threatening her? It no longer mattered. Whether Della told Frederick anything or not was of less importance that finding out the truth. "Why did you tell him that?"

Della shrugged, turning away from Gillian to run her finger along the surface of a marble-topped table. "Because he asked me about his mother's death. I didn't tell him before because he was too young. Now he's old enough to know what she did."

"What *she* did? Don't you mean what Robert did? You told Matt that Robert killed Clarice."

"Only because she made him do it." Della fingered the fringe on the lamp shade, her fidgeting setting Gillian's nerves on edge. "He wasn't a violent person, but she drove him beyond what he could bear. So he ended it."

Maybe that made sense to Della, even if it wouldn't to anyone else. Gillian set aside, for the moment, the idea that Clarice was to blame. If she started arguing about Della's twisted reasoning, she'd never find out anything.

"What did Clarice do that was so bad it could lead to murder?"

"You should know that." Della swung back, fixing her disturbing dark gaze on Gillian's face. "You're the one who keeps feeling her here. Knowing things you shouldn't know."

Della was the one who knew things she shouldn't. How could she possibly know about that tenuous contact Gillian had with Clarice?

"I don't know," Gillian said flatly. "So you'd better tell me."

Della shrugged, touching the red thread. Her gaze slid away. "She put her painting first. Before Lake House, before her marriage. She thought her silly pictures were more important than her duty."

Della wasn't telling her the truth, or at least, not all of it. Gillian could feel the evasion.

"That doesn't seem like much of a reason for murder."

"Reason enough." Della moved toward the door, and Gillian darted in front of her.

"You're not leaving, Della. Not until you tell me why you think Robert killed her. The truth, this time."

"All right!" Anger flared in Della's face, frightening in its intensity. "All right! You want to know, so I'll tell you. She was going away. Deserting him! I found her that day in her room. She was packing. Naturally Robert—" She stopped, abruptly, as if she'd run out of steam.

"You told him, didn't you?" She saw it as clearly as if she'd been there. "You told him Clarice was going away."

Della's expression turned mulish. "It's not my fault. It's hers. She pushed him too far. When he heard what she was doing, he went looking for her."

"That night? The night she died? That's when you told him?"

"Why not? He had a right to know his wife was running away. Going off to New York with another man. He had a right to know that."

"Another man?" Her mind spun. Did Della know that, or was it her malicious imagining? "What makes you think she was leaving with a man?"

Della's mouth clamped shut, but Gillian could see she struggled not to speak.

"You're making that up," Gillian went on, to provoke her. "I don't believe there was another man at all."

Color rushed to Della's cheeks. "Of course there was! Robert suspected it all that summer, and she never denied it. Why else would she go away, if not for a man?"

"Who was it?" Gillian shot the question at her, hoping Della was enraged enough to blurt out an answer.

Della stared at her, eyes glittering. "Who knows? It could have been any of them. They all fluttered around her, like bees to honey. Henry, Theo, Frederick, they were all alike."

Della spun away, as if she'd said all she was going to.

"Which one?" Desperation flooded through Gillian. She had to know the answer. "Which one was her lover?"

"Who knows?" Della paused at the doorway. She smiled, her eyes narrowing. "It might have been any of them. It might have been someone else. It might even have been your father."

The words hit Gillian with the force of a blow, sending her staggering back a step. She knew! Della knew who her father was.

Gillian caught her breath. "I don't know what you mean," she said feebly. "My father . . . "

"Your father was Alec McLeod. Did you think I didn't know? I know everything that goes on at Lake House. Everything." She turned and was gone before Gillian could say a word.

Gillian sank down on the window seat, bracing her hands against the velvet cushion. She knew. Della knew. Maybe she'd known all along. But how could she?

Footsteps sounded as someone came along the hall. Gillian turned toward the window, shielding her face from view. No one must see her now.

The footsteps faded, and she stared out at the valley, leaning her forehead against the cool pane. Della knew, and she'd never said anything, never confronted Gillian about it. Who else had she told? Lockwood, maybe?

It didn't matter, not about Lockwood. She'd hopelessly compromised her job already. The only thing that mattered any longer was finding the truth. Maybe she'd already found it.

Della could be right. Gillian could almost picture Robert finding out that Clarice was leaving him for someone else, charging out into the night, searching for her in the grip of a murderous rage. He might have found her at the dock and accused her of leaving. Clarice wouldn't have backed down. She'd never back down. She'd have thrown her own anger back at him. And then—

No. Gillian still couldn't accept it. Even knowing what she did, she couldn't picture Robert knocking Clarice into the water and then holding her there, feeling her struggles weaken, until she was dead. No, he couldn't.

Unless he found her with another man. The thought bloomed, unbidden and unwelcome, in Gillian's mind. Suppose Robert had gone looking for Clarice and found her at the dock, and suppose she wasn't alone. That shock might have sent Robert over the edge of sanity.

Gillian pressed her hands over her eyes, but she couldn't shut out the pictures in her mind. If jealous rage possessed him, who could say what Robert might have done? But in that case, what happened to the other man? He wouldn't stand by and watch Robert kill Clarice.

Maybe the other man couldn't stop Robert. Once started on this train of thought, her mind wouldn't disengage, no matter how much Gillian wanted it to. Maybe that was why no one had ever seen her father after he left Lake House thirty years ago. Because he'd never left. Maybe Robert had killed him that night, and somehow disposed of his body so that it had never been found.

Hours passed before Gillian calmed down enough to think what to do next. She couldn't talk to Matt. That was the one thing she must not do, not with this terrible suspicion in her mind. If she went near him he might guess, somehow, what she was thinking. She couldn't bring herself to imagine what that might do to him.

Henry. She'd planned to talk to Henry, what seemed an eternity ago. That conversation was much more crucial now than it had been twenty-four hours ago. She had to do something to either allay or confirm these terrible suspicions. Among other things, she was terrified of what she might dream if she went to sleep with this on her mind.

Henry had a suite of rooms on the second floor, near the family quarters. Gillian hurried past the door to Matt's rooms, praying she wouldn't run into him. The hallway was quiet and empty, and she arrived at Henry's door without meeting a soul.

She paused for a moment before knocking, trying to think what she might say to him. What excuse could she give for coming to see him this late? The photographs Henry had taken that day at the gazebo would do as well as anything.

Henry opened the door immediately at her knock, looking at her with a surprise that was quickly and politely masked.

"Gillian, how nice to see you. Please, come in."

The living room of his suite had been turned into a workroom, furnished with a long table littered with proof sheets, papers and books, in addition to the more usual sofa and chairs.

"I'm sorry to disturb you so late." Gillian moved to the table, glancing at the photographs he had spread out there. "I wasn't sleepy, and I started wondering about the photos you took the other day. How did they turn out?" How astonishing that the words came out so casually, given the way her pulse raced.

"See for yourself." Henry slid a folder out of the stack on the table and flipped it open.

Her own face stared up at Gillian, and yet this was not quite the face she usually saw in the mirror. Her image of Gillian Lang was of an efficient, well-groomed business-woman, not this creature with the windblown hair and the dreaming eyes. She couldn't mistake the excellent composition of the photograph, but it made her vaguely uneasy.

"I know," Henry said, smiling. "It's not the way you see yourself. Photographs so seldom are."

He looked down at the picture in her hand, and his gaze suddenly sharpened. He looked from it to her living face, and she read the knowledge in his eyes.

"You know, don't you?" She held out the photograph to him. "You see the resemblance when you look at the picture."

"Alec McLeod," he said slowly. "I don't see it when I look at you, but in the photograph . . . you're his daughter, aren't you?"

Gillian nodded. "I really intended to tell you the evening you talked about him, but it seemed so awkward. I felt as if I were here under false pretenses."

"And are you?" Henry looked at her gravely.

Her cheeks grew warm. "I suppose, in a way. I never would have come if Mr. Lockwood hadn't sent me, but once I was here, I had to try and find out about my father. He never came back, you see. After that summer, he never came back to us."

"I'm sorry, my dear." Henry touched her hand briefly. "I did know that, and I never understood it."

Gillian blinked. That wasn't the response she'd steeled herself for. "Why do you say that?"

Henry looked down at the photograph, as if it prompted his memory. "For one thing, there was you." He smiled slightly. "He and I talked a number of times that summer. I suppose we had more in common than you might think. Every time we talked, he brought out a photograph of you. If ever I saw someone who was besotted with his daughter, it was Alec McLeod."

Her throat tightened. "I'd like to believe that he loved me, no matter what was happening between him and my mother."

"You should believe it. All he talked about was the portrait he'd paint of you when he got home. It would capture your personality far better than any photograph. I told him babies didn't have personalities, but he insisted I was wrong. His daughter, he claimed, was quite unique."

Tears stung Gillian's eyes. "Thank you for telling me."

"I think there's something else you want to know about that summer, isn't there?"

Gillian stared at him. "How do you know that?"

"Your interest in Clarice," he said. "You've been wondering whether your father was involved with her. Whether that's why he didn't come back."

"It is a possibility, isn't it?"

Henry seemed to focus on something far away. "I suppose, but I find it hard to believe. I never saw anything to indicate that they were more than friends." He sighed. "That was such a difficult summer. There always seemed to be thunder in the air. Personal thunder, I mean. Clarice and Robert fought all the time."

"I know."

He looked at her gravely, but he didn't ask how she knew.

"Poor Robert. He thought he was losing her. Maybe it was easier for him to suspect another man than to face what her painting meant to her."

"Clarice might have turned to someone who understood her work, for the sympathy and understanding she couldn't get from Robert."

"I suppose she might have," Henry said slowly, "but I don't like to believe it. They loved each other, those two, even though they never understood each other. And, of course, I loved them both."

"Della told me that she thought Clarice was planning to go away when she died." Gillian tried to phrase it carefully. No matter how sympathetic Henry was, she couldn't tell him that Della had accused Robert of murder. "Do you know if that was true?"

"I'm not sure. I know things became increasingly tense. I thought she might decide to stay in New York, just until after the show. But I never heard anything definite."

That was that, then. There didn't seem to be any way of ever being sure. Each person interpreted Clarice's actions through the lens of his or her own particular view. Gillian wasn't sure any of them really knew what drove Clarice, or even if Clarice herself had known.

"Poor Clarice," she said finally. "Today we like to think we can have it all, although I'm not sure that's true. But thirty years ago, it really wasn't possible, was it?"

"Not with two people as strong-willed as Robert and Clarice, I'm afraid." Henry smiled sadly. "Neither one of them ever heard of the word compromise."

Tears stung Gillian's eyes. It was sad, to think that two people who loved each other so much should hurt each other so badly. "Thank you for talking to me about this." Impulsively she kissed Henry's cheek, and he flushed.

Gillian turned to go, but he stopped her, holding out the folder of photographs.

"Before you go, there's a picture I think you ought to see. It gave me quite a shock when I developed it."

"A picture of what?"

"I don't understand it." He seemed to be talking to himself, rather than to her. He held onto the folder as if not sure he wanted to show her. "It wasn't there on the negative, I checked and double-checked. But when I developed the picture, this is how it turned out."

He handed the photograph to Gillian. She took it, not sure she wanted to look after a buildup like that. She glanced down cautiously.

It had been taken from the trail and showed the whole gazebo, with her sitting on the bench. She should have been alone. She had been alone. But the space next to her on the bench was filled with a foggy presence which might have been the form of a woman.

16

Gillian stared at the photograph until her eyes began to burn. Finally she turned to Henry.

"Do you see the same thing I see?" She held it out to him. His fist clenched as his side, as if unwilling to touch it.

"It looks . . ." He stopped and cleared his throat. "It looks as if someone is sitting next to you. A woman."

"Clarice. That's what you're thinking, isn't it?"

Henry nodded. He turned away from her and stood with his shoulders bowed, looking very old. "I've felt her here so often. I suppose that's why I decided to live here. But I never thought I'd see anything. And then you came. You feel her, don't you?"

"Yes." Gillian put the photograph on the table, suddenly not wanting to hold it any longer. "I've felt her. You knew it that first night, didn't you, when I talked about smelling the jasmine?"

"I've smelled it, very faintly, at times. I thought I

imagined it. But you were a stranger, and you smelled it." He looked at her, startled. "You're not really a stranger, though. You have a link with Clarice through your father. Maybe that's why you sense her here. Why this happened." He touched the photograph.

Gillian stared down at it. She could almost imagine she saw Clarice's sparkling eyes in that foggy shape. "Has this ever happened to you before? With a photograph, I mean."

"Never. I've heard of such things, of course." He smiled faintly. "Ghost photography was quite a vogue in England for a time. Though why a ghost should choose to appear on a photograph instead of to the naked eye, I can't understand."

"There's a lot about the whole situation I can't understand," Gillian said. "If Clarice is here, why? I mean, what's the point of it?"

"Supposedly spirits linger at a place because they died violently, or because there were unresolved circumstances at their death. Some people even believe that the spirits don't know they're dead. They just keep reliving, so to speak, the moments of death." Henry had adopted his lecturing manner, which apparently put him at ease.

Gillian shuddered, remembering the panicky sensations she'd felt on the dock. "That's a horrible thought."

"They say that at times all it takes to get a spirit to leave is for someone to tell them what happened, and to tell them to go."

"Have you tried that with Clarice?" She already knew the answer to that question.

Henry looked suddenly stricken. "No." His voice wavered. "I haven't. I suppose because if it worked, then she'd be gone."

Gillian put her hand on his arm, her heart aching for his pain. "I know how you feel, but wouldn't that be kinder? If you love her, isn't that the right thing to do?"

"I suppose so. But I'm not sure that my telling her would do any good. I'm not important enough to her, you see."

Poor Henry. He'd been cherishing his lost love for thirty years, and she'd never really been his.

"What about Robert? Do you ever have a sense of his presence?" She didn't intend to tell Henry about everything that had happened to her, but she had to bring up the subject, at least.

"No!" Henry looked aghast, as if an encounter with a ghostly Robert was the last thing he wanted. "You don't mean you have!"

Gillian shrugged. "A sense of him, sometimes. It's logical, isn't it? After all, he died violently, too."

"That was a terrible time." A spasm of revulsion crossed Henry's face. "That whole year was dreadful. First Arthur dying in the spring, then Clarice's death, and then Robert. It began to seem the place was jinxed."

"Arthur? You mean Arthur Lockwood, Frederick's brother?"

Henry nodded. "There's no reason why you should have known about it, I suppose. I just thought Della might have mentioned it. She was rather sweet on him, although I'm sure Arthur never saw her as more than a friend."

"She did talk about him, but she just said he'd died long ago. How did he die?"

"A climbing accident on one of the cliffs. Arthur was an excellent climber, but he shouldn't have gone out alone. Everyone told him that, but he wouldn't listen.

Stubborn fellow. All he cared about was his books and his birds and his climbing. The rest of the world could go hang, as far as Arthur was concerned."

"So he died, then Clarice, and then Robert." It seemed there ought to be a connection, with three deaths occurring so close together, but she couldn't think of one.

"I've always thought . . . " Henry began, and then stopped short.

"You've always thought what?" Gillian prompted.

"Robert's car going off the road that way? I never really believed it was an accident. He drove that road from the time he could sit behind the wheel of a car. Why would he suddenly drive off the road? That's what he did, you know. I was one of the first people on the scene. There weren't any skid marks. He just drove off the mountainside."

Gillian shut her eyes, but it didn't do any good. She could still see the car accelerate toward the guardrail, break through, and soar out into space. "So he committed suicide."

"They never said that, of course. Accidental death, that was what they said. Why put the family through any more grief?"

Suicide. And Clarice had been murdered. Gillian had no proof, but she was as sure of it as she'd ever been sure of anything in her life.

"Do you think Robert killed Clarice?" she asked bluntly. Henry had known them both. If anyone had an idea, he should.

Henry looked horrified, but not really surprised. "Of course not," he said at once.

"You've thought that, haven't you? You've thought that he might have killed her."

She saw the struggle in his eyes. "I suppose," he said finally. "The idea is there, sometimes. I don't want to believe it. Robert loved her so much."

"The two things can be very closely connected."

Henry nodded, the movement slow and tremulous. "If Robert did kill her, then I'm positive his death was suicide. He never could have gone on living if he'd been responsible for Clarice's death."

Gillian's mind went over and over the same territory, time after time. By the next day she'd have given anything to be able to think of something else. That wish was unexpectedly granted, when she received a call saying that Frederick Lockwood was on his way back to Lake House. He'd be expecting her report.

Chaining herself to the computer for the morning was the only possible way to finish. That meant that she probably wouldn't see Matt, and since there were too many things on her mind that she didn't want to mention to him, maybe that was just as well.

"Gillian?"

She looked up at the sound of his voice. Her heart jolted as if to remind her that she hadn't dealt with her feelings for him.

"Hi. How are you?" She asked it cautiously. How could he be?

Matt shrugged. He wore a dark suit and tie today, and she had to readjust her image of him. Actually, it didn't make much difference what he wore. He'd always look like a cowboy.

"Okay, I guess. I'm meeting with my attorney today." His smile flickered, sending a little tremor over her skin.

"Feels sort of like going to the dentist. We have to talk over the partnership deal."

"I see." There didn't seem to be much she could say to that. "I understand Mr. Lockwood is coming. He's asked me to have my report finished."

Matt lifted an eyebrow. "And what will you recommend?"

"You already know the answer to that, and so does he. Lake House is a good investment."

Matt shrugged. "I guess that's it, then. Assuming we can come to terms, this will soon be over."

"Not everything. The other matter—"

"As far as I'm concerned, we already know the answers to that, too." He made an effort to keep his voice casual, but his right hand clenched into a fist. "I don't want to talk about it any more. It's over."

Maybe the fact that he stayed so carefully on the far side of her desk told her just how much was over. Ice enveloped her heart. So it was over, before it really started. The last time they touched, they'd both been forced into revelations they didn't want to accept. Matt obviously didn't intend to let that happen again.

Should she try to tell him about the photograph? And about the other things Henry said? That would just hurt him more, and to no good purpose.

"All right," she said reluctantly. "I don't agree, but all right."

Matt stared out the window at the lake. "It's almost the Fourth of July. Maybe, once the anniversary of her death is past, all of this will stop."

"And if it doesn't?"

He shrugged. "I'll be gone, and so will you. There'll be no one left to see or hear it."

❀   ❀   ❀

Gillian walked into the dining room that evening and
was greeted by an unexpected sight. The round table by
the window overlooking the valley was occupied. Matt
sat with Frederick Lockwood and two men she didn't
know, probably the attorneys. It looked as if a deal were
in progress.

She found a seat and picked up the menu card, trying
not to look at them. Lockwood had received her report
earlier, given it a cursory glance, and asked for her opinion. She gave it, thinking all the while that there'd been
no purpose in her coming here, not from Lockwood's
point of view. He'd already decided, probably from the
moment the subject came up, that he intended to bail
out Lake House.

Investing in Lake House wasn't a mistake. Matt
shouldn't feel it was an act of charity on Lockwood's
part. Lockwood might have become involved because of
his long friendship with the family, but the Lockwood
Hotel chain would benefit from the association.

Gillian glanced over the top of the menu. Lockwood
leaned back in his chair, looking perfectly at ease. She'd
never seen him not look at ease, so that wasn't surprising.

Matt, on the other hand, didn't look either relaxed or
happy. Fine, tense lines etched around his eyes. Maybe
he'd been in a suit and tie too long. He fidgeted, as if
he'd be happier on a horse or an oil rig than sitting in the
dining room of his hotel with the man who was probably
going to be his partner.

Loose ends. Whether Matt would admit it or not,
there were too many loose ends. Her time at Lake

House would end soon, and apparently so would Matt's, and they'd both be haunted by things unresolved. His words echoed in her mind. He'd leave, and she'd leave, and then there'd be no one left. If Clarice had something to tell, it would go unheard.

After dinner Gillian couldn't settle anywhere in the House. She was sensitive to the whole place, as if allergic to it suddenly. She wandered outside and walked down to the lake.

She found a seat by the water, apparently the only person outside. Maybe people found the scene of woods and lake too lonely in the dusk. Gillian shivered as the breeze hit her bare arms, carrying the faint, musky scent of the woods. She was lonely, all right, but her loneliness didn't have anything to do with the setting.

The lake gave out a low whispering as water lapped among the rocks. Matt had told her the whispering sound came from caves in the rocks below her, as the water moved in and out. If a body washed into those caves, it might never be found.

She'd come here, weeks ago, thinking she'd find some answer to the riddle of her father's disappearance. Had she found it? She wasn't sure how to reconcile the two images she had in her mind of Alec McLeod. Henry had given her a picture of a young father eager to return to his family, planning for a future which included them.

Opposed to that was the Alec McLeod who might have been Clarice's lover. Who might have planned to run away with her, and who might have died with her.

Gillian moved restlessly, wishing she could be rid of all of it. She never should have come here, when it only resulted in so much unhappiness. Even if she never told Matt what she suspected, it would always stand between them.

She got up, unable to sit still any longer. She was probably dreaming anyway if she thought any relationship between her and Matt could survive. He could never look at her without seeing his parents' tragedy and his own failure.

A rectangle of yellow light spilled out on the porch as she approached the door. It should have been welcoming, but instead it seemed to reach ominously toward her, snaring her. She had a sense that something waited there in the House, and it waited for her.

The downstairs hall was oddly deserted. She started up the wide staircase. Was it darker than usual? Shadows seemed to throng the edges of the steps, and then draw back to let her pass.

She intended to go to her room but ended up, inevitably, in the one place in Lake House that was most associated with Clarice. Her studio.

Gillian walked to the center of the room. The only light was that which slanted in from the open door to the Parlor. It seemed wrong, somehow, to disturb the shadows.

She cleared her throat. "If you're here," she said softly, hardly knowing she was going to do it. "If you're here, I'm sorry. I think you wanted to tell me something, and I'm afraid I never really understood."

The shadows thickened, as if the room listened.

"Clarice, if you hear me, please try to understand. You don't need to stay. It was all over long ago."

A faint disturbance rippled through the room. The air stirred in response to some distant movement.

Gillian rubbed her arms as a chill moved over her

skin. Was this doing any good? Or was she acting like a fool, talking to herself in an empty room?

"Matt and I know now what happened that summer. I'm so sorry that it ended that way." Tears choked Gillian's voice, and she tried to hold them back. She had to think of the words, the right words, that would set Clarice free.

"It's over, Clarice. There's nothing you can do about it now. Matt is all right. You can let go, and find peace."

Peace. The word echoed through the room. And in the echo, the shadows began to move. Gillian took a step toward the door, then stopped. The shadows were thickest there, blocking out the light. She couldn't go through them.

Suddenly the very air in the room took on life. It pressed against Gillian, as if someone had thrown a heavy, wet blanket over her. She sagged, enervated, hardly able to bear the weight.

She stumbled a step or two, and the air began to swirl. It spun insanely around her, and she staggered with it, her hair tossing, her skirt whipping about her legs. She was caught in a tornado. And the noise . . .

Gillian clapped her hands over her ears. Surely everyone must be able to hear the rush of the wind and the voice that screamed inside her head. *No! No! No!*

She pressed her hands harder to her head. She couldn't stand it. If the noise continued another second she'd go mad, she'd—

Suddenly it was still. The rush of air collapsed in on itself, as if its strength disappeared. Gillian stumbled toward the door, reached it, and bolted through to the lights and normalcy of the Parlor.

✴   ✴   ✴

She sat up in bed for a long time that night, arms wrapped around her knees, reluctant to turn out the light. There had been no mistaking the gist of Clarice's message tonight. She wouldn't leave. She didn't want to be at peace. She wasn't done with them yet.

Why? Gillian almost asked the question aloud and stopped herself, afraid she might hear an answer. Why wasn't Clarice satisfied? What was there yet that had to be done, or had to be learned, before she could rest ?

The next day was the third of July. Perhaps that accounted for the odd feeling in the air, a combination of foreboding and expectation. Gillian couldn't settle to anything. The report was finished, and Lockwood hadn't yet asked her to do anything else. He didn't seem in any hurry to send her back to the city either, so she wandered about, at loose ends, wondering whether she should try and talk with Matt about what happened the night before.

She couldn't be sure he'd listen, if she did try to tell him. Frustration gripped her. If Clarice wanted to tell somebody something, why in heaven's name didn't she communicate with Matt? Gillian had certainly proved an ineffective vessel. She'd just succeeded in uncovering unpleasant truths they were going to have to live with.

What had that negative response from Clarice meant? Gillian certainly couldn't doubt that it had been negative. She shivered. Clarice might have meant she wouldn't, or couldn't leave. Or perhaps the negative was aimed at something else Gillian said, but for the life of her she couldn't think what that was.

Was Clarice telling her that they still didn't really know

what happened that summer? Gillian would be glad to be proved wrong, but she couldn't think what else to do.

Finally, as much to get away from her own thoughts as anything else, Gillian changed her clothes and set out for a walk. She ended up on the trail that led to the top of the cliff, the way she'd gone that first day, when she'd found Matt at the top.

She wouldn't find Matt there today. He was closeted with Lockwood and the attorneys. No one told her anything, so she didn't know for sure, but they were probably going over the final details of the agreement. The clock wound down. One way or another, her time here drew to an end.

Gillian came out into the clearing at the top of the cliff. Matt wasn't there, of course. But Della was. She stood on the rim of rocks that overlooked Lake House, far below. She turned to stare at Gillian.

"I didn't mean to disturb you." That vague, unfocused stare unnerved her.

"Come here." Della didn't seem surprised to see her. "I want to show you something."

Gillian edged out onto the rocky surface. She wasn't really afraid of heights, but she'd rather have something to hold on to up this high. Standing atop a height with nothing but the swirl of air around her made her uneasy.

"What is it?" She reached Della's side and looked in the direction she pointed.

"Down there. You can see Frederick's car from here." Della's gaze was intent, no longer vague. "That means he's here, talking to Matt. Maybe signing the papers right now."

"I suppose so." Gillian couldn't tell whether the idea pleased or frightened Della. Today she hid her thoughts behind that smooth, unlined face.

Della swung toward her, reaching out to grasp Gillian's arm. "Did you tell Matt?"

"Tell Matt what?" Gillian scoured her brain for something she might have been supposed to tell Matt and forgotten.

"What I did." Della shook the arm she held, her grip tightening. "I never meant to tell you that, you know. You made me angry. I said more than I should. Matt isn't to know, you understand? Matt isn't to know."

Alarm quivered through Gillian. Della was always a little strange, but this intensity frightened her. She tried to pull her arm free, but Della clutched her tightly.

"I don't know what you mean. I didn't repeat anything you said to Matt."

Della's eyes darkened. She took a step closer, so close Gillian could hear the rasp of her breath. Gillian tried to move back, and found her foot too near the edge of the cliff. Her breath caught in her throat. She didn't like this at all.

"Della . . . " she began. Della thrust her face forward.

"Matt can't know," Della said again. Her eyes glittered. "Matt can't ever know I told Robert about Clarice leaving. He might think I was to blame."

Fear crawled along Gillian's skin. "I won't tell him," she stammered. "I promise." Right now she'd promise anything, just to get out of this situation.

Della's eyes narrowed. "How can I trust you?" She pressed closer, forcing Gillian to the very edge of the cliff. "You're too much like Clarice."

Pure hatred flashed in Della's eyes as she said the name. Gillian's fear escalated to panic. Della's hatred wasn't quite sane. Gillian stood on the edge of a cliff with a woman who looked as if she'd like to kill her.

17

"Gillian! Is something wrong?" Henry's voice was the sweetest sound Gillian had ever heard. She turned, very cautiously, to see him standing on the trail, his face white.

"Everything's fine." She met Della's gaze, challenging her. "Isn't it, Della?"

Della stepped back. "Fine," she muttered.

Legs shaking, Gillian passed her, gained the trail, and grasped Henry's arm.

"Are you going down? I'll walk with you." Maybe her voice didn't sound as shaky as she felt.

"That's a good idea." Henry glanced at Della, but her face was averted. Without a word to either of them, she set off up the trail.

When she was out of earshot, Henry let out a long breath. "What happened? Was Della . . . " He didn't seem to want to finish that question.

"I'm not sure. She was . . . strange."

"You were so close to the edge." Henry still sounded horrified, and his color hadn't returned. "It frightened me."

"It terrified me. For a moment Della looked so angry I thought she was going to push me over."

"She wouldn't!" He clutched Gillian's arm, as if afraid she might collapse. "My dear, you're upset. I know Della can be trying at times, but she'd never hurt anyone."

Trying at times. Henry certainly had a gift for understatement. Della had gone far beyond trying.

"You've known her for years." Gillian searched for the right words. "Has there ever been any suggestion that Della . . . well, that Della could use some help?"

"Psychiatric, you mean?" Henry blanched. "I'm sure there's never been anything serious enough for that. She's always been rather high-strung. Obsessive, you know, about Lake House. Come, let me walk you down."

They started down the trail. Henry held her arm, but he was still so pale Gillian wasn't sure who helped whom. She didn't want to distress his further, but this had to be clarified.

"I'd call her hatred for Clarice a little more than high-strung, wouldn't you?"

Henry swallowed hard, his eyes not meeting hers. "I didn't realize you knew about that." He paused. "I think Della had convinced herself Robert was never going to marry. He left it late, you know. She pictured the two of them continuing on here together, running Lake House just as they had for years. Then he met Clarice."

"Love at first sight?" That's what it must have been, between those two.

Henry nodded. "In a way it was my doing. I'd seen

some of Clarice's paintings in a show of promising young artists, and I met her." Talking seemed to do him good. His color returned. "Robert happened to be in the city, so I took him to a reception at the gallery. Wanting to show off my beautiful young friend, perhaps. They took one look at each other, and it was as if there was no one else in the room."

"How long was it before they were married?"

"A month." Henry gave a slight, sad smile. "Frankly, I'm surprised they waited that long. Clarice insisted on flying out to Texas to tell her father in person. I'm not sure that was successful. Her father never did warm up to Robert."

No, he wouldn't have. "So they were married, and Robert brought Clarice back to Lake House and expected her to take on responsibility that had been Della's." It wasn't hard to guess what the response to that would be.

Henry took her arm again to help her over a rough patch in the trail that she could have negotiated perfectly well by herself. "Robert really wasn't very clever where women were concerned. Anyone who knew them would guess that there'd be fireworks between Della and Clarice."

Fireworks. She shivered at his choice of words.

"And the ironic thing was that Clarice didn't really want to run Lake House," Henry said. "She just wanted to have Robert and her painting, too. Unfortunately as far as Robert was concerned, marriage to him was marriage to Lake House."

"Della tried to break them up, didn't she?"

Henry looked uncomfortable. "Well, I don't know that I'd say that, exactly. Certainly she didn't make things easy. Della's always had a rather malicious streak, and she tends to take sudden dislikes to people for no reason at all."

She'd had plenty of reason to dislike Clarice. That dislike had ripened into hatred. She'd seen it in Della's eyes up there on the cliff, the hatred for Clarice that she transferred to Gillian. If Henry hadn't come along . . .

"How did you happen to appear at just the right moment? I was beginning to think I'd have to tackle Della to get away from her."

"Well, I . . . " Henry seemed reluctant to go on. "I had a feeling." He flushed. "I suppose that sounds strange, but that's what happened. I'd been out walking, but I had started back. Something just . . . came over me. I had to come up the cliff trail, whether I wanted to or not."

Clarice had been busy. "I understand. It happened to me, too." She shivered. "Thanks for giving in to the feeling, Henry. I'm not sure what would have happened if you hadn't."

"It would have been all right. Della wouldn't really harm anyone." Henry seemed to be trying to convince himself.

She didn't press the point. It didn't really matter, did it? Della hadn't hurt her, even if she had seemed to hate her.

The thought struck Gillian with the impact of a blow. It was Clarice Della hated. Alive or dead, Della hated her. She admitted having told Robert that Clarice was leaving that night. What if she had done more than tell him? What if Della had gone looking for Clarice that night herself, and found her?

*　　*　　*

Later that afternoon Gillian sat at her desk, still trying to decide whether to tell Matt what happened with Della. Frederick Lockwood strolled into her office.

"Gillian, there you are. Are you clearing up here?"

"Yes." Actually she'd been sitting there staring into space, but there didn't seem much point in telling her employer that. "Is there something I can do for you?"

That didn't come near the question she wanted to ask. What was happening? What was going on with Matt, with Lake House, with her? Everyone's fate rested in Frederick Lockwood's aristocratic hands.

He shook his head. "Everything's under control. Why don't you simply finish clearing up here?"

"Of course." Gillian bit her lip to keep from asking the questions that burned in her mind.

"By the way, I'm sure you'll be glad to know that our business here is concluded. Matt and I signed the agreement this afternoon."

That was that, then. "Congratulations, Mr. Lockwood. I know you'll find Lake House well worth the investment." And what was Matt going to do? Stay, or go?

Lockwood glanced out the window at the lake. "I'm planning to stay over for the Fourth. You may as well do the same. After you've finished what you're doing, take the rest of the week off." He smiled. "You've done an excellent job, and I know you've put in extra hours. I won't expect you back in the office until Monday."

"Thank you." Being here for the Fourth of July celebration might not be a good idea, but it didn't look as if she had a choice. It also didn't look as if Lockwood intended to tell her Matt's plans.

He started to leave, then paused in the doorway. "There will be some management changes here, of course. If you have any recommendations for the incoming team, pass them on to Brenda Corvo. She'll be staying."

That seemed to give her an opening. "And Mr. O'Donnell?"

"Matt's decided that hotel management isn't for him. I can't say I'm surprised. I understand he'll be leaving for Texas in a few days."

By that evening, Gillian had worked herself into a rare state of depression. This was the last normal day at Lake House. Tomorrow would be the Fourth of July festivities, with their overlay of tragedy. And the next day she'd be gone. Apparently Matt had run out of things to say to her. He hadn't made any effort to see her all day.

Again she had that sense of loose ends dangling, waiting for her to tidy them up. Maybe she should try, one more time, to talk to Matt. He should hear about her experience in his mother's studio. If he wanted to ignore it, that was up to him, but he ought at least to hear it.

And it would give her one more chance to talk with him privately before she left. She couldn't lie to herself about that. She wanted to see him again. Even with everything that stood between them, she wanted to see him again. Unfortunately, Matt apparently didn't feel the same.

Well, he'd just have to take it. Determined, Gillian headed for the staircase. He shouldn't brood all alone about his supposed failure. They had to talk, and she wasn't leaving until they did.

o   o   o

Matt stood on the balcony, watching darkness ripple across the lake like a blanket. He wouldn't do this many more times. Wouldn't look at this view, and if he was lucky, wouldn't feel this way.

Tomorrow night fireworks would explode in the sky. They could hardly cancel a long-standing tradition just because he found it painful beyond belief.

Especially this year. Everything that had happened to him and to Gillian brought his mother's death home in a way he hadn't felt in years. All that grief had been stored away, waiting to be let loose.

Swearing softly, he turned his back on the view and leaned against the railing. Gillian. He wanted to see her again. He wanted to hold her again. It had been all he could do to stay away from her today.

Not here, and not now. Everything that had happened in the last few weeks was building to something. She didn't seem to sense that, but he did. He'd be damned if he'd let that something, whatever it was, hurt Gillian.

The knock at the door raked his nerves. Couldn't he have privacy tonight, of all nights? If it was Brenda with a problem, she could damned well take it to Frederick.

The knock came again, sounding determined. Furious, he crossed the room and threw the door open. Gillian stood there, hand still raised to knock, looking as stubborn as if she intended to stand there all night.

For a moment he stared at her, imprinting her image on his brain.

"Hi." Her determined expression wilted a little in the face of his silence. "Matt, we need to talk."

His hand clenched on the door. This was a mistake. But he opened it wider. "Come in."

As long as he didn't touch her, they were all right. That crazy sense that someone else took them over wouldn't come unless he touched her.

"Are you okay?" Those blue-gold eyes of hers darkened with concern. "I thought I'd see you at dinner."

He shrugged and gestured her to a seat. When she sat on the couch, he deliberately chose the chair on the other side of the hearth rug.

"I didn't feel like joining the crowd tonight. You know we signed the papers today."

"Mr. Lockwood told me." She glanced away from him. "He also said you're leaving."

"There's no point in staying. Frederick's putting in his own management team as part of the deal. I don't plan to be a figurehead."

Bitterness penetrated his voice, and he didn't care. It was like that first afternoon, when he and Gillian had talked in his office. He'd had to face what was happening then, and she'd known what he was feeling, just as she knew now.

There was a difference. Then, they hadn't known anything about each other, beyond that immediate current of attraction between them. Now . . . maybe now they knew too much for casual conversation.

"I'm sorry." Gillian's eyes sparkled. She held back tears. "Matt, I'm sorry it turned out this way."

He leaned back, folding his arms. What he wanted to do was cross the room and kiss away those unshed tears. If he did, it wouldn't stop at that. His blood already pounded, even with half the room between them.

"Don't be. I didn't have a choice. We both knew that from the beginning. Thanks to your digging, I was in a better bargaining position than I could have been."

"I'm glad something I did here was worthwhile." She bit her lip, and the vulnerability of the gesture set his nerves sizzling. "Sorry. That didn't come out quite right. It's just—"

"I know. Look, we didn't expect what we were going to find out about that summer. It's nobody's fault the truth turned out to be pretty damned painful." If she didn't stop looking at him that way, he was going to do something they both might regret.

"That's just it." Gillian flung out her hands. "I'm not sure we do know the truth. Last night—"

"Not another dream." He cut her off. "Gillian, I'm sorry, but I don't want to hear it."

The color came up in her cheeks at that. The sparkle in her eyes turned to anger. "Not a dream, and you have to listen, whether you want to or not. She's *your* mother, Matt. Why do I have to cope with it? And why on earth are we shouting across the room at each other?"

"Because I don't know what might happen if I touched you, that's why."

She took a quick, sharp breath. "I didn't think."

He stood and paced to the fireplace, bracing his hands on the mantel. "Damn it, Gillian, do you think I like this? All right, tell me. What happened last night?"

"I went back to your mother's studio." She stood up too, as if she couldn't sit still any longer either. "Maybe it was stupid, but I thought that if I spoke to her, if I told her we knew everything, maybe she could find peace."

He stared at her. "You . . . " He shook his head. "I can't believe we're discussing this seriously. Okay. I guess I understand why you did that. What happened?"

Gillian rubbed her arms, although the room was warm. He could see the fine, fair hairs standing up on her skin. Something had happened, if just the memory affected her that way.

"It felt as if someone was listening. Maybe it was my imagination. I told her we knew what happened that summer. And that you were okay." She met his eyes. "I thought she might want to know that."

Something hurt inside him at the image. "Then what happened?"

"The whole room went crazy." Gillian's eyes widened in remembered shock. "It was like being in the middle of a tornado. And the noise . . . " She swallowed, the muscles in her throat working. "All I could hear was a voice in my head. I thought I would go deaf with it. It kept shouting, over and over. *No! No! No!*"

Suddenly she put her hands up to her ears, as if she heard that voice again. She shook her head, and the helpless look on her face was a blow to his heart.

He couldn't stand it. In a few quick steps he crossed the space between them and pulled her into his arms.

"Gillian." He whispered her name against the soft fragrance of her hair. "Hey, it's okay. Don't cry. It's over now. Whatever it was, it's over."

She shivered, her whole body trembling with strain. He smoothed his hand down her back, and her warmth penetrated the fabric against his palm. "It's all right, honey. It's all right."

Her arms went around him as if she had to hang onto something. "I'm okay." Her voice was muffled against his chest, setting up vibrations that warmed and teased. "I guess I started remembering a little too vividly."

He tilted her face back with one hand at her throat, and her warm pulse beat against his skin. She smelled of sunshine and flowers. "You shouldn't have tried that yourself. You should have told me what you were going to do."

"I couldn't." Her lips trembled, and he wanted to kiss them until the trembling turned to something else. "Don't you see, Matt? I didn't want you to be hurt by this anymore."

For a moment he couldn't say anything. "So you decided to risk getting hurt yourself?" Anger flashed through him, mixing with desire. "I don't need your protection, Gillian."

She stared at him. "I wasn't trying to protect you. I just . . . I didn't know what else to do." She tried to smile. "You've gotten kind of important to me, you know."

Important. The word branded itself on him. She'd gone in that room knowing something could happen, because of him. And he'd been holding back, telling himself it was safer that way. Safer! When the hell had that started to matter to him?

There wasn't a second between thought and decision. His mouth claimed hers, desire blossoming against her skin like an exotic flower.

Damn. He was done being careful. This was him and Gillian, no one else. Whatever he had to do to keep the others at bay, he'd do. He'd be damned if he'd let anyone, living or dead, come between them tonight.

18

Dismay gripped Gillian as Matt's lips sought hers. They shouldn't do this. They both knew the risk was too great. To be taken over, to be invaded in that way by someone or something else . . . that was unbearable.

His kiss was warm and persistent. Slowly her fear ebbed, vanishing as her body kindled to his touch. This was Matt and Gillian, no one else. As her conviction grew, hunger swept through her like wildfire, wiping out the traces of fear. No one else touched her now, just Matt.

Gillian stroked his back, finding hard, smooth muscles through the nubbly cotton of his sweater. She urged him closer against her. He groaned, raining a trail of kisses down the line of her throat, and she tingled everywhere their bodies touched. The faint, musky aroma of his after-shave teased her, like the scent of the woods after a storm.

"Just us," he whispered, and his breath was warm and moist on her throat. "Nobody is going to come between us tonight."

"Are you sure?" She arched closer, smothering the faint sparks of doubt.

"I'm sure," he growled. Then his soft laugh tickled her skin. "This may be the strangest conversation any two lovers have ever had."

Her breath caught on his words. "Lovers?"

He drew back a little, and the air cooled her skin where his kiss had been. His chocolate eyes were rich with promise.

"Oh, yes." His fingertips traced the throat of her shirt, slightly rough against the silk, the friction whispering softly. "I've been planning to make love to you since the morning I found you at my breakfast table."

"Liar. You were furious with me."

"Not furious. Frustrated. You sat there all prim and businesslike, ready to do battle. But there was butter dripping from your fingers, and I could see your pulse beating right here." He kissed her throat, then the curve of her shoulder, igniting her skin in instant response.

"You terrified me." Attempting to think was like grasping smoke when Matt's lips were doing dizzying things to her. "You looked as if you wanted to throw me in the lake."

"Only if I went with you. What I really wanted was to do this." He kissed her again, caressing her mouth even as he stroked the curve of her breast, sending desire licking like flame along her veins.

"It's a good thing you didn't." Her breath was out of control. "Every time you've touched me since—"

He stopped that sentence with his mouth. "Not every time," he said. "This time I intend to have you all to myself. There's nobody else here." His tone challenged her to argue. "Nobody."

"Nobody," she agreed, her lips against his.

The last remnant of doubt burned away in the heat of his kiss. His confidence raced into her, as if when their bodies touched their minds melded.

Matt's tongue stroked the curve of her mouth, then dipped inside. Rational thought was swallowed up as the sensation blossomed inside her. She clung to him, exchanging kiss for kiss, breath for breath, caress for caress, until she could no longer tell where she left off and he began.

He tugged impatiently at her shirt, then slid his hands under it. The feel of skin against skin escalated the passion that licked along her nerve endings.

"I have a nice big bed in the other room." He punctuated the words with kisses. "I want to see you in it."

"Why don't you show me?"

Matt swung her up in his arms. She buried her face in the curve of his shoulder, drinking in the faint musky aroma and the heat that penetrated his sweater. He carried her across the room.

A moment later the bed gave under her body, the quilt sliding away as Matt pushed it. The cotton sheet was cool, then warming where her body touched it.

Matt leaned over her for an instant, his eyes darkening with arousal. Then the bed gave as his warm weight covered her. He kissed her, long and slow and thorough.

"Mm." He drew back at last, looking at her with a lazy smile. "Now this is what I had in mind." He stroked her hair, spreading it across his pillow. "This is what I've been seeing in my dreams."

"Have you?" Her mind flickered away from her own dreams. She wouldn't remember that now.

She slid her hand under his sweater. His stomach was smooth and taut, his chest all hard planes and crisp hair.

Her fingertips seemed to grow more sensitive with every touch.

His breath stilled, and then he stripped his sweater off, tossing it aside. He captured her hands, pinning them against his chest with one hand while he undid the buttons of her shirt with the other.

Cool air from the open window touched her over-heated skin. Gillian brushed aside the momentary impulse to cover herself. This was what she wanted, to be here with Matt. This was what they'd been building toward every day they were together.

Matt pulled the silk shirt free of her. It slithered to the floor as he reached for her skirt. She helped him, their fingers entangling, and in a few moments the fragile barrier of clothes was gone from between them.

Matt paused, arched over her, looking at her as if memorizing every inch of her body. Her skin heated at the frank pleasure in his face. Then he was against her, and conscious thought vanished in flame.

She was on fire everywhere they touched, and only the very thing that caused the fire could possibly put it out. She found herself thinking muzzily that she'd have to fight fire with fire.

Desire blazed through every inch of her, searing in its intensity. Then he thrust into her, and the flames united in a single fierce, consuming blaze.

Gillian woke to the softness of an unfamiliar bed. She stretched lazily. Her body was warm, as if it still glowed with pleasure.

She turned, the cotton sheet rustling. Matt had pulled it over them when the air from the window cooled their heated bodies. The night was so still she could hear the soft lapping of the lake outside the window.

Matt's arm was a warm, sweet weight across her breast. She pressed a kiss into the smooth skin of his shoulder, her lips lingering as the scent and warmth of his skin enveloped her. Her heart overflowed with tenderness so piercingly sweet that she had to blink back tears.

Gillian moved carefully, not wanting to wake him. She raised herself on her elbow so that she could see his face.

The moonlight that streamed through the open window painted his face with silver and shadow. She spread her palm flat on his chest. His heart beat against her hand, strong and steady.

I love him. Surprise and inevitability mixed. *I love him.*

The feeling was so new and so surprising that Gillian found no need to share it, not yet. All she wanted in the world right now was to watch Matt sleep and to savor the fact that she loved him.

Matt stirred. Perhaps he felt her gaze on him, even in his sleep. He frowned, turned restlessly, and flung out an arm.

Suddenly, to her shock, he began shaking his head. "No!" The word burst from his lips, frightening in its clarity. "No, no!"

"Matt!" Alarmed, Gillian shook him. "Matt, wake up. What's wrong?"

He groaned, a sound so deep and heart wrenching that it frightened her. Then he lurched up onto his elbows, eyes opening, still shaking his head as if to shake off the remnants of his dream.

"Are you all right?"

He looked at her with eyes that didn't seem to see her. Slowly they focused, and the staring gaze softened.

"Gillian. What . . . " He thrust his hand through his hair. "Sorry."

"There's nothing to be sorry about." She ran her hand down his arm, to assure herself that he was all right. "You must have had quite a nightmare." She tried for a lightness she didn't feel. "I'm not sure that's very complimentary."

Matt still looked faintly dazed, and some remembered horror lingered in his eyes.

"I'm the one with the dreams, remember?" she said, touching his face.

He caught her hand in his and pulled it away. Fear tinged Gillian's concern. What was wrong? Matt looked at her as if she were a stranger.

"I'm sorry," he said again. He seemed to pull his composure around him like a blanket. "I must have scared you."

She looked at him steadily. "It only scares me if you try to shut me out. I thought we were in this together, Matt. What's going on?"

"It's nothing to do with . . . with what happened between us." His fist clenched the sheet. "It's an old dream. I don't know why I had it tonight."

Some of the fear inside her ebbed. She wanted to touch him, but the memory of the way he'd pulled her hand away still stung. "Tell me."

He shook his head. "I don't want to talk about it."

The bleakness in his face hurt her. "Matt, I . . . " Without thinking she touched his shoulder, and he jerked back.

"Leave it alone, Gillian. Please."

She stared at him, pain battling anger for control. He had no right to hold out on her now. "Whatever it was, it's here between us. I think I have a right to know."

"All right!" The words burst out of him. "You want to know? You won't like it."

Something cold touched her heart. "I still want to know."

His face hardened into a mask. "I told you how my mother came to talk to me the night she died, how she told me she might be going away." His mouth twisted. "I didn't tell you the rest of it. I didn't tell you that my father came in later, too, to say goodnight. And I told him."

Her heart hurt at the pain in his eyes. "Matt . . ."

"I asked my father why she was going away. He didn't know about it, and I told him!"

She must have known, at some subconscious level, that he'd been holding back something like that. Guilt, the guilt he talked about feeling—it wasn't just Robert's. It was his. And it was so unnecessary.

"Matt, don't." She clenched her hands to keep from touching him. "It's not your fault."

He looked at her as if he hated her. "Don't you get it, Gillian? I told him. If my father went out that night and killed my mother because she was leaving him, it was my fault."

The words dropped between them like stones. Gillian swallowed hard. She had to get through to him, and she didn't know if she could.

"It was not your fault. You were a little kid, for heaven's sake. You said something perfectly innocent, and—"

"Innocent! If I hadn't said anything, my mother might still be alive."

"That's crazy, and you know it." Gillian's voice was sharp. "In the first place, you don't know that Robert killed her. And even if he did, you weren't responsible. If it was going to happen, it would have happened anyway. Besides, you weren't the only one who told him. Della told him that night that Clarice was going away."

Matt stared at her. She hoped to see some sign of relief in his face, but it wasn't there. "Della?" he repeated. "Della told him? How do you know?"

"She told me. I don't think she meant to, but she was angry, and she let it slip. Della found Clarice packing that day, and told Robert."

She was breaking her word to Della, but it didn't bother her in the least. Matt's feelings were far more important right now. He had to let go of this guilt that he carried.

He shook his head. "I should have known. But it doesn't matter. It doesn't wipe out what I did."

Gillian clenched her teeth to keep from screaming at him. "You didn't do anything wrong. You have to stop thinking that way. Do you imagine your mother would blame you, if she knew?"

"Probably not, but that doesn't change anything. Look, Gillian, I know you want to help, but there isn't anything you can do. I'd stopped thinking about it, until this summer. Once I leave Lake House . . . "

Once he left her. That was the unspoken commentary under what he said. If Lake House reminded him so painfully of that childhood betrayal, what about her? Every time he looked at her and thought about the events of this summer, he'd remember. Pain closed around her heart.

Matt swung himself out of bed, picked up his robe, pulled it on. He walked to the balcony door and stood looking out at the lake, his back and shoulders rigid.

"This isn't turning out the way either of us thought, is it?" He didn't turn to look at her as he spoke. "I wish things could be different, Gillian. I really thought . . . well, I shouldn't have let this happen, not here."

Gillian wrapped her arms around her knees and tried to still the shivering that set in, starting deep inside her. "That sounds like regret. And good-bye." Her voice choked on the words.

"Not good-bye." He turned toward her then, but he carefully didn't touch her. "I don't want to say good-bye. You mean too much to me. But as long as we're here, we'll be haunted by everything that happened. Once we've left Lake House, I'll meet you anywhere you say. It'll be different then."

Even as she nodded, Gillian felt the cold, dead resignation inside her. He meant it, of course, but it wasn't going to happen. He'd never be able to look at her without remembering this summer, and that other summer thirty years ago. And that meant there was no chance of a future for them. No chance at all.

19

Gillian worked like an automaton the next day. It was the only way she could keep from thinking, and the only way she could keep the pain at bay. The problem was that it didn't work, not entirely. Grief kept seeping in around the edges of the barrier she'd erected in her mind, and she couldn't do anything about it.

The day dragged endlessly. The Fourth of July celebration went on without her. Games, a water carnival, an endless array of food—none of it had any appeal for her.

Gillian had a sandwich and an iced tea at her desk and kept working, compulsively. No one bothered her. Everyone was out, joining in the celebration.

The recommendations Mr. Lockwood had told her to leave with Brenda took longer than she'd expected, maybe because she couldn't seem to concentrate. Apparently Brenda Corvo would get what she wanted. She now worked for Lockwood Hotels. She should be glad that someone, at least, would have a happy ending.

As for her . . . well, she'd already packed. When she finished this, she could leave. She didn't have to stick around for the inevitable fireworks tonight. She could drive down the mountain, stop at a motel somewhere for the night, begin the painful process of getting over Matt.

A figure drifted by her open doorway, then turned and came in. Gillian looked at Della warily. She couldn't forget that episode on the cliff.

She had told Matt what Della did. If he'd said something about it to Della, she might be in for a difficult time.

There was something on Della's mind, but it didn't appear to be confrontation. Without speaking, she wandered around the office, touching things and then putting them back, always in a slightly different position.

Gillian's hands stilled on the keyboard. She couldn't possibly work with Della in the room. Maybe she should force her to come to the point of this visit.

"Is there something you want, Della? I'm rather busy right now."

Della's dark eyes shifted nervously, as if she was afraid to meet Gillian's gaze. "I just . . . Henry talked to me. He said I need to apologize to you."

She said it as a child would, forced into an apology by an irate parent. It was hardly sincere, but politeness demanded that Gillian acknowledge the words in some way. She looked at Della and realized that the time for polite exchanges was past.

"Why did you do that, Della? You frightened me. Was that what you wanted? I could have been hurt."

Della's eyes flickered. Frightening her was probably exactly what Della had had in mind.

"I wouldn't have hurt you," Della muttered. "I wouldn't hurt anyone."

"You wanted to hurt Clarice," Gillian pointed out. "You did hurt her. You tried to break up her marriage."

"That was different." Remembered anger flared on Della's face. "You don't know what it was like. We'd been so happy. Then she came and everything changed."

"Robert was married. Naturally things would be different." Didn't she see that?

"All of a sudden everything revolved around her. Robert behaved like an idiot. Anything Clarice wanted, Clarice had to have. After all the years I gave to Lake House, my feelings didn't count for anything."

"It made you angry," Gillian said softly. Della was angry now, and angry people sometimes let things slip that they wouldn't otherwise say.

"Yes, it made me angry!" Della's eyes blazed. "It would make anyone angry. Everyone fluttering around her, praising her, talking about how wonderful she was all the time. And when she got pregnant . . . well, you'd have thought no woman had ever had a baby before. That was her job, that was what she was supposed to do! Give Robert an heir to carry on at Lake House!"

Della might have been talking about royalty, to hear her. Did she have the slightest idea how absurd that sounded? Probably not. Della really did see Lake House that way, like some medieval stronghold that had to be defended to the last man.

"You hated the attention Clarice got," Gillian said. If she kept Della talking, she might learn something, assuming there was anything left to learn.

Della gripped the edge of the desk. "She had to be the center of everything. And of course all the men played right into her hands. Especially that last summer. You don't need to think your father was immune to her. He wasn't."

The barb hurt, but not much. Maybe Gillian was getting used to the idea. "What about your friend, Arthur Lockwood? Were you telling me the truth when you said he didn't care about Clarice?"

Della's lips tightened, but her blazing eyes answered the question. "It didn't mean anything." The words burst out. "Arthur just admired her painting, that's all. Not like those others. They wanted to take her away from Robert."

"You used that, didn't you? You played on Robert's jealousy to come between them." Anger swept through Gillian. "How can you say you wouldn't hurt anyone?"

"That was different," Della said again. She'd probably been saying that to herself for the last thirty years. She leaned toward Gillian, as if she really wanted her to understand. "I was trying to protect Robert, and Matt, and Lake House."

"Matt!" Gillian was suddenly furious. "How can you say that? I suppose you were trying to protect Matt when you started that rock slide. He could have been killed!"

Della recoiled, stumbling back a step from the desk, denial written in every line of her body. "No! What are you saying? I didn't do that!"

"Of course you did. You were angry with Matt because of the problems at Lake House, and you wanted to hurt him. For heaven's sake, Della, didn't you realize how serious that could have been?"

"I didn't do it!" Desperation came into Della's eyes, and her hand twisted in the red thread necklace she wore. "I didn't! I wouldn't do anything to hurt Matt." Something that looked like horror flickered across her face. "I wouldn't dare do anything like that."

"Why?" Gillian shot the word at her. "Why wouldn't you?"

Della shuddered, gripping the red necklace. "I wouldn't dare." Her eyes were wide and unfocused. "I wouldn't dare hurt Matt. Clarice would do something terrible to me if I tried to hurt Matt."

"Clarice . . ." Gillian's voice trailed off. Della was terrified. She couldn't possibly be faking that. "You really think Clarice could do something to you?"

Della seemed to make an enormous effort to get a grip on herself. She shrugged, but fear still haunted her eyes. "Clarice is here. You know that." Her gaze rested on Gillian, something speculative in it. "You feel her, I know you do. You more than anyone must know what kind of power she has. I wouldn't do anything to hurt Matt. I couldn't."

"I'd like to believe that," Gillian said slowly. "But if you didn't do it, who did?"

Della made a fluttering gesture with her hands, then drifted toward the door. "You'll find out," she said. "Or Clarice will. Maybe it's too late, anyway."

Gillian stared at the empty doorway once Della was gone. There were goose bumps on her arms, she realized, and she rubbed them irritably. *Too late.* What did Della mean by that? That it was too late because Matt was leaving? Or something else?

It would do no good to chase after Della and demand an explanation. Any answer she gave was as likely to be fantasy as the truth.

One thing Della had said had convinced her. There was an unmistakable ring of truth when she said she wouldn't hurt Matt. Della really was terrified of what Clarice might do to her.

Gillian was too agitated to sit still. She put her hand on the desk to push her chair away. If she—

Her hand rested on something small and hard and round. Gillian moved the paper that covered the object. The Florentine ring, which she'd left safely locked in her suitcase upstairs, lay on her desk.

She picked up the ring. It was warm to the touch. "Playing games?" she asked aloud, and immediately felt foolish. Did she expect Clarice to answer her?

If Clarice wanted to get a message to her, she was certainly going about it the wrong way. Gillian had no idea what she meant to convey by moving the ring around, except to frighten her.

Well, she wasn't frightened. Defiantly, Gillian thrust the ring on her finger. She'd had enough of hiding it away. The reason for that was long since gone, anyway. If Clarice wanted to move the ring again, she'd have to take it off Gillian's finger.

The setting sun turned the lake to molten gold by the time Gillian finished writing up her recommendations for Mr. Lockwood. She printed them out and then sat frowning at the papers.

She'd come into this too late. If someone had found out about the reservations mess earlier, Lake House could have had a successful winter season. That might have made a difference to Matt. Perhaps he'd be staying then.

Or would it all have turned out the same anyway? Maybe Matt could never be happy here, even if he'd been successful.

Gillian swung her chair around to look out the window at the crystal lake and the white cliffs. It was so beautiful here, so apparently peaceful. It hurt to think of Matt being driven away from this place by the tragedy of the past and his own sense of failure and guilt.

Guilt was certainly the strongest impetus to his leaving. Gillian looked down at the Florentine ring, the symbol of guilt. It looked alien on her hand, but she felt nothing from it. If Clarice wanted to tell her something with the ring, she was failing.

Her father was the only connection Gillian could see to the ring. Apparently the terrible suspicion about what happened to her father that had occurred to Gillian hadn't entered Matt's mind. If it had, he would have said something the night before. It was another barrier between them.

Gillian tried to swallow over the lump that formed in her throat. Here she was, back again at the thing she didn't want to think about.

Did Matt really believe they'd be able to come together once they were away from Lake House? In the clear light of day, whatever faint hope she might have cherished during the night had vanished. Any relationship between them was already doomed by something that had happened thirty years ago.

She shoved her chair back angrily and gathered up the papers. Keep moving, that was what she had to do. Maybe she could outrun the pain for a while, at least. She was going to be a long time getting over this. A very long time.

She went down the hall to find Brenda. The door to the assistant manager's office stood slightly ajar. Gillian tapped on it, then pushed it open and glanced inside. Brenda wasn't there, but the mug of coffee still steaming on the desk and the glowing monitor made it apparent she'd be back soon.

Gillian crossed to the desk, leafing through the papers in her hand. She'd prefer to go over these with Brenda, rather than just leaving them.

A paragraph caught her eye that needed an explanatory note, and she sat down in Brenda's chair, picking up a pen. Too bad these things hadn't been taken care of a long time ago. Too bad efficient Brenda hadn't found them for herself. Maybe Brenda had been hoping all along that the difficulties at Lake House would turn out just the way they had, giving her an opening into another corporation.

No, that didn't make sense. Brenda couldn't have known that she'd be kept on when the new management team came in. It was just as likely that the new team would make a clean sweep of the present personnel. Brenda was lucky she wasn't busy updating her résumé right now.

That thought took Gillian's gaze to the monitor in an automatic response. Updating her resume? No, that certainly wasn't what Brenda was doing.

Gillian frowned, staring at the monitor. Brenda seemed to be preparing some sort of report for Mr. Lockwood, too. Well, that was logical enough. Brenda would want to get in on the ground floor of any changes. She'd want to impress Lockwood with the fact that she wasn't to blame for the problems at Lake House.

The problems at Lake House—was that the subject of Brenda's report? It appeared to be a long list of names and dates. Curious, Gillian paged up.

The list she stared at sprang into focus in her mind, as if she'd turned a kaleidoscope to come up with another pattern. No wonder it looked familiar. It was just like the one she'd made up herself, when she'd tabulated the false reservations.

The door swung open, and Gillian looked into Brenda's startled face. Expressions chased across it:

annoyance, anger, then the realization of what she'd left visible on the monitor.

"It was you." What possible motive could Brenda have? "You were the one who sabotaged the reservations."

Brenda crossed the room slowly, probably to give herself time to think. Only the faintest hint of irritation gave itself away on her face. She stopped at the desk, looked at the monitor, and shrugged.

"I could deny it, I suppose, and you'd never prove anything. But it doesn't make much difference now." She brushed back her wing of glossy bangs. "It's too late to do anything about it."

"But why? I don't understand. What did you have to gain?"

Brenda smiled. "You really are slow on the uptake, aren't you? I thought you'd have guessed by now. I've been working for Lockwood Hotels for the last year, making sure that Lake House had enough problems that Matt would need help. You and I have the same boss, Gillian dear, even though you never knew it."

20

Brenda had been working for Lockwood Hotels
for the last year? So much for Gillian's assumption that
Frederick Lockwood didn't have it in for the son of his
old friend. Her head spun. It still didn't make sense.

"I don't understand. A year ago? But Matt didn't
approach Mr. Lockwood until a few months ago. Are
you saying that Frederick Lockwood hired you a year
ago to cause problems for Lake House? That doesn't
add up. Matt could have done any number of things
other than go to Lockwood for help."

Brenda shrugged, her shoulders moving under the
green Lake House blazer. Gillian fought a thoroughly
irrational desire to tear it off the woman.

"Mr. Lockwood didn't confide in me. I don't know
what his intentions were. I only know that he paid me,
and paid me well. And, of course, promised me a future
with Lockwood Hotels."

"And you decided to buy that with disloyalty to your employer? What makes you think Lockwood is ever going to trust you? You've already made it clear that you're for sale to the highest bidder."

An odd look crossed Brenda's face. That thought had obviously never entered her mind.

"Mr. Lockwood knows he can trust me." Brenda said it firmly, as if to shore up the doubt Gillian planted. "That's more than he can say for you. It's pretty clear where your loyalties are. Matt O'Donnell got you on his side with a few kisses."

Heat flooded Gillian's cheeks. Brenda hadn't guessed the half of it.

"I haven't given Matt anything that betrays Lockwood's trust. It's too bad neither you nor he can say the same. You messed up the reservations." She glanced at the monitor. "It was easy for you, wasn't it? You had access to every part of the system."

"Before Matt came I virtually ran the place! Of course it was easy. Matt never suspected a thing."

No, Matt wouldn't, Gillian thought. He believed in things like loyalty and friendship.

"You made it look as if Andre was skimming. You knew how volatile he is. The slightest hint of suspicion and he'd stalk out in anger. But that didn't work, did it?"

Brenda shrugged. "Not everything worked, no. But enough did. Mr. Lockwood is satisfied with me."

"Was it part of Lockwood's plan for you to kill Matt? That's what you could have done with that rock slide you started." Anger burned along Gillian's veins.

"I didn't mean that to happen." Brenda's cheeks flushed. "I didn't even know he was out there. I saw somebody coming up the trail—you, as it turned out. I thought a near miss with a rock slide would convince some of the guests that Lake House was dangerous. I was as shocked as you were when Matt was caught in it."

Gillian had to fight the urge to throw something. "I'll bet you were. Mr. Lockwood wouldn't have thanked you if that had turned into a police investigation, would he? Your part in this might have come out. I'm sure he doesn't have any illusions that you'd protect him in that case."

"You have such high standards." Brenda's tone and her look were contemptuous. "Grow up, Gillian. The only reason Lockwood sent you here for this job was because you weren't smart enough to figure out what was going on."

Gillian clenched her fists. All that talk about how Lockwood trusted her to do the evaluation. He'd known all along what she was going to find. He'd probably planned to use it for leverage in his negotiations with Matt.

"He was wrong, wasn't he?" Gillian shoved the chair back. "I did figure it out."

Brenda's eyebrows lifted. "Not in time. The deal's already signed and sealed. Lockwood gets the half interest in Lake House he wanted, I get a position with Lockwood Hotels, and you . . . you're probably out on your ear once I talk to Mr. Lockwood."

"And you think that matters?" The woman was incredible. She actually thought Gillian would want to continue working for Lockwood after this.

"Suit yourself." Brenda's smile was satisfied. "I have what I want, and it's too late for you to do a thing about it."

"Maybe so. But I wouldn't rest too easily on my perch, if I were you. Somebody will come along to knock you off it, sooner or later."

She brushed past Brenda, out of the office. She was wasting her time bandying words with Brenda Corvo. The sooner Matt knew what had happened, the better.

Or was it too late? If Matt had proof of Lockwood's activity, might that be enough to overturn the deal? Assuming, of course, that Matt even cared. He might still want to walk away from the whole situation.

Even if he did choose to leave, Matt had to know the truth. He had a right to know what his new partner was capable of.

Gillian hurried down the hall, glancing into Matt's office. It was dark and still. She hadn't really expected him to be there. With the Fourth of July picnic going on, he'd probably been outside most of the day. She looked at her watch. It was later than she'd thought. She'd probably find him out on the lawn where they were serving.

As she rounded the corner by the reception desk where Fred sat, looking bored, Henry came hurrying down the stairs. "Gillian! Why aren't you out enjoying the picnic? Surely Frederick doesn't expect you to work this late."

She grasped his arm. "Have you seen Matt? It's important that I talk to him."

"I haven't seen him in some time. He's been avoiding the crowd as much as possible, I think." A shadow crossed Henry's face. "I'm afraid the Fourth of July doesn't have a happy connotation in Matt's mind."

"I've got to find him." If that sounded shrill, she couldn't help it. Apprehension gripped her. She had to find Matt, right now. She didn't bother arguing with herself about it. The feeling was too strong for that.

Fred leaned across the reception desk, clearing his throat.

"Is something wrong, Ms. Lang?" His round face seemed to reflect her worry.

"I have to find Mr. O'Donnell." She tried to still her racing pulse. "Do you have any idea where he is?"

Fred nodded. "I saw him starting out the path around the lake about a half hour ago. I haven't seen him come back."

Danger! The word screamed inside her head. Matt was in trouble, she knew it. The knowledge raced along her veins and pounded in her blood.

"I'm going after him." She spun toward the door. Henry caught her hand.

"Here, take my flashlight. It'll be dark soon. You shouldn't go out without one. Do you want—"

He stopped suddenly, staring down at her hand. Gillian followed his gaze. He was staring at the Florentine ring, the oddest expression on his face. A tremor skittered along Gillian's nerves.

"Where . . . where did you get this?"

"It was with my father's things." She tried to pull her hand free, but Henry held her fast. "Please, Henry, I have to find Matt."

"But . . . " He looked at her with an expression of total bewilderment. "I don't understand. How did it get there?"

"What do you mean?" Something trembled against her skin like a warning. This was important. This was something she had to know.

"The ring was mine." Henry still wore the bewildered look. "I lent it to Alec because he was planning a portrait of Clarice in Renaissance dress, and he thought it suited the subject."

"Yours!" Gillian's mind rocked. The ring was Henry's.

It had never been Clarice's. That meant all the assumptions they'd made about its meaning were wrong.

"It doesn't matter." Henry tried to smile. "It shocked me to see it, that's all. With everything that happened at the time, I didn't realize until long afterward that I'd never gotten it back." He pressed Gillian's hand. "You keep it."

There wasn't time to argue or to assess what this meant. The urgency pounded through her.

"I'm sorry." She pulled away from him. "I have to find Matt. We'll talk later." She darted out the door.

Torches burned on the lawn in the gathering dusk, and people thronged around the picnic tables under the trees. Gillian pushed her way through the crowd. Matt had gone out the lake path, toward the gazebo, where she felt Clarice's presence so strongly. Toward the dock, where Clarice died.

Panic surged through her at the thought, sheer panic. It seemed to come both from within and without, as if she felt someone else's fear along with her own. She ran past the tennis courts and into the woods, the feeling intensifying. Danger, Matt was in danger. She could sense Clarice's presence, could almost hear another set of footsteps beside her own.

The ring had never belonged to Clarice. The thought resounded to the beat of her footsteps. *Never belonged to Clarice, never belonged to Clarice.* That meant that she hadn't given it to Gillian's father. The object that had convinced her of her father's affair was meaningless.

Maybe that was why Clarice kept drawing the ring to Gillian's attention. She wanted Gillian to know that. But if not Alec McLeod, then who?

Gillian gasped for breath, slowing her pace as the trail

grew rougher. The yellow circle from the flashlight bobbed erratically. She raced past the gazebo. There was no peace there now, no pleasant sense of anticipation. Just a palpable increase in the tension that pressed on her. *Hurry, hurry!*

Downhill now, and she had to be careful. If she fell, if she couldn't go on, there would be no one to help Matt. Fresh terror surged through her at the thought. He was in danger, and there was no one else to help him . . . no one but her, and the silent, unseen presence that raced beside her.

Stumbling, clutching her side as she gulped in the cool night air, Gillian reached the boulder field. Her feet slid on the gravel, and she felt a stir around her, as if the very air held her up.

She had to keep going, had to keep going or it would be too late. The words echoed in her mind. *Too late.* She couldn't be too late.

The trail swung around a cluster of rocks. The beam of her flashlight reflected from dark water. The lake was just ahead of her, and the dock where Clarice died. Somehow she'd known all along that was where she was going.

Gillian swung the flashlight frantically. Where was he? He had to be here, he had to be, she couldn't be too late . . . and then she saw them.

Two figures were on the very edge of the dock, silhouetted against the silver-gray sheen of the water. One of them lay crumpled, dead still against the rough wooden boards of the dock. Even as she raced forward, she saw the other figure raise something, ready to strike.

"No!" The scream tore from Gillian's throat. She raced across the dock and threw herself on Matt's still body. Her hands grasped him frantically.

Breathing. He was still breathing. Only when she knew that could Gillian turn and look at the dark figure that loomed over them. She saw the upraised walking stick. She looked without surprise into the face of Frederick Lockwood.

$\overline{2}\overline{1}$

"*Gillian.*" *Lockwood said her* name heavily, with resignation. "Somehow I had a feeling you would cause me trouble. You've been surprisingly persistent."

The coldness with which he spoke sent a tremor down Gillian's spine. During that mad dash through the woods, she'd felt that no harm could come to Matt once she found him. Now, that idea seemed ridiculous. If she stood in Lockwood's way, he'd simply remove her.

"You've hurt him." She ran her hands over Matt's chest, searching for signs of injury.

"Just knocked him out." Lockwood spoke as casually as if he did this every day. "It's better that way, don't you see? Better if he's unconscious when he goes in the lake."

She swallowed hard, trying to force her numb brain to think. Then she glanced at the heavy walking stick, still raised and ready to come down on her head. It must be weighted, the way Lockwood handled it. For a brief instant she pictured it crashing into her skull.

She wasn't going to defeat Lockwood physically. Their only chance was if she could delay him, hoping that Fred or Henry would be concerned enough to come looking for them.

Hope surged through her. Lockwood didn't realize other people knew where she'd gone. That might be a tiny advantage, if she could play this right.

"I don't understand." She looked up at Lockwood, and it didn't take any acting to produce a tremor in her voice. "Mr. Lockwood, what's going on? What happened to Matt?"

Lockwood smiled, the movement barely visible in the gathering darkness. "Very nice, Gillian. But I'm afraid it's a little late for an innocent act. You already know much too much."

Yes, of course she did, and Lockwood knew it. He certainly didn't intend to let her survive this night, either.

"You're going to make it look as if Matt drowned himself." Her steady voice surprised her. "You hope people will assume he committed suicide."

"Why not? That's what they thought about his mother, isn't it? Poor Matt. Thirty years to the day after his mother's death, feeling like a failure, he killed himself the same way his mother did. No one will doubt it."

Her breath caught. "You killed Clarice, didn't you? It wasn't Robert, it was you."

"So you've been thinking Robert was responsible. I suppose Matt thought that, too." Lockwood shrugged. "Logical. Everyone knew about Robert's temper, and his jealousy. No, my dear, in answer to the question you're about to ask, Clarice and I were not lovers. I tried, of course, but she was depressingly moral."

So Robert's jealousy had been unfounded. "The only thing she loved besides Robert and Matt was her art," Gillian said slowly. "That's it, isn't it? That was the only thing Robert had cause to be jealous of."

The air around her stirred, touching her skin with warmth. She'd finally gotten the message Clarice tried so hard to give her.

"Clarice made it easy for me," Lockwood said. He didn't seem to sense the presence Gillian felt so strongly. If he didn't have the ability to feel Clarice, perhaps that meant that her spirit was helpless against him.

"Easy?"

"Clarice's pride wouldn't let her defend herself against Robert's accusations. So when she died, people thought they knew why." He hefted the stick. "No one thought of me, just as no one will suspect me once Matt is dead."

"No!" She put herself between Matt and the stick, knowing it was futile. "You can't!"

Lockwood looked at her coldly. "Then I'll have to deal with you. Just as I dealt with your father that night. History seems to be repeating itself."

Her father. "You knew." Lockwood knew who she was. Maybe he'd known all along.

"Della told me. She is a fool, but sometimes a useful one. Alec McLeod's daughter is in the wrong place at the wrong time, just as he was."

"Did he see you kill Clarice? Is that why you had to kill him?" She risked a glance back along the trail. No sign yet of the thing she prayed to see. No lights bobbed along the trail from the House. She had to stall Lockwood, and hope for a miracle.

"Nothing so dramatic," Lockwood sounded slightly

reproving, as if murder were acceptable, but not melo-drama. "I'd already taken care of Clarice and was headed home through the woods. No one should have suspected I was on the property that night. And then I ran into McLeod."

"Once it was known that Clarice died that night, my father would remember. He'd say he'd seen you."

"He invited me into the cottage for a farewell drink. He was packing, getting ready to go home. He'd decided he couldn't stand being away from his family any longer." Lockwood touched the side of her face with the heavy stick. "You, my dear."

Gillian held herself steady by an exercise of will she didn't know she possessed. "You killed him, there in the cottage. Then you took his things away, so people would think he left on his own."

"He's buried under the rocks, if that's what you're wondering. That's why I had to interfere in Matt's plans for Lake House. He was going to clear the area to build cottages. I couldn't let that happen."

"You paid Brenda to make sure Matt had too many financial problems to go ahead with his plan."

Matt moved, very slightly, under her hand. He was regaining consciousness. She carefully restrained herself from looking at him. If only he didn't move, didn't make a sound . . . If he did, Lockwood would strike now, and they'd have no chance at all. She tried to send a message through her touch. *Be still. Please, be still.*

"Hiring Brenda Corvo was a necessary evil. I didn't want anyone else involved, but she's so avaricious her-self it will never occur to her that I had any motive other than the obvious one of taking over Lake House."

"Why kill Matt?" Panic surged through her, and she

forced it back. "You already have what you want. You have a partnership in Lake House, and Matt's going away."

"It's too much of a risk." Lockwood sounded as judicious as if he were considering which stocks to buy. "I'd always be wondering when Matt would decide to interfere. It's better this way. Under the partnership agreement, Lake House passes to me entirely with Matt dead."

Matt's hand moved, a fraction of an inch, pressing against hers. She had to buy time, time for Matt to recover enough to have a fighting chance, time for help to reach them.

"But if you weren't Clarice's lover, what was the point of the whole thing? Why did you have to kill her?"

Lockwood smiled. "Playing for time, Gillian? I'm afraid time is about up, for both of you. But I don't mind satisfying your curiosity before you die. After all, I owe you. You found the painting for me."

Painting . . . the canvas under the floorboards at the cottage. "It was you, that night. You attacked me and took the painting."

"I'd been looking for it for years." For the first time a trace of agitation crossed Lockwood's face. "Who would have thought Clarice would be so clever?"

"What did she do? What was in the painting that was worth her life?"

"Unfortunately Clarice was in the woods painting the day my brother had his tragic climbing accident. She saw him on the cliff. She knew that he wasn't alone that day, the way everyone thought."

"You killed him." The certainty of it struck hard. Poor Arthur, with his birds and his climbing. He'd never have turned Lockwood Hotels into anything.

"He shouldn't have inherited." Envy poured through Lockwood's voice like corrosive acid. "The fool ran the business into the ground with his neglect. It should have been mine from the beginning. I was the one who had the talent to make it a success."

Was Matt listening, or had he lapsed into unconsciousness again? "If Clarice knew, why didn't she tell?"

"I was able to convince her it was an accident." Lockwood's face twisted. "At least, I thought I convinced her. Then I found that she'd included two recognizable figures in the painting she did that day. As insurance, she said. That was when I knew I had to kill her."

His voice grew colder on the words, and his hand tightened on the walking stick. Her mind raced frantically for something, anything, to delay the inevitable attack.

"But you—"

"Enough conversation, my dear." The heavy stick prodded at her. "Move away from him."

"No!" Gillian clutched frantically at Matt, trying to keep herself between him and the stick. She felt him move, felt his muscles tense, and knew he was going to try and stop Lockwood.

"Then you'll have to be first," Lockwood said calmly. He swung his arm. The rush of air hit her, and the walking stick began a deadly arc toward her head.

The world exploded. Matt shot up, shoving her aside so violently she rolled against the edge of the dock. He surged upward, toward Lockwood. Lockwood swung wildly, and the stick caught Matt a glancing blow. It sent him to his knees again, but he managed to grasp the stick with one hand.

"Run, Gillian!" He grappled with Lockwood, trying to wrest the heavy stick from his hand. "Run!"

Matt was younger, stronger, but he was still only half-conscious. He stumbled. Lockwood jerked the stick free. He struck at Matt, his face twisted with fury.

"No!" Gillian screamed, staggering to her feet. She had to help him. She had to.

Something rushed into her. In an instant she was Gillian, feeling her own terror, and she was Clarice, facing death at Lockwood's hands. It was Clarice who screamed now.

"No! Robert, help me!"

The night shattered at the sound. Lockwood, his deadly swing arrested, turned toward her, shock and hatred battling on his face. He looked at something beyond her, and his expression froze into terror. Gillian turned, somehow knowing what she'd see.

It advanced toward them over the dark surface of the lake, sending waves of grief and fury battering against them. The water roiled under it. The gray, smoky form twisted and turned, as if it fought furiously to transform itself into human form once more. Second by second it thickened, becoming more solid, more real, surging toward them.

Lockwood stumbled backwards. He held the stick up in futile defense against the thing that advanced on him. His face went white with indescribable terror.

Matt. She had to get to Matt. She crawled toward him. It was like struggling through a hurricane. She forced her body forward into a gale that sucked the very breath from her lungs. Gasping, half-sobbing, she reached him, her arms going around him. They clutched each other, watching helplessly.

Lockwood made it to the edge of the dock. His running feet hit the path. He looked around frantically, as if for help, but there was no help. There was only the twisting gray cloud, coming inexorably closer, anger and grief emanating from it. It reached Lockwood, seeming to envelop him. Just for an instant, Gillian saw Robert's face.

Lockwood screamed shrilly, the sound almost inhuman. He turned and raced across the boulder field, dropping the stick, running erratically, screaming as he went.

He stumbled, his arms windmilling wildly. Then he fell. The sound of his head hitting the rock was sickeningly final.

22

The smoky form spiraled in on itself. A sensation of triumph washed over them, and then it vanished.

"It's all right," she murmured. "It's all right."

Matt couldn't hear her. He'd slipped into unconsciousness again. Breath coming in shaky sobs, she cradled him against her breast.

Light split the night sky, and a shower of red and gold stars floated down toward them. The lights from the sky echoed other pinpoints of light that flickered through the woods. The fireworks had begun, and help was on the way.

Several exhausting hours later, Gillian slipped into Matt's hospital room. She paused just inside the door. He was so still. Maybe he was sleeping, maybe she should come back later. . . . Then he turned his face toward her and held out his hand.

"How do you feel?" The question was a feeble expression of the love that flooded her heart, threatening to overflow. Careful, she had to be careful. She wasn't sure what Matt might feel after this devastating night.

"Pretty damn foolish," he muttered, and the growl reassured her. "I don't need to be here. Find me some clothes, and let's get out of this place."

"Not yet." She sat down beside him. "Be glad the doctors insisted no one could talk to you. There are two police officers outside who want some answers. Henry is delaying them so I can get to you first."

Matt's face tightened. "Lockwood?"

"He's dead."

"I thought so." His hand closed over hers, and she could see his mind grappling with the situation. "What did you tell the cops?"

"A carefully edited version of the truth," she said. "I found out about Lockwood's tactics, went to tell you, and found him attacking you. He ran when he saw people coming from the House and realized he'd never get away with it. He fell." She took a deep breath. "I didn't think they'd believe the real story."

"Ghosts." A spasm of grief or pain crossed his face. "No, they wouldn't buy that. Did they believe you, or am I about to be arrested for Lockwood's murder?"

"Of course they believed me. Henry and Fred have already told them you were unconscious when they arrived. And Brenda admitted her part in the sabotage. All you have to do is tell them what happened, and leave out . . . well, how it really ended."

"Right." He was still for a moment, his expression dark. "Was I hallucinating?"

Gillian shook her head, her throat tight. "He came. Clarice called for him, and this time he came."

The lines deepened in Matt's face. "He couldn't rest. That was what I've felt all along. I thought the grief and guilt was because he'd killed her, but it wasn't. He couldn't rest until he had justice for my mother's death."

"They loved each other. I saw that in my dreams. I just didn't understand until it was almost too late." She struggled to speak over the lump in her throat. "They loved each other, but their pride drove them apart. They died before they could make that right."

"No wonder they couldn't be at peace." Pain filled Matt's eyes. "They had everything, and they let it slip away." His fist clenched. "Damn. They lost each other . . . "

"No," she said quickly. She couldn't let him think that for another second. "Not anymore. While I was waiting for help, I saw them again." Her tears overflowed, dropping on their entwined hands. "Just for a moment, I saw them. Clarice was at the gazebo, waiting for him. They held each other, and their faces were filled with so much love." Her voice choked. "Then they were gone. I don't think we'll see them again. I think they're all right now."

Was she crying for Clarice and Robert, together at last, or for Gillian and Matt? She wasn't sure. She didn't know what Matt felt now. Were they still caught in the tragedy they'd shared, or were they free of it?

"Don't cry." Matt reached up to wipe away her tears, his hand warm against her cheek. His own eyes were bright with unshed tears. "They have their happy ending at last, thanks to you. I just wish . . . "

He stopped, frowning, and her heart seemed to stop, too.

"What do you wish?" she whispered.

His head moved restlessly against the pillow, turning

away from her. "It's not right. Your father was an innocent bystander. You lost the chance to know him,
because he was in the wrong place at the wrong time."

"I don't feel that." She searched for the words. "I
came here to find the missing piece of my life, and I've
found it. Before . . . well, before there was just a blank
where my father should have been. Now that space is
filled. He was talented, and loving, and he cared about
me. I know that now. He cared."

"You should have had the chance—" Matt began
stubbornly, and she put her fingers over his lips.

"You can't take responsibility for what happened to
him." She had to make him accept it. "I don't know if my
parents would ever have been happy together. Maybe not.
But at least I know now my father was going to come back
to me. That's all I need. That's what I came here to find."

Matt's fingers interlaced with hers. "I wish you could
have known him. And them," he said softly.

"Yes." Her lips trembled, and she pressed them
together. "Maybe I do, in a way."

His grip tightened painfully. "What about us? Do
Matt and Gillian get to have a happy ending, too?"

Suddenly her heart was beating somewhere up in her
throat. "You're the one who wasn't sure," she reminded
him.

"I'm sure now." His dark eyes were filled with
promises. "I love you, Gillian Lang. I don't care if we
were brought together by ghosts or fate or pure chance.
What I feel for you is the most real thing I've ever felt in
my life. I can't lose you."

"Then you won't." She pressed their clasped hands
against her cheek, her heart overflowing with love. "Not
in this life. Not in any other. I promise."

Someday Soon by Debbie Macomber

A beautiful widow unwillingly falls for the worst possible new suitor: a man with a dangerous mission that he must complete—even if it means putting love on hold. Another heartwarming tale from bestselling author Debbie Macomber.

The Bride Wore Spurs by Sharon Ihle

When Lacey O'Carroll arrives in Wyoming as a mail-order bride for the unsettlingly handsome John Winterhawke, she is in for a surprise: he doesn't want a wife. But once the determined Lacey senses his rough kindness and simmering hunger for her, she challenges Hawke with a passion of her own.

Legacy of Dreams by Martha Johnson

Gillian Lang arrives at Lake House, a Victorian resort hotel in upstate New York, determined to get answers to questions about the past that have haunted her. As she is drawn to the hotel's owner Matt O'Donnell, her search for the truth unfolds a thirty-year-old tragedy involving both their families and ignites a dangerous passion that could lead to heartbreak.

Bridge to Yesterday by Stephanie Mittman

After falling from a bridge in Arizona, investigator Mary Grace O'Reilly is stunned to find she has been transported one hundred years into the past to help hell-raising cowboy Sloan Westin free his son from an outlaw gang. They face a perilous mission ahead, but no amount of danger will stop them from defying fate for the love of a lifetime.

Fool of Hearts by Terri Lynn Wilhelm

Upon the untimely death of her father, Lady Gillian finds herself at the mercy of her mysterious new guardian Calum, Marquess of Iolar. While each attempts to outwit the other to become sole heir to her father's fortune, they cannot resist the undeniable desire blazing between them. A witty and romantic novel.

The Lady and the Lawman by Betty Winslow

Amanda is ready to do whatever it takes to uncover the mystery behind her father's death—even live in a brothel in a rugged backwater town in Texas. More disturbing than her new lodgings is the undercover Texas Ranger assigned to help her, with his daring and hungry kisses proving to be the most dangerous obstacle of all.

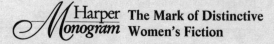

GLORY IN THE SPLENDOR OF SUMMER WITH

HarperMonogram's

101 DAYS OF ROMANCE

BUY 3 BOOKS, GET 1 FREE!

Take a book to the beach, relax by the pool, or read in the most quiet and romantic spot in your home. You can live through love all summer long when you redeem this exciting offer from HarperMonogram. Buy any three HarperMonogram romances in June, July, or August, and get a fourth book sent to you for FREE. See next page for the list of top-selling novels and romances by your favorite authors that you can choose from for your premium!

101 DAYS OF ROMANCE
BUY 3 BOOKS, GET 1 FREE!

CHOOSE A FREE BOOK FROM THIS OUTSTANDING LIST OF AUTHORS AND TITLES:

HarperMonogram

____LORD OF THE NIGHT Susan Wiggs 0-06-108052-7
____ORCHIDS IN MOONLIGHT Patricia Hagan 0-06-108038-1
____TEARS OF JADE Leigh Riker 0-06-108047-0
____DIAMOND IN THE ROUGH Millie Criswell 0-06-108093-4
____HIGHLAND LOVE SONG Constance O'Banyon 0-06-108121-3
____CHEYENNE AMBER Catherine Anderson 0-06-108061-6
____OUTRAGEOUS Christina Dodd 0-06-108151-5
____THE COURT OF THREE SISTERS Marianne Willman 0-06-108053-5
____DIAMOND Sharon Sala 0-06-108196-5
____MOMENTS Georgia Bockoven 0-06-108164-7

HarperPaperbacks

____THE SECRET SISTERS Ann Maxwell 0-06-104236-6
____EVERYWHERE THAT MARY WENT Lisa Scottoline 0-06-104293-5
____NOTHING PERSONAL Eileen Dreyer 0-06-104275-7
____OTHER LOVERS Erin Pizzey 0-06-109032-8
____MAGIC HOUR Susan Isaacs 0-06-109948-1
____A WOMAN BETRAYED Barbara Delinsky 0-06-104034-7
____OUTER BANKS Anne Rivers Siddons 0-06-109973-2
____KEEPER OF THE LIGHT Diane Chamberlain 0-06-109040-9
____ALMONDS AND RAISINS Maisie Mosco 0-06-100142-2
____HERE I STAY Barbara Michaels 0-06-100726-9

To receive your free book, simply send in this coupon **and** your store receipt with the purchase prices circled. You may take part in this exclusive offer as many times as you wish, but all qualifying purchases must be made by September 4, 1995, and all requests must be postmarked by October 4, 1995. Please allow 6-8 weeks for delivery.

MAIL TO: HarperCollins Publishers
        P.O. Box 588 Dunmore, PA 18512-0588

Name_____

Address_____

City_____State_____Zip_____

Offer is subject to availability. HarperPaperbacks may make substitutions for requested titles.

H09511